THE SIBERIA JOB

THE SIBERIA JOB

BASED ON A TRUE STORY

JOSH HAVEN

THE MYSTERIOUS PRESS
NEW YORK

THE SIBERIA JOB

Mysterious Press
An Imprint of Penzler Publishers
58 Warren Street
New York, N.Y. 10007

Library of Congress Control Number: 2023902462

Cloth ISBN: 978-1-61316-407-5
eBook ISBN: 978-1-61316-408-2

10 9 8 7 6 5 4 3 2 1

Printed in the United States of America
Distributed by W. W. Norton & Company

For my parents

FOREWORD

I t's a dubious luxury for a novel based on real events to have those events continue to unfold as the book makes its way into print. The writing of this novel was prompted by the untimely and unusual death of a man involved in the transfer of one of the world's most powerful and profitable companies—a Russian energy company—from state to private ownership after the end of the Soviet Union. Because this novel is based on real events, the first draft used the company's real name. Unfortunately, people connected to the company keep getting murdered (at least five in the last six months), and that's made publishing a book about it a slightly more delicate issue. And anyway, this isn't a work of journalism, it's a novel based on real events, so certain things about the company, including its name, have been changed.

As it happens, nearly all Russian energy companies follow the convention of choosing names that use the word *gaz*, which means gas, or *neft*, which means oil, or both. Rosneft, Gazprom, Transneft, Northgaz, and Rusneftegaz comprise an incomplete list. So to strike a neutral tone, for the purposes of this novel, our company will be called *Gazneft*.

What I can say about Gazneft without giving its identity away is that it is one of the largest publicly traded energy companies in the world and one of the largest companies of any sort in Russia. It's a major supplier of energy to NATO countries. Russian energy exports helped pay for Russia to invade Ukraine, which meant that as Europe rushed to help Ukraine fight off Russia, it also paid for Russia to keep fighting. This got the rest of the world wondering what was going on, who was controlling what, and who was controlling whom. Meanwhile, an unprecedented series of sanctions hit Russia. Switzerland violated its own neutrality to join them. And yet, aside from losing a few of their yachts, Russia's political elite seemed to weather the storm well.

People began to notice the deep ties between Russia's energy infrastructure and the West's political elite. People heard that a former foreign minister of Austria had worked for Rosneft and a former German chancellor had worked for Gazprom. That a former Austrian chancellor and a former American Assistant Secretary of State had worked for Lukoil, and that a former French prime minister had worked for two Russian energy companies, Zarubezhneft and Sibur, simultaneously. "Oligarch" was the word of the day and to say the geopolitical situation was muddled and confusing would perhaps be an understatement.

The genuinely crazy story herein will do little to clear any of that up. Sanctions have caused Gazneft's share price to plummet to levels not seen since its IPO and, as of my writing this, Gazneft shares aren't trading at all. The bizarre story of Gazneft's IPO, and the way in which many of those shares came to be owned by their current oligarchic owners, is the story of this novel.

(And while Gazneft does represent a specific company, I suspect its story could be generalized to many denationalized companies whose corrupt and murder-y acquisition by a small number of men created Russia's oligarchy.)

One last disclaimer, as regards this book being fiction based on a true story. For the reasons I've already given, and other reasons that will be obvious if you read the book, I don't want to be too specific about what's real and what isn't. Don't assume it's the crazier parts—the Caspian Sea fishing trip, for instance, or the club-feud kidnapping—that are made-up. It was mostly the banal, technical stuff that seemed most likely to get people into trouble. Those two bits of borderline absurdism, and many others, really happened. Post-Soviet Russia was the Wild Wild West of the East.

—Josh Haven

CHAPTER 1

JUNE 2, 1994

London has more bars—pubs, places to drink adult beverages—than just about any other city in the world. There's an endless supply; an endless variety of quaint or ancient or Victorian or Churchillian or sleek and ultramodern. There's also a bar in every hotel restaurant in the city. Some of them are pretty famous; they serve diners who want an aperitif or a nightcap or an excuse to put on a tux. They're not "drinking" bars. The only reason for actually drinking at a hotel bar in London is if you've already emptied the minibar.

John Mills was fed up—to the back teeth—with London, the world, banking, business, his job—his former job—with being away from the United States, away from his wife and their home in Texas. So he'd quit a very good, very high-paying job with a top investment bank and bought a plane ticket to Dallas Fort Worth. His flight left in the late morning. Including time to pack all the junk he'd been lugging around for three years—from Texas to Tokyo to India to London—he still had time to get drunk, tell the world of multinational finance to go to hell, sober up, and be at Heathrow in time to sleep for ten hours on the plane.

It was one in the morning, and the only people in The Goring Hotel's dining room were the barman and a crowd of raucous businessmen—stockbroker types in striped shirts and white collars—celebrating something. John was in the sort of mood where the sound of happy people having a good time makes you want to throw empty bottles at them. John didn't have an empty bottle. He had an empty glass. He held it up for the barman to see. The barman came over and filled it up again, with some obscenely expensive Irish whiskey. John wondered how much longer he'd be able to afford the good stuff, having quit his job.

The barman finished pouring, John thanked him and, before he could walk away, said, "Can I ask you something?"

"Certainly, sir," said the barman.

"Why is there a hotel in London named 'The Goring'? It'd be like having a hotel in Pearl Harbor being named 'The Admiral Yamamoto.'"

The barman began to walk away. John called after him. "Why not just name it the Hotel Wernher von Braun and stop beating around the bush?"

The barman ignored him. He was pouring another round for the stockbroker guys; apparently, the final round. The host, speaking lightly accented English, had called to the barman for slivovice—Czech slivovice—nothing else would do—for a final toast. John wondered if, once they closed their tab, the humorless Goring barman would issue a last call and begin closing up. The

Hotel Admiral Yamamoto—how could someone not laugh at that? Philistine.

John wasn't sober enough to eavesdrop so he didn't catch much of the slivovice man's lengthy toast; only that the group seemed to have struck it big on some trade or something. The men—six of them, all pretty young, late twenties to late thirties—all drank their plum brandy and, after some handshakes and hugs, began to file out of the restaurant.

John waved the barman back over. "You got a pack of Camel filters back there?"

"No, sir," said the barman. The slivovice guy was counting out money as he walked toward the bar. Probably coming to settle up and pay his czech. John laughed inwardly.

"What have you got?" said John, to the barman.

"Nothing, sir. I'm afraid I'm out of cigarettes," said the barman. "We'll restock in the morning."

"Perfect," said John. "A fitting end to the day." He finished his drink.

"Can I offer you one of mine?" said the slivovice guy.

"I'd appreciate that, thank you," said John. "What're you smoking?"

The slivovice guy was walking down the bar toward John, pulling a pack out of his breast pocket.

"Laikas," he said, flicking the bottom of the pack to pop a cigarette out, holding it out for John.

"Huh," said John. "Never had one before. You bring these from home?"

"No," said the slivovice guy. "They don't sell these in the Czech Republic. Only in Russia, and—apparently—London. I saw them at a newsstand. I was curious."

"How are they?" said John, accepting a light from a nickel-plated Zippo.

"Fine," he said. "Not very good, not very bad. Fine."

John took a drag and nodded his agreement, then added, "Any cigarette, when you haven't got one, is delicious. Thank you."

"Don't mention it," said the slivovice guy. "Mr. . . . ?"

"Mills," said John, extending his hand. "John Mills."

"Petr Kovac," said the slivovice guy. They shook, and John waved over the barman. "Can I offer you a drink, Mr. Kovac?"

Petr Kovac looked at his watch, then shrugged. "Yes, thank you. Call me Petr."

John nodded, held up two fingers to the bartender and said to Petr, "Slivovice?"

"Perfect."

◆

An hour later, they had moved from the bar to a table, taking the circular slivovice bottle with them, and were exchanging life stories—the clichéd two sides of the same coin—John, the born and bred capitalist, a multinational investor, and sick of it; Petr, the born and bred socialist who had only recently taken the plunge into the new free markets in his home country—and had just made his first million dollars.

With Communism gone and Czechoslovakia on its way out, the new, pseudo-interim government needed to privatize formerly state-owned socialist businesses; the whole country had to restructure.

With the help of the International Monetary Fund, the Czechoslovakian government had issued stock vouchers to every Czech and Slovak. They were negotiable—transferrable—and entitled the bearer to a percent of ownership in whatever company a voucher applied to, if presented at an eventual voucher auction. The simple math example was, if a hundred people showed up to the voucher auction, each with one voucher, then they'd each get 1 percent of the company's newly issued stock.

In post-Communism, no one had any idea if socialist Czech industries would survive privatization, let alone the split of Czechoslovakia into two independent countries.

But Petr had had the idea that, if a little hard capital flowed into the country, they'd do just fine. He also didn't share the fear that his country would dissolve into a bloody civil war, as Yugoslavia had. The Balkan wars were raging just two hundred miles south. But Petr was willing to bet (literally bet, everything he owned) that Czechs and Slovaks didn't really dislike each other, that they wanted independence but would be happy to part as friends, that a split would be peaceful and the conclusion would be two countries ready for prosperity.

He'd scraped together all the money he had and had flown to London to spend it trying to meet a few market guys in the City and sell them on his idea: buying up vouchers en masse. He exuded an air of not only confidence, but competence.

He got five guys to put in half a million pounds each—pounds sterling—and went back to the Czech Republic with a suitcase of cash—in American dollars. He'd bought a car and drove around Prague, and Pilsen, and Brno, and Ostrava, and the countryside in between, buying up the vouchers of anyone who wanted to sell.

Most of the people who sold to him thought he was insane, trading hard currency—stable, real money that wouldn't lose 80 percent of its value overnight—for near worthless slips of paper in

rundown Communist claptrap companies. Petr and his little investment fund ended up owning big chunks—5, 10, 20 percent—of
hundreds of Czech industries. Everything from bus companies to
glassworks. Today they'd liquidated part of their holdings. The
two-and-a-half-million-pound investment had turned, in about
two years, into stock valued at nearly a billion Czech koruna—or
about twenty million British pounds. And now Petr was one of
the wealthiest men in his country.

John had had a very different kind of day. An ordinary day, until the
midafternoon, when he began to read the American morning papers
with his lunch. There'd been a piece about a classmate of his, another
Harvard Business guy, who'd just capitalized a new hedge fund.

Henceforth he would be his own boss, managing half a billion
dollars. And that was fine—John didn't begrudge anyone's success,
financial or otherwise. The reason this specific news item bothered
him was that this particular classmate of his was an idiot. A total
goddamn idiot. There had been tufts of grass on Boston commons
with higher IQs. But there he was, head of his own fund, answering
to no one but the people whose money he would certainly be losing
over the next few months. It was galling.

John had put the paper down and stewed for a little while, in a
big pot of self-loathing. If a Cro-Magnon like this ex-classmate of
his was running his own life, making his own decisions, then why
wasn't John? Why was he still sitting on a step on the corporate
pyramid? Could it be that a man who was routinely outwitted by
inanimate objects had more gumption than John had? More confidence in his ability to swim when others sank?

John felt the stirrings of an existential crisis. Too young for a
midlife crisis, right? He was thirty. Already thirty, but he'd never
climbed a mountain or fought a bull or been in a car chase. He'd

boxed in college and been an Eagle Scout before that, but he'd never been a soldier, never shot at anyone or been shot at. He'd spent his life as an office drudge, pushing other people's paper. It was time for a change.

John leaned way back in his chair, lit a cigarette, and looked at the ceiling. A few cigarettes later, his boss, the head of the European investment portfolio, knocked on the glass door in the middle of the big glass front of John's office, and stuck his head in.

"John, sorry, you can't smoke in here."

"Really?" said John, puffing out a lungful of blue tobacco smoke.

"Really."

"Well, heck," said John tossing the cigarette into a half-drunk cup of coffee. "I quit."

". . . What?"

"I cordially tender my resignation, Alan. Spread the word." John stood up and began to clear out his desk drawers. A few minutes later, the head of the London Branch in toto was in John's office, offering to install an opaque glass front and a separate ventilation system so that John could smoke without anyone knowing about it. John politely declined, shook the boss's hand, and left the building with a small cardboard box of personal items. A photo of his wife, his Rolodex, a few books—that was it.

He'd gone back to the hotel where he lived, asked the concierge to arrange his flight home, called his wife to tell her the news—as expected, she was thrilled to hear it; she'd had to go back to Texas to take care of her parents and was sick of being five thousand miles away from him—packed his bags, and hit the bar.

"Jesus," said Petr. "That's quite a day."

"Yep," said John, accepting another Laika.

"But congratulations. You've got what we call in Prague, chutzpah."

John laughed.

"What will you do now?" said Petr, lighting another Laika of his own.

"Start my own fund, I expect," said John. "I was at our Tokyo office until a couple years ago. There was a guy over there—a guy who'd started with a sewing machine factory and ended up with a manufacturing empire—we got to be good friends. He'd been a sailor in the Imperial Navy during the war—he was actually at Midway—had a long list of remarkable stories to tell. It's not often you get to hear about history firsthand. Especially the Japanese side of the war; it's not talked about much over there, aside from the occasional Yasukuni Shrine argument. Anyway, he told me if I ever wanted to strike out on my own, he was in for a million. I've got some other contacts. Plenty of them, really. I think I can raise the money—I just need to decide what to do with it."

Petr nodded.

"Any more voucher privatizations going on?"

Petr shook his head. "Only Russia."

John exhaled a puff of smoke. "What's wrong with Russia?"

"Well, look at it like this—when Communism in Europe collapsed, all these countries started fresh—us, Hungary, Poland, Lithuania, and so on. They were the winners. They had defeated the specter of the USSR. They were able to go forward with the national unity and brotherhood you get from winning a war.

"But Russia, they hated Communism, but better to be Communist winners than capitalist losers . . . you know what I mean? They like that Gorbachev and Yeltsin mean they don't get thrown in gulags anymore, but they hate Gorbachev and Yeltsin for cutting off their balls. If you know what I mean. They don't have Václav Havel, or Lech Wałęsa. They have a government they don't respect, no clear authority, no sense of pulling together for a new beginning. They feel . . . screwed. By the West, by the satellite countries, by their government, by each other.

"And remember, Russia isn't a nation-state like Czech or Slovakia or Poland. 'Russian' is a nationality and 'Russian' is an ethnicity, but not all Russians are Russians, you know? You also got Belarusians, Tatars, Bashkirs, Chuvashes, Avars, Chechens, Mordvins, Darghins, Kazakhs, Armenians, Udmurts, Ossetians, Ingush, Tuvans, Uzbeks, Laks, Kalmyks, Jews, Georgians, Karelians—Koreans, in the Far East. You see? I could go on for half an hour. And mostly, they all hate each other. Some have gotten out, to their own nation states—Belarusians to Belarus, Uzbeks to Uzbekistan, Jews to Israel, et cetera. But mostly they're still there, and it gives the country characteristics of a giant Yugoslavia.

"Then add to that an enormous army, which is now mostly not getting paid, an enormous secret police force—also now largely not getting paid—and the largest black market in the world. Investing there, it's not like investing in Estonia. It's like one of those lawless mining towns in the American Old West. Like that Humphrey Bogart movie, yeah? But instead of a town, it's the largest country in the world. You talk about free markets—this is the freest market in the world. If someone screws you, you got no one to call for help."

John was nodding along. He knew all that. And he knew Petr was right. It was why he hadn't put any of his company's money into Russia. . . .

But this voucher thing . . . Russia had some of the most valuable companies in the world. And the Russian economy—the

Russian people—needed hard currency a damn sight more than the Czechs had.

"Have you spent a lot of time in Russia?" said John, after a moment.

"Not a lot, but enough. Before the vouchers, I sold Czech office supplies around the western USSR."

John nodded. "Do you speak Russian?"

"Yes."

"Fluently?"

"Yes."

John nodded again, and scratched his chin. After a moment, he refilled his glass, and Petr's, took a sip, and savored it. "Petr . . . let me ask you. When you were growing up, and you heard about those Old West mining towns in America, Gold Rush towns—did you think, *man, I'm glad I wasn't there, that sounds like it would have been dangerous?*"

Petr swished his glass, waiting for John to continue.

"Or," said John, "did you think, *damn, I wish I'd been there with a six shooter and a cowboy hat and a goldmine.*"

Petr swished his drink another moment, and then drank it down.

CHAPTER 2

The night concierge was able to change John's ticket to Dallas into a ticket to Moscow. John told his wife that there was going to be a little delay in his getting home—gave her a précis of the plan—that he just wanted to have a look around, see what the Russian business climate was like; see if there were any opportunities.

She told him she loved him, to be careful and come home safe, which made John feel a little more like a gold prospector on his way out to them there hills, where people didn't need no stinking badges. Which, if he were honest, was about 50 percent of his reason for going. It made him feel a little heroic—or at least, a little courageous. He promised her he'd be careful, said he loved her, and then jogged to the gate, where Petr had been standing, pointing emphatically at his watch. Everyone else had boarded.

The two men didn't talk much on the flight; they both had bad headaches to sleep off—though not nearly as bad as they might have been, after John got his first experience in the freest of free markets. Petr had been rubbing his temples for about half an hour after takeoff, head back, eyes closed, when they popped open, and he pulled out his wallet. He leafed through the cash inside it and turned to John.

"I've only got sterling . . . can you change a twenty-pound note?"

"Uh, sure, why?" John pulled his own wallet out, pulled out an American twenty and gave it to Petr, waving away the twenty pounds.

"I want to try something."

They were flying Aeroflot, the Russian airline that—because of its international business—was handling the collapse of the USSR reasonably well. Well enough that the plane didn't seem too ramshackle, though John couldn't help but wonder what kind of safety inspections it could possibly be getting. The attendant call button didn't work—not a great sign—but Petr waved for a stewardess, who came over in a neat blue blazer, flower-print dress, and a polite, international smile.

She said something in Russian to Petr, Petr said something in Russian to her. She shook her head no. Petr said something else. She cocked her head to one side and thought about it for a moment. She said something to Petr; he held up John's twenty dollars. She nodded and walked to the back of the plane.

"What did you say to her?" said John.

"I asked if there was emergency oxygen on board."

A moment later, the stewardess returned with a bright yellow bottle that looked like a little scuba tank. The valve at the top was connected to a brown rubber face mask that looked like it was a relic of the fifties. Petr handed her the twenty, she handed him the bottle and walked away.

Petr squinted at the Cyrillic instructions, then put the mask over his mouth and nose, opened the valve, and took a deep breath. He did this five or six times, then lay his head back and took a deep breath of normal cabin air.

"That's very nice," he said, then rolled his reclined head toward John. "No more headache. Try it."

John did. It worked like a charm. By the time he was done, Petr was asleep. John was only a minute or two behind him.

They woke up when the airplane bounced off the runway in Moscow. It bounced again and then shook like a blender as it rolled to a stop over a landing strip badly in need of repaving. There were a few minutes of taxiing, and then a twenty-minute wait while a set of rolling stairs was located for the passengers to exit by.

The Moscow international airport terminal was all neon lights and linoleum, wood from when it was cheaper than plastic, and brutalist seventies abstract sculptures. John and Petr presented the visas Petr had obtained at the Russian embassy in London that morning (after a generous gratuity to hurry the process along). The unsmiling, expressionless passport officer—in a military-esque uniform—looked at each of the men carefully, then at each of their visas and each of their passports, stamped them, and slid them back through the little slot at the bottom of his window. John thanked him. The man waved for him to move along.

They retrieved their luggage from an unceremonious heap of bags and went outside again. There was a line for taxis. It was a warm summer day, slightly overcast; the taxis were all Ladas, and when they reached the head of the line, they stuffed their things into a cab's trunk and climbed in the back. Petr said they were going to the Hotel Metropol. Not speaking Russian, John followed along as best he could.

The driver quoted a price. Petr said it was absurd. The taxi driver told him he could get out then. Petr shrugged and opened his door. The driver quoted a new price. Petr rejected it and made a counteroffer. The cab driver was deeply insulted, and made a rebuttal, which Petr rebutted. Finally they settled on five pounds, though Petr said the driver would take four dollars instead. John handed Petr a five, who held the bill up and said he would pay when they arrived. The driver insisted on being paid in advance. Petr opened his door again. The driver started the engine and pulled away from the curb, with the door still open. Petr shut it, and John shook his head in amazement.

The airport—Sheremetyevo—was about twenty minutes north of the giant ring road around Moscow. Unlike any major international airport John had ever visited before, the drive took them through undeveloped forest. It was like Sheremetyevo was a dacha in the country. The ring road marked the edge of Moscow. Moscow's outskirts were every bit as dreary and depressing as they looked in spy movies.

From the ring road to the city center—where the famous Hotel Metropol sat a block from Red Square, two blocks from the Kremlin—the city went through a magical transformation.

The Ladas were replaced by Mercedes. Or at least, half of them were—half the cars looked like they'd been built in the fifties, and the other half were Mercedes and BMWs and one Lamborghini Diablo. Most of these looked brand new and were immaculately waxed and shined. Everywhere, new buildings were being built. Also everywhere were half-built new buildings, with construction halted. There were blocks of cement and plaster buildings next to blocks of glass and flashing lights, like little Times Squares. Every surface was plastered with advertising. Every sidewalk was filled with people buying and selling. It made John think of the stalls along the Seine in Paris.

There were frumpy women in babushkas and hard-worn men in hard-worn raincoats scattered among men wearing gold chains and white suits, and a bevy of long-legged, short-skirted women who looked like they belonged on catwalks in Milan.

At the Metropol, the Lada taxi pulled up at a red carpet. Its door was opened by a valet in a livery overcoat and white gloves, and Petr handed the five-dollar bill back to John and said, "Don't pay him until I get our luggage out of the trunk." Petr and the white-gloved valet unloaded the bags, John handed the cabbie the five, the cabbie waved for John to get out of the car, and then sped off into the thick Moscow traffic.

Inside the Metropol, the lobby was abuzz with activity—a three-way mix of foreigners, who were obvious by their clothes, nouveau riche Russians, even more obvious by theirs, and stunningly beautiful women—some of them affixed to the sides of escorts, some clearly available to be escorted.

A wide staircase ascended from the slightly sunken doorway; the steps were marble, the fixtures were brass, the coffered roof was supported by brightly polished wooden columns. The red carpet was a little threadbare.

The valet deposited their bags at the reception desk, where a man in a poorly tailored but still—somehow—expensive-looking suit greeted them in English. He talked them up from two rooms to the two-room Hermitage Suite. He was the first person in Russia that John had seen smile.

Petr paid in advance for two weeks with two fifty-pound notes, and the reception man rang a handheld bell he had sitting on his desk. When no one responded, he shouted "Slava" at a suited man in his late twenties who was deep in conversation with one of the girls. Slava brought a luggage trolley over, loaded it with John and Petr's bags, received a Russian instruction and a pair of keys from the reception man, and led the way to an elevator. It had an operator on a small stool inside; Slava said something to him and the elevator began to ascend. Bumpily.

They emerged on the top floor, into a hermitage-esque hallway. The elevator operator—a kid of about sixteen—held his hand out for a tip. Slava smacked the hand away and led John and Petr to big double doors at the hallway's end. Inside was a lavish suite with bedrooms on opposite sides of a large sitting room. All the furnishings looked prerevolution.

John and Petr looked around and Slava said, in heavily accented English, "Will the suite be satisfactory?"

John looked at Petr, who nodded.

"Perfectly, thank you," said John, pulling a five-dollar tip out of his wallet.

"Is there anything else I can provide you with? Food, drink, reservations for dinner in our restaurant?"

"Are reservations necessary?" said John.

"No," said Slava.

"Then I think we're fine," said John, looking at Petr, who again nodded.

"Would you like to speak to one of the girls from downstairs?"

"Uh, no," said John, slightly taken aback by the question.

"How much are they?" said Petr.

"Of course, you may negotiate with them, but perhaps fifty dollars for the night."

"Thanks," said Petr. "Not right now, but we'll be in touch."

Slava nodded, placed two keys on a small table by the door, and withdrew.

"I can see you're concerned," said Petr, when he'd left. "I'm not going to get a prostitute."

"You're a bachelor," said John. "It's none of my business."

"What it is," said Petr, lighting a cigarette and tossing the pack to John, "is a very good indicator of the strength of the local economy. Last time I was here, you could have the best one for ten dollars a night."

"Huh," said John. He lit a cigarette of his own. "Maybe we should start trading hooker futures."

Petr laughed.

CHAPTER 3

P etr was the guide, and their first stop was a club called the Hungry Duck, already becoming famous as the Studio 54 of Moscow. Petr suggested it would be a good place for up-to-the-minute gossip on the voucher issuances and, besides, he knew the owner, a Canadian named Doug Steele. They'd met in Prague while Doug and a friend tried to get visas to go to Russia. This was right around the time Yeltsin had had to fight off a coup, and Doug had been stranded for a while before someone at the Canadian embassy was able to come up with the name of the right Russian embassy worker to bribe.

After bouncing around Moscow awhile, Doug's friend had gone home but Doug had fallen in love with the city and decided to stay. He'd opened a bar called the Moosehead with a trio of partners from the Caucasus—a Kalmuck and a two Chechens. One day, the Kalmuck had disappeared with all the club's capital. The Chechens had held Doug responsible because Doug had introduced them to the Kalmuck. Doug had squared things by giving the Chechens

THE SIBERIA JOB 19

his third of the club and walking away—that's when he'd started the Duck, and now the Chechens wanted half of that too.

At least, that's what Doug had said on the phone, when Petr called and asked if they could give him dinner at the Metropol. Doug had laughed and said, "Yeah, I'm not going to be out and about for a while. There's a contract on me."

John, who'd listened to the conversation over speakerphone, assumed Doug was joking. Apparently, he wasn't. He'd suggested they meet him at the Duck, where he was holding court like normal. Petr had never been before but Doug told him how to find it—directions that proved unnecessary because the cab they caught outside the Metropol (another Lada) knew exactly where it was. He pulled up at an archway leading into a somewhat dilapidated-looking courtyard, which was filled with men standing around in knots, smoking and drinking and checking their watches. At the far end was a narrow door with four large bodyguards in front of it, in two sets of two. Petr and John wended their way through the crowd and approached the guards.

The four guys looked like they were straight out of an eighties Schwarzenegger movie, with tailored leather coats, gelled hair, and steroid muscles. Before Petr could say anything, the man directly to the right of the door said, with practiced dismissive rudeness—and in English (did they look so obviously Western?)—"No men."

"We're here to see—"

"No men. Come back in an hour."

"We're here to see Doug Steele," said Petr. The man took a step forward.

"See him when you can get in. Come back in an hour."

"We came to meet him now. Go check with him," said John, sticking a cigarette in his mouth. "You have a lighter, or only matches?"

The man looked over his shoulder and said something to one of the other men. The man stepped in through the door; John could see him walking down a narrow stairway into a basement. He must have opened a second, soundproofed door, because, for a moment, thumping music spilled out into the courtyard, and then went quiet again.

"Lighter?" said John, making a striking gesture with his thumb. Without changing his expression, the big Schwarzenegger guard pulled out a Zippo, flipped it on, and held it out to John. John lit his cigarette, exhaled a puff of smoke, and said, "Thanks—care for a smoke? Laikas."

"You don't have American cigarettes?"

"No, but these are okay."

"Yes, fine. I'll take one," the man said. John held out the pack. As the man put the cigarette in his mouth, John took out his own lighter, flicked it on, and lit the man's cigarette. The man gave John a funny look; his colleague reappeared, said something in Russian, and the Schwarzenegger guard stepped aside.

"You can go down," he said. "Mr. Steele is at his table in the rear corner, that way." He gestured left.

"Thanks," said John.

"*Spasiba*," said Petr, as the two men walked past the guards, down the stairs, and through a heavy, recording-studio-style padded door.

On the other side of the door, the thumping music was back—but the scene was not at all what John had pictured. He'd assumed "no men" meant the club had too many guys in it and they weren't going to let in any more until a few left. In fact, the opposite was true—there were no men in the club at all. Just hordes of Russian girls, most of them very attractive, dancing, drinking, chatting—and watching a male stripper.

John and Petr looked at each other, and then back toward the center of the room, where the male stripper was pulling a girl up on stage and slipping her shirt over her head.

It looked like, beside John and Petr, this stripper was the only man in the room. The bartenders were girls too; so were the cocktail waitresses. Then Petr tapped John's shoulder and pointed to a corner booth visible on the other side of the stripper and his squeeze, where a rather unassuming man was smoking and reading a newspaper.

Petr leaned in close to John's ear and shouted—to be heard over the thumping—"THAT'S DOUG." John nodded, and they began to head that way, pushing through the mob of dancing, shouting girls. A few of them shrieked happily when they saw the two men moving amongst them, and John was pretty sure he got groped once or twice before arriving at Doug's table.

Petr and John sat down on either side of Doug, whose back was to the corner. It was a round table with a round bench around it, and it took some shimmying to get close enough to Doug for the men to talk.

When Doug saw them he half stood up—as much as he could in the booth—and reached a hand out to shake Petr's.

"Petr! So good to see you, guy, it's been a while! What brings you to Moscow? And you must be John—" Doug stuck his hand out again, and John shook it. "You want a drink? We've got some fantastic Pilsners, if you want a taste of home."

Petr nodded. "That'd be great." Doug waved to a drop-dead gorgeous waitress, put up three fingers and shouted, "Urquell."

"What the hell's going on here?" said Petr with a big smile on his face and a wave toward the sea of girls.

"This, friends, is the greatest marketing idea since P. T. Barnum popped off. It's ladies' night—which means ladies only until ten o'clock, no cover charge, free local beer, and male strippers. They party to their hearts, content without worrying about impressing guys—and then at ten o'clock, we let the guys in. At which point some of the girls leave, and the rest stay in a hunting ground of happy, horny girls. We could charge men a month's salary to get in here and they'd still be lining up around the block."

John laughed and nodded—P. T. Barnum–esque indeed. On stage, the girl and the stripper were both naked, except for the stripper's leather vest; he was holding her up, her legs were wrapped around his waist, and they were either having very public sex or else doing a very good imitation of it.

The waitress returned with three draft beers.

"So, what brings you to my door, boys?" said Doug, taking a sip. He was wearing a chic black suit and no tie, but John felt instantly at ease with his Canadian accent and manner.

"The Russian government's been issuing vouchers for stock auctions, for stock in state-run companies. You heard about it?"

Doug laughed. "Of course I've heard about it—they're absolutely everywhere. I bet half the girls in here right now have some in their purses."

"We want to buy some," said Petr. "Or at least, we want to find out if it's possible to buy some—buy a lot—in bulk."

"It's definitely possible," said Doug. "It's not my area, but they're definitely negotiable—I see people on street corners selling them, I've seen little kiosks set up to sell them. I'd say you have to know where to look but, honestly, they really are everywhere."

There was a type of "Ladies and Gentlemen—The Beatles!"-esque scream from the girls as a Black stripper in gold sequins jumped onto the catwalk.

"What about banking?" said John. "Is there a bank you trust for us to wire money to?"

"Hmm," said Doug, nodding his head thoughtfully. "Well—wait, hold on a sec." He put a finger up to shush them; at the same time, the Black stripper was silencing the crowd. He put his hand to his brow in a perfect, formal military salute . . . and the Russian national anthem began to play.

The women in the room all started singing it. Some of them looking serious, some of them laughing—when it got to the chorus, the lyrics briefly became chaotic as some of the women sang the words *"partiya Lenina"* and the others sang something different. John had heard the anthem thousands of times over the years, at the Olympics and so forth—rarely with the words, though. It hadn't occurred to him they'd have to be changed, to be decommunized.

The anthem ended and the music gracefully transitioned into Pat Benatar singing "Heartbreaker." Doug resumed: "There's one guy you can talk to about banking—I don't use him personally, because I'm not moving money in and out of the country, but I definitely trust him. He's an interesting guy, a real character, name of Benny Sheldon. He just backpacked into town one day, after the wall fell, looking for a soup kitchen to volunteer at. He couldn't find one—there literally aren't any, that I know of, in Moscow.

"At the time he was living at a hotel with a shitty gym, so he decided to start an American-style gym so he'd have a place to work out. It's called the Moscow Beach Club, got super popular. He missed American food, so he started an American-style diner, along with the only bar in town that I don't own that's worth going to—it's called Uncle Guilly's. And he started making a lot of money—he came from the banking world, Goldman Sachs maybe? Anyway, he needed a bank he trusted so he started one, with a couple Russian kids who had big plans but didn't know shit about the technical side. It ended up as part of the Dialog finance group—it's called Troika Dialog? Heard of it?"

Petr nodded his head yes.

"Is that a basketball joke?" said John. "'Triple-Double?'"

"Huh," said Doug. "I don't know, hadn't thought about it. Anyway, he's the guy to talk to. I'd take you over there myself—I could use a good steak, and Guilly's has got the only good ones in town—but, you know, there's this whole murder-contract thing."

"It would be embarrassing for us to get you killed," said Petr, with a smile, and a sip of his beer.

"Yeah, don't worry about it," said John. "You've already been extremely helpful; we owe you one."

Doug was looking at his watch, then tapping his fingers on the table.

"You know I haven't been out of this place in almost a week?" he said. He tapped his fingers a few more times. "Screw it. I'll take you over there. Don't talk to anyone on the street between my car and his front door, though, ha ha."

John half wanted to tell Doug not to come—out of concern for him, and concern for himself—he didn't particularly want to get caught in cross fire—but when a man's willing to risk assassination for a steak, no red-blooded American could, in good conscience, try to dissuade him.

Outside the Duck, the courtyard was even more packed with men than before, all counting down the minutes till ten o'clock when they'd be let inside. Doug said something in Russian to one of the guards and then waved for John and Petr to follow him toward the street—he was walking very fast through the groups of fecund smoking Russian men. They passed under the arch, out of the courtyard and back onto the street. None of them saw two men break away from one of the groups.

John felt a hand on the back of his collar and a kick to the side of his right foot, and suddenly he was falling backward; beside him Petr was falling too. He hit the ground hard, trying to figure out what was happening—a man was stepping over him and grabbing Doug. Another man was stepping over Petr and pulling open the door to a car. Doug connected a mean right hook to the face of the guy grabbing him; the guy responded with a jab to the gut, and then a sort of judo-twisty-thing, throwing Doug into the side of the car. Now he was pushing Doug into the open door; the other man was inside the car, pulling.

John and Petr were dazed, but not too dazed to figure out what was happening. They were pushing themselves back to their feet when a smallish swarthy man came running up the street in the other direction and delivered a full-body tackle to the man pushing Doug into the car. The swarthy man and the pusher crashed hard into the ground; John could hear the pusher's head crack on the cobble sidewalk. And now Doug was pulling away from the guy inside the car who'd been pulling him in. The guy had a death grip on Doug's left hand. Doug grabbed the car door with his right and slammed it as hard as he could onto the puller's arm. The man screamed. Doug opened the door and slammed it again. The car tore away from the curb, down the street, around a corner, and disappeared.

John and Petr were both back on their feet now, and Doug was hugging the swarthy guy. Petr leaned up against a wall to catch his breath; John knelt down and checked if the guy with the cracked head was alive.

"He's got a pulse," said John. "He needs an ambulance."

"They'll come back and get him in a minute," said Doug. "Guys, this is one of my bartenders, Asdrubal."

"Hola," said Asdrubal.

"He's Cuban," said Doug.

"My shift's about to start," said Asdrubal in lightly accented English.

"Thank Christ," said Doug. "You guys should go before we call someone. Here." He pulled out a pen and a business card and wrote an address on the back. "Show this to a cab driver and he'll get you to Guilly's. Say hi to Benny for me."

"Thanks," said Petr. "Sorry about all that."

"Sorry?" said Doug, laughing. "You got nothing to be sorry about. I need to bite the bullet and start paying someone protection money, I guess. Anyway, get going; if the cops pick you up for questioning it's going to be expensive as hell to get out of spending the night in jail."

"Thanks," said John. Petr was already flagging down a cab.

CHAPTER 4

Uncle Guilly's could hardly have been more different from the Hungry Duck. Instead of the giant crowd, the thumping, pulsating girls, the strippers, the sequins, Guilly's looked like it belonged in a London pub's guidebook. A 1938 edition. Stepping inside, it was like John had gone back in time—one week, to when he was in London going to old pubs. It was warm and inviting; the clientele were mostly men, sitting in pairs at the few dozen tables or at the bar; everyone was drinking beer; several were eating steaks. A youngish guy in a tidy suit was playing darts with a youngish guy in a Hawaiian shirt.

Petr pointed to him. "You think that's Benny?"

They walked over to him, skirting around the tables.

"Mr. Sheldon?" said Petr, who was first to reach him. The man in the Hawaiian shirt was just about to throw. He looked at Petr, then back at the dart board, hit a double sixteen, said to his opponent, "That's sixteen closed—that's game, I think," and then to Petr, "Yeah, I'm Benny Sheldon." He stuck his hand out and Petr shook it. He shook John's hand next and asked what he could do for them.

◆

At a booth opposite the bar, John and Petr sat on one side, facing Benny on the other. He had his hands laced behind his head and was looking up at the ceiling, thinking something over.

"Yeah," he said after a moment. "I don't see any problem handling that kind of money; we're pretty heavily capitalized—in dollars—and we've got a solid reputation with everyone. From the beginning, our deal has been no corruption, no bribes, no shady business of any kind. And it turns out that even the corrupt and shady bribe-takers decided that having a bank people trusted was good for everyone. Good for the country, and good for them—I don't think they're being altruistic, exactly, but we're definitely opening the door to foreign investment. I mean, there's already a huge amount of hard stuff in Russia—dollars, pounds, yen, et cetera—but people are still bringing it in duffle bags, you know what I mean? You can't build a thriving economy that way. Foreign money coming in is good for everyone. Basically, we're trying to help Russia build a trade surplus.

"As for vouchers, we're already doing a huge amount of that—mostly registering them for people, you know, taking them to the auctions and then the formal stock issuances, but also buying them. And I'd say probably . . . half? maybe more? of the people who work for me are just doing voucher paperwork, all day, every day, 'cause we have people dealing in stacks of like, ten thousand vouchers, coming here from Kyiv with a whole town's worth of the things, and every single voucher needs to have an individual, hand-filled-out form. Each one has a nine-digit number on it. It's like if before you could put money in the bank, you had to hand-copy the serial number off every bill."

John and Petr were nodding along; Benny was looking at one of his waiters, who had a hand raised to get his attention.

"Sorry to monologue and run, boys, but I got to head back to the back and check a shipment. US Prime from Chicago."

"US Prime?" said Petr. "Are you buying mortgages?"

Benny laughed. "Beef." He dropped a business card on the table as he stood. "If you want to bank with us, give me a call—here or at the office. And let me know if you want to buy a health club."

"The Moscow Beach Club? Doug mentioned it," said John. "You're selling?"

"Yeah," said Benny. "It's getting too dangerous. Tired of seeing mafiosos come in with gold-plated Colts."

"Fair enough," said John, and with a final "Later, guys," Benny walked away toward his kitchen. John turned to Petr: "So, what do you think?"

"I don't think I want to own a beach club in Moscow."

"Mm. But do you want to bank with him?"

Petr lit a cigarette. "What do you think of him?" he said, after a slow exhale.

"I like him," said John. "And Doug likes him."

Petr nodded. "Well—let's do a test transfer, see how it goes. Before you get to work raising capital, we need some seed money . . . what do you think, fifty thousand each?"

"How much of that's going to be eaten up getting an office in place?"

"I really have no idea—real estate prices in Moscow, they say, are crazy."

"Yeah," said John, scratching his temple with his thumb. "How about this: we set up a test wire to Benny's bank, and then I find us an office while you start talking to your business contacts about where the voucher deals are. I've got to say I'm a little worried about how many people seem to be doing this already."

Petr shook his head. "They're locals. We can beat their returns—if we don't get"—he put a finger-gun up to his head and mimed pulling a trigger—"first. But, yes, tomorrow I will begin to speak to my friends here. We will ferret. Ferret?" John nodded. "Ferret out the deals."

John nodded again. "Good, sounds good."

"Can you handle finding an office though, not speaking the language?"

"Yeah, sure," said John. "I'll get a translator; shouldn't be too hard. It's a buyers' market."

"Yes," said Petr. "So . . . it's still early?"

"Not for me," said John. "I'm wiped out. I'm going back to the hotel and calling my wife, let her know things look sort of promising here."

"I wouldn't tell her about the Hungry Duck kidnapping thing."

John smiled. "Good advice. You going to stay out?"

"For a little while, maybe. Maybe go back to the Hungry Duck, check on Doug. Maybe tell Benny we're going to try him out?"

"Thanks," said John. "You don't mind if I leave you here?"

Petr smiled. "It's okay, I know how to entertain myself."

John nodded. "I'll see you back at the Metropol then."

CHAPTER 5

The next morning, John was sitting in his and Petr's shared sitting room. He was drinking coffee, eating a Danish, and reading a newspaper—all of which had been procured for him, for a modest fee, by the indefatigable bellman Slava. The door to Petr's bedroom opened and an utterly stunning, long-legged, pale-eyed brunette stepped through it. John must have looked surprised, because she smiled mischievously and said, "Pardon me for interrupting you—have you seen my dress?"

She was carrying a pair of high heels, one in each hand. Aside from a pair of panties, she was nude.

"I'm afraid not," said John.

"Oh, it's okay," said the girl, opening a French door onto the terrace. "Here it is." She stepped onto the balcony and reentered more or less fully clothed in a satiny and very short, strapless party dress. At the same time, Petr emerged from his bedroom, smiling.

"John," he said with a hint of ironic glee, "guess what? I found you a translator!"

John looked at the girl, who was bent over, putting on her shoes. She smiled.

"I hired her for twenty-four hours, so . . . you've got like eighteen left to find us a good base of operations, yeah?" Petr was pouring himself a cup of coffee from Slava's silver pot.

John laughed, shaking his head. "Well, perfect." He took a sip of his own coffee, and looked at the girl. "You want to change into something a little less formal before we get going?"

"It's okay," she said. "I have an overcoat. And maybe," she gestured to her revealing outfit, "it will come in handy."

John nodded. "Sounds good."

◆

Calling the Moscow property market crazy had been an understatement. After several hours on speaker phone calls, with the girl Yekaterina translating, John was finally able to track down a broker who had office space that was both uncommitted and not astronomically expensive. It was utterly bizarre—twenty miles south, John and Petr probably could have purchased entire towns for a few hundred American dollars, but in Moscow the buyer's market—the real estate buyer's market, anyway—had been turned on its ear.

No matter how wild-wild and west a country is, as long as it has the largest nuclear arsenal in the world, people are going to be sucking up to its government. And it seemed that every NGO and lobbying group and multinational in the world—even the ones who weren't ready to put a penny into the venture side of the market—wanted an office adjacent to the Kremlin. They wanted a foot in the door.

According to the landlord who drove John and Yekaterina out to the office space he had on offer, most of the offices in Moscow were totally empty, just waiting for people to decide Russia seemed stable enough for it to be worth putting in fax lines and setting up Bloomberg terminals. Or whatever.

It was a good twenty minutes from the center of the town, on a run-down street. It was a large, boxy, depressingly Soviet-looking building that took up most of the block. John wondered what it had been before falling vacant. Too many spy novels had made him picture most innocuous Moscow office buildings as having some sort of Lubyanka Prison in the basement. More likely, he figured, the building was one of the near infinite bureaucratic offices that had found itself without any money or workers or purpose after the collapse of Communism.

"Who were the last tenants?" said John to Yekaterina.

"Tenants?" said Yekaterina.

"Who used to work here?"

Yekaterina translated the question for the rental agent.

"Speakerphone telephone company," said Yekaterina. John nodded.

"Is the place set up with utilities? I mean, electric, water, heating. Phone lines?"

Yekaterina asked, then answered the question. "He says, yes water, no everything else. But he has someone who can turn them on, and someone to install phones, for a low price."

They had stepped into the building's low, unimpressive lobby. Everything was done up in wood veneer or green paint where one or the other hadn't begun to peel. John walked past a receptionist's desk into a hallway and stuck his head into the first office. It had the same depressing decor and a little furniture that looked as if it belonged in a 1950s American high school. All the same, there was no draft, and it seemed dry and basically habitable.

"Which offices is he renting?" said John.

Yekaterina got the answer. "All of them," she said.

"How much for this one, to start with?"

Yekaterina asked the realtor, who seemed to do some math out loud, looking at the ceiling, and then said, "One thousand dollars American," in English.

"For how long?"

Yekaterina asked. "One month," she said.

"You're joking."

"He says he's not joking. He says it's a good deal for this close to Moscow center."

"Will that include utilities once they're on?"

"He says no."

"How much with utilities?"

"He says two thousand a month, with electricity, water, and heat. But not phone. He doesn't do the phone."

"Tell him I'll give him five hundred for the office with utilities."

"He says no."

John shrugged and began to walk out toward the street.

"He says you won't find a better deal, but on second thought, the thousand dollars does include electricity, water, and heat."

John said, "Tell him I'll take it for two months with an option to extend, but no deposit until everything gets turned on. Including him sending his phone guy out here."

"He says that's okay. He says if you wait here, he will send the telephone guy, and tomorrow collect the deposit. He says failure to pay the deposit is very serious crime in Russia, but he'll let you pay tomorrow."

"Tell him sure, that's fine."

She told the rental guy. He answered. She said something else. They had a short conversation in Russian.

"What's going on?" said John.

"I have to go now, he offered me a job."

"What?"

"He offered me a job."

"Doing what?"

"Secretary. Full-time."

"What am I supposed to do for a translator out here in the sticks?"

"The sticks?"

"Out here away from the center of town."

"He says the telephone man speaks English. He will have him here in one hour."

◆

The telephone guy did speak English, after a fashion—though he didn't arrive for about six hours. When he showed up, John was asleep, stretched out on his back on top of the reception desk, with his jacket for a pillow. The telephone guy shook him awake.

"Which room for phone?"

John held up a hand to indicate he needed a minute, then shook himself awake and slid down from the desk. "Over here," he said, and led the way. John sat down at the office desk while the telephone guy worked unscrewing jack caps and then running cable from one that worked.

"What's your name, sir?" said John after a few minutes, both out of Texas politeness and festering boredom.

"Andrei," said the telephone guy.

"I'm John," said John. Andrei looked up at him and nodded his head.

"Thank you," by which he meant—John thought—good to meet you.

"Have you been a telephone man since before the end of the Soviet Union?"

"I was everything," said Andrei. He was a youngish guy, early twenties, dark hair, strongly built, and quite tall.

"Where did you learn English?"

"*Cheers*," said Andrei.

"Huh? Cheers?"

"*Cheers, Cheers*, you know, Boston, Bean Town, where everybody knows your name. Sam and Diane and Frasier."

"Oh," said John. He chuckled. "That's great. How did you see *Cheers* here?"

"Radio broadcast from Finland."

"Radio?"

"Yeah, just sound, no picture. Good, to help focus on the words."

"Huh," said John. "Very impressive."

"Yes," said Andrei, removing a beige, plastic rotary phone from his toolbox and putting it on the office desk.

"Andrei, do you know anything about vouchers? Business privatization vouchers?"

"Yes," said Andrei.

"How much?"

"Everything," said Andrei.

"Where's the best place to buy them?"

"Voucher market."

"There's a voucher market?"

"Yes. At convention center, by GUM store."

John tried to suss that out. "By a gum store?"

"By *the* GUM store," said Andrei, stressing the definite article as if to stress he knew how to use it. "By *the* Red Square, but on *the* other side. GUM is *Glavny Universalny Magazin*. Means 'primary universal store.' Convention center behind it has *the* voucher market inside."

"Can you show me?" said John.

Andrei shrugged. "Yes."

"Great, thanks. Wait one second while I call my partner. Is the telephone on?"

"Yes."

"Great," said John. An operator connected him to the Metropol, but there was no answer at his and Petr's suite. He left a message for Petr with the desk, suggesting they meet at the hotel for dinner, and then he walked with Andrei out to Andrei's work Lada. On the way, he asked Andrei if he'd like a job as a translator and guide. Andrei thought about it for a moment before saying yes. John suggested either doubling Andrei's current salary or an hourly rate. Andrei suggested fifty dollars American, a week. They shook on it.

The convention center was gray and run-down but it had the surging energy of the New York Stock Exchange. Here again was the weird combination of shiny-suited men and dowdy babushkas. Also some more-serious-looking guys in quieter, better-cut suits, and some uniformed policemen and soldiers—though John couldn't tell if they were on or off duty.

People were walking in with tied bundles of vouchers in gunny sacks. Guys were walking with phalanxes of security guards carrying light machine guns and briefcases filled, John assumed, with cash. Walking farther into the room, John started to figure that the place was organized in a sort of concentric series of trade levels.

The lowest level, at the outermost "ring" of tables, were low-level Moscow workers and peasants from the countryside, who were trading handfuls of vouchers for canned goods, dry goods, bottles of vodka, toiletries. It was like a series of food-stamp bodegas but the food stamps were stock vouchers.

The guys at the tables trading vouchers for vodka, et al, were then turning around and selling their vouchers to the next "ring" of tables; they were selling bundles of tens or hundreds of vouchers to guys who were assembling them into bundles of thousands. The guys with bundles of thousands were selling to private speculators—mostly, it seemed, the flashy-dressed young men—but at the same time, negotiating deals to sell their bundles of thousands farther inward, to a small ring of big shots who were buying hundreds of thousands or millions of vouchers, and dividing them into individual piles by type and business (Andrei explained).

Here were the well-tailored suits—and some of the vulgar ones—and some of the model-esque girls, in high heels, on people's arms—negotiating huge deals. This is where the briefcases of money were going. Standing just close enough to eavesdrop on one of the deals, John asked Andrei to translate.

"The guy in the shirt is selling vouchers for machine manufacturing companies. The guy in the suit is arguing over the price. The guy in the shirt wants ten dollars a voucher. The guy in the suit says he won't go above nine-ninety."

"What kind of machine manufacturers?"

"No, machines—*mashinas*—it means *automobile*. The company they're arguing over makes springs, for the wheels, you know."

John nodded; Andrei continued. "They settled on nine-nine-five, and the guy buying will raise the number he'll buy by an extra two hundred vouchers." The negotiating parties shook hands, and the guy in the suit turned and said something to a security man standing next to him. Then he put a briefcase on the table next to the vouchers, opened it, and began to remove bundles of American money.

"How much is the guy buying?"

"Forty thousand, two hundred and one vouchers."

John watched the man count out forty stacks of what must of have been thousand-dollar bundles, in twenties. The two men then began to count—the guy buying the vouchers counted them; the guy selling counted the money.

"They're looking for counterfeits," said Andrei. "Both of them."

John pulled a pen out of a pocket along with a crumple of notepaper he always carried. He began to jot down notes on the transaction and the prices, and spoke to Andrei while he was writing.

"Andrei—I want to get the name of every company whose vouchers are being sold back here—any company with more than a thousand vouchers for sale. Start asking the guys what they have and what the prices are. Can you do that?"

"Sure I can," said Andrei—then, after a moment's hesitation, added, "boss."

"Just call me John," said John.

CHAPTER 6

Back at the Metropol—after sharing a laugh about the prosti-translator that John had lost—John and Petr began to compare notes. John had assembled a list of companies that could be bought, and Petr—after trawling through his Russian business contacts—had assembled a list of companies whose assets were suspected to be underreported, whose stock would therefore be undervalued, and whose vouchers would therefore be a good investment. They checked their lists against each other's and found a half dozen companies on both. And instantly a plan began to come together.

First things first. They would buy up as many of the cross-referenced undervalued vouchers as they could. Then Petr would begin hunting for vouchers for the undervalued companies not on John's list, and John would begin raising money to pay for them.

John told Petr he'd hired Andrei to stay on as a sort of man-of-all-work—driving or translating or fixing things as needed. Petr agreed he'd be a good man to have around. Petr called Benny to arrange to set up a wire account and John called Sheremetyevo Airport to book the first leg of his round-the-world investment fundraising tour. His flight would leave at nine A.M.

The last thing John did before knocking off for the night was to call Andrei and arrange for Andrei to drive him to Sheremetyevo and then come back to take Petr to their office. Petr suggested they go back to the Hungry Duck to celebrate the birth of their investment group. John declined with a yawn and asked Petr to try to avoid getting kidnapped or anything.

◆

John woke up to Andrei knocking on the door—the front door of the suite. John stepped out of his bedroom at the same time Petr stepped out of his, visibly hungover, and scowling.

"Tell whoever's knocking on our door," said Petr, stopping to take a breath. "Tell him that when this fund is capitalized, I'm going to hire Doug's Chechen friends to kill him."

"It's okay," said John, "it's just Andrei. He's taking me to Sheremetyevo."

"Oh," said Petr. "Right, I remember." He turned to go back into his room. "If you're going to Sheremetyevo, though, I suggest you put on pants."

John chuckled and opened the door. It wasn't Andrei.

"Hi," said the guy on the other side of the door. "I'm George Menshikov. I wonder if I could talk to you about your investment fund."

". . . What?" said John.

"I heard, yesterday, from an acquaintance of mine, that Petr Kovac and his partner John Mills are starting a nationalization-voucher investment fund. I wanted to know if I could talk to you about it."

"You're an American?" said John.

"Yes, dual citizen. I take it you're John Mills."

John nodded. "*Who* are you?"

"George Menshikov."

"Yeah, I heard you the first time—I mean, who *are* you? Are you an investor? Sorry, I'm a little foggy here, I just woke up like fifteen seconds ago. You know, when you started knocking on the door."

"I'm with *Forbes*," said Menshikov. "I'm a writer. A journalist."

Petr had been standing in the doorway of his bedroom. Now he walked over to stand beside John.

"A journalist?" he said.

"Yes," said Menshikov.

"We're busy," said Petr, and closed the door. "Some other time perhaps," he added, loudly enough for Menshikov to hear him in the hallway.

"Uh . . . okay," answered Menshikov.

"Some press would help the fund," said John—quietly enough for Menshikov not to hear him in the hallway.

"Not in Russia," said Petr, and walked back to his room.

CHAPTER 7

By the midnineties, Tokyo was among the richest and most cosmopolitan cities in the world and flying into it at night was like landing at the edge of a Times Square the size of Rhode Island. John landed at Narita International Airport just before eleven, local time. His was the last flight in before Narita closed for the night as part of a compromise on noise pollution that had sort of ended decades of not-quite-terrorism from left-wing student groups. The airport was consequently quiet and sleepy, and so was John, who was in his hotel—the Imperial Hotel, very fancy but a shadow of its former, Frank Lloyd Wright–designed self—by midnight.

He called his wife to let her know he'd made it, then slept till a six A.M. wake-up call. He was carrying coffee out to a cab by six-thirty, and by eight he was rolling up the cherry tree–lined driveway of his elderly industrialist friend Soichiro Yamamura.

The Yamamura estate—made from whole cloth by Soichiro himself—was possibly the most beautiful place John had ever been, and certainly the most peaceful. It was quintessential old Japan in design, with the quaint and unassuming wooden buildings, the paper walls and sliding doors, the immaculately tended rock gardens, the ever-blooming trees, the koi brooks and half-moon bridges, and in the near background, Mount Fuji.

Soichiro, a perennial early riser, was at his breakfast table on a lawn edged by cherry trees, cross-legged on a mat on the ground, in khakis and a collared shirt with rolled-up sleeves, reading *The Wall Street Journal*. The table was laid with American breakfast foods and—for use only when Soichiro was in private or with close friends—forks.

It was a curious mix of East and West. Particularly the forks. John had never seen another member of the Japanese upper class eat with one in Japan. John had finally asked Soichiro one day why he didn't use chopsticks. He'd said that Japan is the most sanitary country in the world in every way but eating with wooden utensils. John asked why he didn't use disposable chopsticks. Soichiro said it was bad for forests. John suggested metal chopsticks, and Soichiro asked him, what was he, a chopstick detective? Anyway, only Koreans used metal chopsticks. John had dropped the matter there.

"John!" said Soichiro, as a servant of some sort led him over to the breakfast table. "So good to see you. I was surprised to get your call; please have a seat."

"Soichiro, it's good to see you too. I'd almost forgotten how lovely your place here is."

"Well, you should visit it more often," said Soichiro, pouring John a glass of orange juice.

"I should," said John. "Maybe I'd be able to work out how it is that you never seem to age." Soichiro was seventy but looked fifty and had the energy of a thirty-year-old. "I'd say it must be the healthy Japanese food but I get the feeling you eat more bacon than I do."

"Hot baths, cold baths, long swims, and fresh air, young John."

"It's not quitting smoking and drinking and fried foods?"

"You know what Freud's son, the painter, said about that. If you quit smoking it doesn't make you live longer, it just makes it feel longer." John laughed. "How was your flight?"

"Good," said John.

"No trouble at Narita?"

"None."

"Good," said Soichiro. "Haneda used to be the main international airport, you know, until the late seventies. They insist on using Narita now for international flights, out of bloody-mindedness, I think. The government won't give in to the student idiots, which is a good thing, I suppose. But at some point I wonder if it's worth the trouble. And what happened in Tel Aviv can happen here, you know, with the Japanese Red Army." He was talking about the Lod Airport massacre, where three Japanese far-left terrorists had flown to Israel and murdered twenty-six random people at Lod Airport and injured eighty others to strike a blow against international capitalism or something.

"It's terrible," Soichiro continued. "We have it going both ways. The Marxists tried gassing a suburb of Tokyo a few weeks ago, and then you've got the right-imperialist neo-Samurai murdering politicians on live TV and attempting coups. It makes me long for the simple, peaceful days of World War Two." He smiled to show he was joking, and John chuckled.

"Yeah, I bet," he said.

"Well, enough small talk," said Soichiro. "If Tokyo is going to become Belfast, we should try to enjoy life while we can. I gather you're starting your own fund?"

"I am," said John. "Are you familiar with the privatization vouchers being issued in former Eastern Bloc Communist countries?"

"Yes," said Soichiro. "Vaguely."

"I'm working with a guy named Petr Kovac who made a killing using vouchers to buy undervalued assets in Czechoslovakia. We're going to try to duplicate his success in Russia, on a much bigger scale."

"What are the terms?"

"Petr and I split fifty percent."

Soichiro put down his fork and dabbed his mouth with a napkin. He was silent for about twenty seconds, before returning his napkin to his lap.

"I'm in for five million."

"Just like that?"

"Just like that," said Soichiro. "Now, have some breakfast."

◆

The next morning, around five A.M., John landed at LAX. It was two years after the Rodney King riots but, if LAX was any indication, the city was still a mess. The thought popped spontaneously into John's head that the floors at Narita had looked cleaner than the tabletops in the LAX food courts.

Stepping out into the smog, John was annoyed with himself for thinking so much better of Tokyo than Los Angeles—as if he were letting the American side down. But Los Angeles was *sui generis* and John had never been a huge fan. He did have a good friend out here, a guy he'd made a lot of money for at Merrill Lynch, who'd decided to use his windfall to start an independent studio. Now he was even richer and an "artistically" respected Hollywood big shot to boot.

John stole a few hours of sleep at the Chateau Marmont and, by noon, was rolling up into the Hollywood hills to one of those giant stilt-houses that looks down at LA the way the Olympian god looked down on Greece. "Looking down" in both the literal and metaphorical sense. Generally speaking, anyway. In spite of the corrupting influence of money and power—not to mention Hollywood—Donny Dietrich was a good guy and John liked him.

John's cab dropped him at Donny's gate. John pressed the call button and a scratchy intercom voice told him to find his way to the pool, which was nestled in the center of Donny's circular mansion like the yolk in a fried egg. Donny was there, waiting, lying out on a pool chair, barefoot, in linen shorts and a New Jersey Devils home jersey with its sleeves cut off. He had a little intercom box on the ground next to him, which apparently doubled as a radio, and was playing a Beach Boys song.

"John!" he said, swinging his feet down from the pool chair and slipping them into a pair of New Jersey Devils flip flops. "How the heck are you?"

"Oh, pretty good, pretty good," said John, taking off his sport coat to come a little closer to matching Donny's level of sartorial formality. "How's the movie business?"

"It's great, loads of fun," said Donny, reaching out to shake John's hand, and pointing him toward a plastic table and its chairs, all in wild, transparent colors, sort of like a reduction of abstract, extremely ugly stained glass. Very chic.

Donny followed John, rolling a drink table with him. "You know who Quentin Tarantino is?" he said, starting to mix something fruity.

"Uh . . . no," said John, sitting down on the neon-lime chair.

"He's a writer-director who's breaking huge. Anyway, I've just found the next Quentin Tarantino. He's gonna break huge too."

"Is that a Hollywood name?"

"Quentin Tarantino?"

"Yeah."

"No, I'm pretty sure that's his real name."

"Don't think I've ever heard of someone named Quentin, outside of Quent McHale."

"Who?"

"McHale's Navy?"

"Oh, right."

"And Captain Quent, of course."

"Of course," said Donny, handing John a drink.

"What is this?" said John, taking a sip.

"An alcoholic beverage."

"What's in it?"

"One part alcohol; two parts beverage."

"It's good."

"Well, enjoy it, 'cause I have no idea how to remake it. I don't even know what's in some of these bottles . . . the fruit juice could be grapefruit, peach, watermelon? I think one of these is Hawaiian punch. And for all I know the alcohol is grappa—I don't drink that much. I only have this for guests."

"Oh, well, don't drink on my account."

"Oh, no, I like drinking, but if people in this town see you with a can of beer they figure you're on the way out and stop answering your calls."

John laughed.

"So what can I do for you, John, or is this a purely social call?"

"No, it's business."

"Are you trying to sell a screenplay? 'Cause I'm full up at the moment, but I suppose you could take a shot at being the next-next Quentin Tarantino."

"I'm here because when you cashed out of the Merrill Lynch fund you told me to stay in touch if I ever went private."

"You're starting your own fund?"

"I am."

"Awesome."

"You want in on it?"

"Absolutely. I've got too much liquidity right now, which is never a good idea in Hollywood—you start to get ideas about financing art movies out of your own pocket. Action stuff's a good investment but, God, if you knew how close I came to backing a movie about Queen Victoria the playgirl . . ." Donny shuttered.

"The playgirl? Have you ever seen a photo of Queen Victoria?"

"Yep. But she's the chick they named Victoria's Secret after."

"Seriously?"

"Seriously. But do you want to talk lingerie or do you want to talk cash?"

"That reminds me, I want to buy something for my wife before I head back to LAX."

"Do you think she'd like a complete skeleton of a Tyranno-saurus rex?

"Uh . . . no."

"Shame. I think Nic Cage is selling one."

◈

John had figured on spending more time with Donny before getting on his next flight, but Donny had jumped in so quickly that he'd begged off—not something you'd do with a normal investor, but . . . well, Donny was a good guy, and John told him his wife had had to leave London to take care of her father, who'd been sick, and John hadn't seen her in almost two months. Donny just laughed and asked what he was still doing in LA, drove John back to the Chateau Mormont to grab his bags, and then drove him to the airport.

John had been on a plane home by a little after nine in the evening. He could've made a flight an hour earlier, but it had taken Donny and him a while to figure out how to get both himself and his bag into the passenger seat of Donny's 25th Anniversary Edition Lamborghini Countach, which appeared to have been designed to accommodate no more than a single unencumbered Oompa-Loompa.

At LAX John had called his wife to tell her he was coming but that his plane wasn't getting in till around midnight and not to bother picking him up. He knew she was wiped out taking care of her folks and he didn't want her driving two hours to get him and then two hours back.

But when he walked into the arrivals terminal, heading for the taxi stand, there she was, holding up a little sign with "J. MILLS" written on it. They had one of those reverse-Casablanca airport embraces. John gave her a little smack on the rear for being such a headstrong, uncontrollable, cowgirl sort of a wife, and then fished the keys out of her hip pocket. They walked back to the car holding hands.

John was originally from Oregon, and he never got tired of Marsha's accent. He listened to her give him the news from the home front and felt very glad to be back in Texas. She asked to hear everything about the Russia deal, and it wasn't till they were on Route 35 heading home that she told him she had some news of her own. He asked what it was, and she said—rather smugly—

"We're going to have a baby."

John turned so aggressively to look at her that he almost drove the car off the road. They were coming up to a truck stop. He pulled off the highway and then onto the grass by the side of the exit ramp so he could embrace her. An eighteen-wheeler honked at them as it rolled past.

It was an idyllic day with Marsha, back home in Texas. John did nothing but sit around the house, eat (at long last) some real food, and admire his wife. But an idyllic day was all he could spare—one idyllic day, and it was back on the road again, back to Dallas Fort Worth for the next leg of his fundraising world tour. It was a three-hour flight to Washington, DC—specifically, to Washington National Airport, which, at least, was a damn sight better than flying into Dulles. A quick stopover at the Hay-Adams to drop off his luggage, and then to K Street, to meet with Jim Schultz at his corner office in one of the most influential law firms anywhere in the world.

◆

Jim Schultz was the consummate Washington insider. Few outside the Beltway had ever heard of him, but he'd been directly involved in more major geopolitical events than nearly anyone alive. He'd been hired by the FBI straight out of the University of Texas and had worked on counterespionage throughout the Second World War. Schultz was in Dallas the day JFK was shot and, in the succeeding maelstrom, had been drafted as an advisor by LBJ. That was the beginning of a tour de force through every subsequent administration, Democrat and Republican. His straightforward and pragmatic common sense was currency in DC.

In the late seventies, Carter made Schultz his top trade rep and sent him off to booming industrial Japan. It was the first trip of what would become two decades of on and off trade-work there, during which he would eventually meet young banker and fellow Texan John Mills. Schultz was considerably older but took an instant shine to John—who was, by then, rapidly making a name for himself by rapidly making money for other people. They stayed in touch and, like Soichiro and Donny, he'd told John to keep him in mind if ever he started a fund of his own. Which was why John was heading to Schultz's office on K Street.

After Japan and a successful trade deal, Schultz continued pinch-hitting in various international arenas, finally winding up as a special envoy and trade ambassador to the Soviet Union. When Yeltsin had fended off a Communist coup in the early years of post-Soviet Russia, Schultz was standing beside him. Literally standing beside him, on the tank with which he faced down the Communist conspirators. So, as John headed to Schultz's office on K Street—to the law firm he'd joined after the first Bush left office—it was with the knowledge that Schultz understood the vast potential of the Russian market.

"You're investing in Russia?" said Schultz, as he shook John's hand. "You want something to drink? Coffee? Tea? Vodka?"

"Nothing, thanks," said John. "I know you're busy, I won't keep you too long. Yes, we're investing in Russia. You want in?"

Schultz laughed from his belly and took a seat on a couch, waving John to a couch opposite.

"No fucking way," said Schultz.

"What?" said John.

"Do you know what it's like over there? I mean, big improvement from Communism but the teething pains are intense. Until they get used to a free-market economy, any money you pour into a Russian business is going right down the drain. I'd advise against it."

"Too risky?"

"Much too risky," said Schultz. "You're going to be investing in companies that are being privatized through the IMF voucher system. They're going to be sold to random Russians for a tiny fraction of their value. Everything you invest is going to get eaten up in the transfer."

"Uh-huh," said John. "That's why we're not investing in companies; we're investing in vouchers."

Suddenly Schultz looked more interested. "Wait, you mean you're not investing in Russia, you're investing *in* Russia? I mean to say, you're going to be opening a Russia office? You can't buy vouchers internationally."

"I know. And yes."

"Huh," said Schultz. John said nothing, letting him ruminate.

"It'll be dangerous," said Schultz.

"Yeah," said John.

"And I don't mean financially. I mean, it may be very dangerous to your . . . you know. To your person. Someone may take a shot at you."

"Yup."

Schultz resumed his rumination.

"But then, once the shares become internationally negotiable, you'll clean up."

"That's the idea," said John.

"Well, I'll give you this much, Mills: you've got spunk. A hell of a lot of spunk."

John nodded. "Yes, I have."

"Well," said Schultz. "Well—well, Jesus. If you're willing to risk your life, I think I can risk a little money. *Qui audet adipiscitur.* Where do you want me to sign?"

John began pulling paperwork out of his briefcase. *"Qui audet adipiscitur?"*

"The motto of the British SAS: 'Who Dares Wins.'"

◆

John felt as if he'd barely closed his eyes, back at the Hay-Adams, when the telephone opened them again. His room was dark; he had no idea what time it was. He reached his hand toward the insistent ringing, and, on his third attempt, got hold of the handset.

"Hello?" said John, through a deep yawn. "Who is this? And do you know what time it is? That's not a rhetorical question. I don't think the Hay-Adams uses luminous digital clocks . . ."

On the other end of the phone, Petr began to shout—not because of a bad connection, but out of uncontainable excitement: "We've got sixty percent of Kursk Tobacco! Sixty percent! We have a controlling interest in the third largest tobacco company in the former Soviet Union!"

John snapped upright in bed—"Kursk Tobacco . . . that was on your list, right? Heavily undervalued?"

"Yes! They're basically the top distributor to Asian Russia, and the ex-commie-stans, and the Caucasus countries. They're goddamn huge."

"Jesus Christ," John was out of bed and kicking away the bedclothes that he'd dragged with him, tangled up around his ankles. "Benny must be greased lightning—you got cash on the wire from Japan already?"

"No!" said Petr. "I mean, yes, the money from Yamamura's already in the bank and Benny's got cash to cover it, but I haven't touched it yet—I got fifteen thousand vouchers at that warehouse for sixty thousand dollars. Only one other guy showed up at the auction, carrying ten thousand vouchers, so he got forty percent and we got sixty."

"My sweet lord," said John. "The estimated assets value you got on Kursk Tobacco was—"

"Thirty million dollars, give or take."

"So we just spent sixty thousand dollars, and bought *eighteen million?*"

"We sure goddamn did—soon as the stock becomes negotiable."

"Jesus God Almighty," John sat down on the side of the bed. "I can't believe it. When can we meet with the company directors?"

"I've got it set up for next Monday. Can you get back here by then?"

"I'll be there, don't worry. I've got two more stops planned. Though . . ."

"Yeah—screw your other stops John, between this deal and the LA-Tokyo money, we're set up. We could make this a billion-dollar fund without giving away another bit of equity."

"Jesus," John repeated. There was a brief silence while they considered the implications. "Hey Petr, you want to hear something *really* great?"

"Huh?" said Petr.

"I'm gonna be a father!"

CHAPTER 8

The boardroom of Kursk Tobacco looked like every other "nice" office John had seen so far in Russia—wood veneer and Soviet Deco wall clock. It was in a "nice" office building not far from the Kremlin. John and Petr were sitting on one side of a long table. On the other side was a solemn-looking, slightly overweight Russian man.

"Gentlemen," he said in English. "I understand you wish to exert some control over the operations of the company."

"Yes," said Petr.

"That is, of course, your right as majority shareholders. Or at least, it will be your right, as majority shareholders once you sign our investiture documents. But the minority shareholders wish to make something clear before you do."

"Who are the minority shareholders?" said Petr.

"They wish to remain anonymous," said the man. "But you may think of them as *Bratya*."

"*Bratya?*" said John

"Literally, it means 'brothers,'" said Petr, who was looking uncomfortable.

"What does it mean not literally?" said John.

"Mafia," said Petr. John nodded, and for a moment no one said anything.

"Are they trying to keep us from taking possession of our share in the company?" said John, finally.

"No," said the man. "In fact, they can see many advantages to your being majority shareholders of Kursk. But they wish first for you to understand the responsibilities that will go along with your ownership."

"Which are?" said John, after a pause.

"Kursk has an unusual business model. You will be legally liable for it. Not that there is any cause for concern."

"What's the business model?" said Petr.

"It is generally understood that Kursk manufactures and distributes cigarettes."

He paused and, after a moment, Petr said, "Okay?"

"But it is does not only manufacture Kursk cigarettes."

". . . I don't follow," said John.

"Kursk also manufactures, uh . . . Marlboros, Camels, Lucky Strikes, Parliaments, Pall Malls, Newport, Winston. Kursk manufactures maybe one in three of Western cigarettes sold in Eastern Russia and Central Asia."

"You make counterfeit cigarettes?" said John

"And now you do too," said the Kursk man.

"Jesus," said John.

"Are you saying that's how you generate your revenue? Fake name-brand cigarettes?"

"No," said the Kursk man. "Not at all. No, Kursk is legitimately a very profitable business. And illegitimately, a much, much more profitable business. But here is the issue: your new partners do not intend to modify this business plan. With Westerners—if Czech counts, too, as Westerners—uh, nominally?—yes, nominally running the company, your partners believe it could help to expand these operations to new markets. Mutually beneficial? Everyone earns, you see. But as I said, you will be liable to Russian courts. If you do not wish to participate in this business model, your partners will then buy you out. The choice is yours."

John and Petr looked at each other. Each saw the other was at a loss. Petr turned back to the Kursk man.

"Buy us out for how much?"

The Kursk man produced a billfold, from which he removed a bank check. He slid it across the table. Petr picked it up.

"One thousand dollars."

"Yes," said the Kursk man. "As I say, your new partners feel either choice will be satisfactory to them, but assuming you do not wish to remain their partners, they do not wish to overpay."

"Uh-huh," said John. "And if we offered to sell to a third party?"

"As the lawyer for Kursk, I can tell you that we handle these matters of stock strictly in accordance with Russian law. The stock is not publicly negotiable, so if you were to attempt to sell it to a third party, it would be simply remand to the company."

"Uh-huh," said John.

"So what shall I say, gentlemen?" said the Kursk man, holding up his hands. "Welcome, or farewell?"

John and Petr looked at each other, then John turned back to the Kursk man. "Obviously we're going to need some time to discuss this."

"Of course," said the Kursk man. "Take twenty-four hours."

CHAPTER 9

John had suggested they go to Uncle Guilly's to talk about things over a steak. Petr had suggested the Hungry Duck instead. They flipped a coin and ended up at the Hungry Duck. Early in the day, the club was mostly empty and, at Doug's suggestion, John and Petr had hired a couple "masseuses" working the bar to actually give them massages.

Seated backward on a chair, John was getting his shoulders worked over by a slip of a girl, built like Audrey Hepburn, who squeezed and kneaded with the iron grip of Hulk Hogan. Beside him, Petr had pulled two tables together and was laid out on top of them, face down, with his head dangling over the leading edge, while a pair of beautiful prostitutes worked on knots in his back and legs. He reached for a glass of scotch on the floor beneath him, sucked a sip out of it through a cocktail straw, and replaced it on the floor. He looked up at John.

"At the risk of stating the obvious," he said, "it would be a very, very bad idea to become involved with the Russian mob."

"Agreed," said John, languidly. His eyes were closed, and his shoulders no longer felt like bones and muscle. They might as well have been made of Jell-O. Petr looked up at him.

"Are you with me?" said Petr, sucking up another sip of scotch.

"Yes."

"Really?"

"Yes."

"You don't look it."

"No."

"You look like you've swallowed a fistful of Valium."

"I bet."

"Give me a sign you're listening."

John yawned, and said, "You were born by C-section, weren't you?"

"Yes," said Petr. "How did you know that?"

"People who've had C-sections have rounder and more symmetrical heads than the rest of us because your soft infant skull didn't have to go through a birth canal."

"I didn't know that. Yes, it is a very nicely shaped head I have, isn't it?"

"Uh-huh. And you're a patriot."

"I don't think that took any deduction."

"No, I mean you're a *real* patriot. You were willing to die for your country."

Petr chuckled. "What makes you think that?"

"You wanted to be a soldier."

"You don't have to 'want' to be a soldier in Czech and Slovakia. There's conscription; every man becomes a soldier."

"Yes, but even though you write with your right hand, every time someone puts a glass above your knife and spoon, you move it to the left side of the plate. Makes me think you're naturally left-hand dominant, but that you trained yourself to be a righty. Since all Soviet rifles are designed for righties, the easiest way not to worry about facing combat is to be left-handed—but instead of taking the easy way out, you actually wanted to fight. You loathe Communism, so you certainly weren't eager to be on the front lines for a puppet Soviet government. So I figure you were thinking there might be another Prague Spring."

Petr laughed.

"It could just be that my parents were superstitious and thought the left was the devil's hand, though."

"Not if you went to state nursery care."

"And how do you know I went to state nursery care?"

"You told me."

Petr laughed and said, "Fine, you pay attention."

"I sure do," said John, opening his eyes slightly. "What were we talking about?"

"The pros and cons of taking possession of our interest in Kursk Tobacco."

"Well, the cons are—ummmm." John was swept away for a second as a knot in his shoulder unraveled. "The cons are pretty self-evident. What are the pros?"

"You two look like you're in pretty good shape," said Doug, walking past. "Maybe I should make this place a pre-party massage parlor."

"Wouldn't get any arguments from me," said John.

"Who's your friend?" said Petr, looking up at Doug. At Doug's elbow was a tall, grizzled man who looked like a defensive tackle in a dark suit.

"My new security guy. We're just closing the deal."

"Does he speak English?" said Petr.

"Not a word."

"He looks like Russia's answer to Don Corleone."

Doug smiled and shook his head. "Not the mob—he was a colonel in the KGB. Very well-connected inside the FSB—that is, the new KGB. After the little attempted-kidnapping incident the other night, I got a phone call from the head of the Chechen group that's unhappy with me. The guy says, 'Look, one way or another, we're going to get what we want, or you're going to die. And just so you understand, it will never end. If I fail to kill you, it will become my son's mission to kill you. If he fails, it will become his son's mission to kill you. It will never end.' So I figured maybe it was time to bring in reinforcements."

"It's a good idea," said John, opening his eyes again to get a look at Doug and his new colonel, closing them again as the massage continued uninterrupted. "Maybe we should hire this guy."

"Oh yeah?" said Doug. "What's your problem?"

"We just secured stock in a company—stock that's worth eighteen million dollars, US. But if we convert . . . if we put it down on the books, we're agreeing to front a gigantic black-market tobacco operation, with the Russian Mafia as our operating partners."

"Oof," said Doug.

"Yeah," said John.

"We know we need to walk away," said Petr. "But it's easier said than done, walking away from eighteen million dollars. American."

"Why don't you sell it to someone else?" said Doug.

"It's nonnegotiable. Apparently, if we try to sell it to a third-party, the stock automatically revests in the pool of current owners' shares."

"That wouldn't be a problem," said the KGB colonel, "if you sold it to someone who was already part of the company's management."

Petr looked at Doug. "I thought you said he didn't speak English."

Doug looked at the KGB guy. "I thought you said you didn't speak any English."

"I exaggerated."

"You exaggerated?"

"I speak some English."

"How much?"

"All of it."

"Very funny."

"This is why I'm so good at my job," said the ex-colonel. "I'm extremely subtle."

Doug rolled his eyes.

"It is Kursk Tobacco you're speaking of, yes?" said the ex-colonel.

John nodded. "You're not about to say you're on their board of directors or something, are you?"

"No," said the ex-colonel. "But I could be. I would be a very valuable partner for them. Maybe more, even, than you."

"So *you* want to buy the stock from us?" said Petr.

"Yes."

"How much?"

"Zero dollars. But I will pay you in billion-dollar information."

"Thanks, we've already been offered 'nothing' for the stock."

"Shall we talk privately? I think you'll be interested in what I can propose."

Petr looked at Doug. Doug gave him a discreet thumbs-up.

"Okay," said Petr, with a look at John, who nodded. "Can we use your office?"

"Sure," said Doug. "Just remember to duck if you see a red dot on one of your foreheads.

◆

"So—" said the ex-KGB guy.

"What's your name, by the way," said John, cutting him off.

"Colonel Semyon Sergeyevich Krylenko."

"Is that a courtesy title, or are you still in the FSB?"

Krylenko didn't answer. After a minute, John said, "Okay. Go on?"

"So," said Krylenko, "I'm a poor civil servant. Cash poor. Since the collapse, I do a great deal of private security work. I am the best at what I do. Partly because I take the long view of things. Mostly I get paid in stock, you understand? Someday it will be negotiable. But what it means in the nearer term is that if I learn of a really fantastic investment opportunity, I am forced to find someone else to put up the money. Mr. Steele mentioned he had some friends in town launching a Russia investment fund. That's why I wanted to make your acquaintance."

"This meeting wasn't coincidence?" said John, who had taken a seat on the edge of Doug's desk.

"Nothing's a coincidence," said Krylenko.

"You couldn't possibly have known we were coming here today," said Petr.

"Well, yes, *this* meeting was a coincidence, but we would have met in the next day or two, one way or another."

"Fair enough," said Petr.

"In any case," said Krylenko. "There's another company I handle security for. They're about to issue vouchers and have voucher auctions. They've hired me to make sure the public auctions are kept secret from the public."

"That's illegal, isn't it?"

Krylenko shrugged.

"What company is it?" said John.

Krylenko shook his head. "The price of the information is your shares of Kursk Tobacco."

"Oh—that's all you want? Eighteen million dollars of stock? Maybe we could throw in some tickets to Euro Disney to sweeten the pot."

Krylenko shook his head again. "No, it's not all I want. I also want fifty percent of the realized post-auction stock in the company we're about to talk about."

"Fifty percent," said Petr. "Plus Kursk Tobacco.

"Yes."

"This must be pretty good information," said Petr.

"Yes."

"How much would you say the stock we could get would be worth?"

"Depending on how effective your operation is . . . as much as five—maybe ten—billion dollars."

"Five to ten billion dollars?" said John.

"Yes."

John and Petr looked at each other, then back at Krylenko.

"Seems unlikely," said John.

"If you're expecting to clear two-point-five to five billion dollars on this," said Petr, "taking your fifty percent—what do you want the Kursk stock for?"

"Call it a deposit. In case you screw me on the other end."

"If we screw you, I'd just assumed you'd have us both killed," said Petr.

"Oh, yes, I certainly would," said Krylenko. "But even if I do, that won't get me the stock. With Kursk, at least, I could retire. You understand?"

"But you had no idea about our Kursk problem before meeting us today," said John.

"No," said Krylenko.

"But you already wanted to meet us," said John.

"Yes."

"So your original plan was just to propose a fifty-fifty split."

"Yes."

"So maybe if we give you the Kursk stock, we knock it down to a thirty-three by three split."

"No," said Krylenko. "But what I will do is this. I'll tell you the name of the company. It won't really matter, because without me, there's no way you'll be able to make the auctions work for you. If the name doesn't impress you, we all walk away with no further obligation to one another. If it does, we shake hands, you give me Kursk, and I tell you how to become permanent fixtures on the *Forbes* billionaire list."

John ruminated a moment, looked over at Petr and gave him a conditional thumbs-up. Petr returned it.

"Okay," said John. "Shoot."

"The company, gentlemen, is Gazneft."

John's eyes opened wide. So did Petr's.

"They're not doing a voucher issuance. I've checked."

"Yes they are," said Krylenko. "But they are also—how do I put it?—lying. Lying through intentionally misleading statements. What they're *actually* not doing is issuing vouchers in Moscow or Leningrad. The IMF deal with the Russian government requires that they issue privatization vouchers. But the directors would prefer to maintain ownership themselves. So, they've come up with a . . . a clever system. They're issuing region-specific vouchers, for the regions in which they operate. The official justification is—or will be, when people find out this has happened—that they wished to guarantee ownership of their gas reserves to people who live on the land where the gas actually is. And they've already issued tens of thousands of vouchers in these areas. Many of the people they've issued them to are illiterate; virtually all are desperately poor—none will have any way of getting to the actual auctions, which are being held at specific times on specific days, announced in tiny ads on the last pages of local newspapers, just before they actually happen, and in the most remote possible locations within the legal territory, in non-gas-producing tiny towns where *no* vouchers were issued.

"So those few people who both grasp the meaning of the vouchers, and see the announcements, will have to have private transportation. Which, outside of the big cities, is mostly ox carts and dog sleds. No, so you see, they won't make it, and the only people who will actually succeed in showing up at these auctions will be representatives of the current management. If they're the only ones who show up, all they need is a single voucher to present at each auction, and they will take control of that auction's entire stock issuance. If you show up too—well, the more vouchers you have, the larger a percentage you'll get. If he shows up with a hundred and you show up with a hundred, it'll be fifty-fifty. If he shows up with a hundred and you show up with ninety-nine thousand and nine hundred, you'll get ninety-nine-point-nine percent of the stock issued. You follow me?"

John and Petr were slack jawed. Looking from Krylenko to each other, to blank spots on the roof and walls, staring at nothing while they did mental arithmetic.

"What's the total value of Gazneft's gas reserves?" said Petr.

Krylenko paused for dramatic effect. "About twenty billion, American."

"Jesus *Christ*," said Petr, quietly.

"How much of that are they issuing through vouchers?" said John.

"Two-thirds," said Krylenko. "About fourteen billion worth, the share that is reserved for Russian purchase, nonnegotiable outside. The rest will be offered next year for European, American, Japanese, et cetera, so you will be in the market entirely on your own. I assume your fund is based in Russia. Legally."

"Yes," said John.

"Good. You wouldn't be able to register the stock otherwise. All part of the design to control who gets it. So—shall we settle Kursk?"

John nodded to Petr, and Petr said. "Very well. It's yours. I'll let our banker know."

"Good," said Krylenko. "So, the Gazneft auctions will be happening sequentially, to assure them opportunities to correct the process if anything is going wrong. It won't be smooth sailing once they catch on to what you're doing. From my end, I'll help you where I can. But this is the crucial data: The first set of vouchers were issued in Bashkortostan, in the Volga federal district. The auction will take place in Baymak, at the town hall. All of them will be at town halls. The second issuance has been in the Omsk Oblast. The auction will take place in Tara."

John was making notes as Krylenko spoke; Petr was standing at a map on Doug Steele's office wall and trying to follow along.

"Where's Tara?" said Petr.

"North of Omsk, where the Tara River meets the Irtysh River."

"Good," said Petr, poking the map. "Okay. Continue please."

"The third issuance is happening in the Irkutsk Oblast. East of Novosibirsk," he added, for Petr's benefit. "The auction will happen in Tayshet. The fourth issuance will be in the Jewish Autonomous Oblast."

"The what?" said John and Petr, at almost the same time.

"You don't know about the Jewish Autonomous Oblast?"

The two non-Russians shook their heads.

"You should study your history more. There aren't actually any Jews there. It was where Stalin planned to deport them all. Partly to weaken the so-called intellectual class, which Stalin thought would be a threat to Marxism, and partly in hopes they would create trade with China and Japan and Korea. Which, apparently, would not be a threat to Marxism. It borders China, west of the Sea of Japan. Before the deportations could happen, the war started. The Germans killed all the Jews of Belorussia and the Ukraine—which was most of them in the USSR—so there weren't enough left to send to Eastern Siberia. But they kept the name. And one of the official languages is Yiddish."

"Huh," said John.

"The auction will happen in Lazarevo. The final issuance will be the Magadan Oblast, on the Sea of Okhotsk. The auction will be in Susuman."

Krylenko paused to let John finish writing. Petr looked over his shoulder, turning away from the map. "Got it?" he asked.

"Yup," said John. "When will the auctions happen? We need dates."

"They will happen on five consecutive Sundays, at six in the morning. 'To ensure they do not conflict with the activities of those citizens who wish to attend religious services.'" He shook his head. "The first, in Baymak, will happen this Sunday."

John and Petr looked at each other. It was Wednesday.

"Yes," said Krylenko. "You'd better hurry."

◆

Fifteen minutes later they were in their office, where Andrei was managing a large team of Benny Sheldon's people, hard at work filling out voucher paperwork. Most of them were sitting on the floor. No one had had time to buy furniture yet.

John pulled Andrei out into the hall.

"Andrei, we've got a bit of a time emergency here, so I've got to do this rapid fire," he said, as he closed the office door behind them. Petr was pacing; John continued, "You went with Petr to the Kursk auction, correct?"

"Yes," said Andrei, who didn't look rattled at all, despite the obvious agitation of his bosses.

"Could you handle the next auctions by yourself?"

Andrei looked from John to Petr and back to John.

"Yes."

"You know the schedule for all the auctions for the vouchers you and Petr were buying while I was away?"

"Yes."

"And you know how to register them afterward?"

"No. But Mr. Sheldon can explain to me."

"Perfect. We need to head out of town, so you have to manage everything here yourself. You're in charge. If anyone gets in your way, kill him."

Andrei's expression didn't change.

"That last part was a joke."

"I suspected this," said Andrei.

"Okay, good. Now—I need you to tell me the fastest way to get . . ." He pulled out the list he'd made at Doug's office, ". . . to all these places. Starting with Baymak, by Sunday. Is that possible?"

Andrei looked over the list for a moment.

"Yes and yes," he said. Petr exhaled.

◆

As John and Petr emerged from the office building, heading for the idling cab they'd asked to wait for them, they were met at the door by George Menshikov.

"I'm a reporter? With *Forbes*?"

"Yeah," said John. "I remember. Can't talk right now."

Menshikov followed the investment duo from the door to the curb, where they found the cab empty. John and Petr scanned up and down the street, looking for the driver.

"There he is," said Petr, pointing toward the door of a tobacconist, where the cabbie was lackadaisically opening a fresh pack and lighting up.

John stuck a couple fingers in his mouth and let out an ear-shattering whistle. "Hey!" he shouted to the driver. "We're in kind of a rush here!"

The man shrugged. He didn't understand English. Petr began to remonstrate with him in Russian.

"I was hoping you could comment on the mass profiteering by Russian businesses and businessmen, monopolizing vouchers for the privatization of Russian industry. I understand your fund is investing in vouchers—with an American multinational money guy and the top Czech voucher expert. I'd like to ask about your plans, your involvement. Big things are happening and you two are clearly part of them."

"What?" said John, who'd only half heard him. "I'm sorry, Mr. Menshikov. Some other time, we're in a hurry."

The cabbie was climbing back into the driver's seat; John jumped into the back, and Petr pulled open the front passenger door. Menshikov put his hand on the door frame, momentarily blocking Petr from getting in. Petr—who had a couple inches on Menshikov and a good fifty pounds—peeled the offending hand away and brushed the reporter back—adding, with the unique apathy of an ex-Communist Slav, "Fuck off."

Petr jumped into the cab, and as he pulled the door closed behind him, Menshikov could hear him saying, "Okay, Mario Andretti, go-go-go," as the cab pulled away from the curb. It sped off into the Moscow traffic.

"Babes in the wood," thought Menshikov, wondering if they knew what they'd gotten themselves into.

◆

What John and Petr needed was a train, and by the time they had persuaded the ticket lady to figure out what track the right one was on, they had only a few minutes to get aboard. When they got to the platform, they found the ticket lady had given them the wrong instructions and they had to make a mad dash back into the tunnels of Kazansky Rail Station, reemerging, after another mad dash, at the right platform—more or less. The platform had passengers waiting on it, but no train. Petr grabbed a passerby and coughed out the question, "Chekmagush?", the station Andrei had told them to head for—the primary city and rail stop of Volga District-Bashkortostan. The man didn't understand, and Petr began to cough. John, who'd now had a moment to catch his breath, repeated the question, and got an answer in Russian he didn't understand.

"He says this isn't the right place, it's that train there," said Petr, pointing to the adjacent platform. They needed to go back down into the tunnels and come up one platform over. But the train's giant diesel-electric locomotives were already rumbling.

John was sweeping his eyes back and forth over the tracks. "They're not electrified—come on." Each man was carrying only a small duffle bag; there hadn't been much time to pack. John was glad of that now. He dropped down off the low platform and ran across the intervening tracks. He grabbed hold of the service ladder that ran to the train's roof, past a closed door that would open at right-side platform stops.

Halfway up the side of the car, John tried the door. It was latched on the inside. He banged on its window. The few people visible through the door's window—figuring out which cabins they were in; looking for seats—ignored him. He climbed the rest of the way to train's roof, with Petr behind him. Crouched down—instinctively keeping his center of gravity low enough that he wouldn't slip, fall fifteen feet, and crack his skull on a concrete buckler—he crossed the train's roof, grabbed the top of the far-side service ladder and began to climb down. His searching feet found all but the top few rungs were blocked by the open train door. He dropped the remaining two yards to the platform.

He landed beside a ticket-taker lady who was nonplussed for only a second and then—apparently—not concerned at all when Petr dropped down beside John a moment later. A show of that old Russian sangfroid.

"Is this the train for Chekmagush?" said John, in English.

"Chekmagush? *Da*," said the ticket-taker lady.

"Thank God," said John. Petr handed her the tickets. She looked at them, said something to Petr in Russian, and handed them back. Petr was pulling out his wallet.

"What was that?" said John.

"She says the railway company no longer has the right to sell tickets for this train, that it is under new management, and we have to buy tickets from her."

"Is she scamming us?"

"I have no clue," said Petr, handing over a few American bills. "It's not expensive here; she takes dollars."

The lady accepted the bills, pulled out two small blank business cards (that's what they looked like, anyway), wrote something on each of them, stamped them, and handed them to Petr—who handed one to John.

Petr posed the lady a final question, in Russian, and then let her wave them aboard; a line was forming behind them.

"Okay, we're good," said Petr. "She says Chekmagush is twenty-nine hours from here. First class is to the right. We're car four. Compartment one." John followed Petr up the wooden steps—a step stool to compensate for the train being higher than the platform. The steps, though, went up higher than the door into the train. So John and Petr stepped down off them, into the compartment between cars, turned right, and headed for car four.

They were starting near the back of the train and it was a long walk, beginning in third class. And third class was surprising—much nicer than John had expected. It was crowded, filled with filled-up booths—large families eating and talking, on well-worn vinyl-cushioned benches facing each other in pairs. The aisle was narrow, because the benches were all long enough for a normal-sized person to lie flat on them, and each booth had two more "benches" to fold down above it.

In some parts of the car, and the next nine cars they walked through, university kids and family matrons were already making the benches up into beds. Some single men appeared to be renting freshly pressed sheets from the small attendants' rooms at the end of each cabin.

Each cabin had a line outside it, a line of people either renting sheets or getting hot water from a large water heater. A water samovar, really, that seemed to be a feature at the end of every train car. There was a steady stream of people carrying glass mugs back to their booths, with tea bags already brewing in them. Each of the cars had the feeling of a mini-shtetl—clearly a lot of the people knew each other, this presumably being their regular train. Old men were already playing chess, and here and there a paper airplane flew from a kid camped out in a top bunk.

More than a few people were already sound asleep, despite the bustle. As John and Petr crossed from third class into second, the train started to move.

Second class was an obvious upgrade from third, though not a dramatic one. Instead of six beds to a booth, there were four to a compartment, one upper and one lower on each side of the small but not too small rooms. The second-class cars were a lot quieter, and looking in a few of the open doors, John could see the cabins were roomier than the booths had been, and their bench-beds wider.

Ten second class cars, and John and Petr were nearing car four.

"Did Communist trains always have different travel classes?" said John.

"They did for all of my lifetime," said Petr. "You expect party members to travel with onion farmers?"

John laughed.

"I do like this tea thing," said Petr, looking into a stewardess cabin, where a stewardess looked up from a paperback and smiled at them. "Free hot water and mugs. The Russians love their tea."

First class began at car number eight. It was another clear upgrade—now the cabins were even larger; downright roomy, in train terms—instead of cabins on either side of a central corridor, there was a corridor running along the edge of double-wide compartments. And looking inside, the compartments were a damn sight nicer than the modern Amtrak sleeper cabins John had traveled in a few times. Not as nice the 20th Century Limited–style cabins that he remembered from his early childhood—the end of the glory days of American train travel. But still—twin beds, two to a cabin, made up as sofas with plush vinyl pillows as the backrest, a small table, and even a bit of room to move around in.

"Why is first class at the front of the train, where it's noisiest?"

"No idea," said Petr. "Bureaucracy? Or maybe first-class customers like arriving a few seconds early."

A few more cars crossed, and they arrived at car four. They found compartment one, went inside, each plopped down on a sofa and sighed a breath of relief. After a moment, Petr lay down, with his feet to the door. John prepared to light a cigarette, then noticed the small no-smoking sign over the door—clearly a recent addition to the worn but rather homey patina of the train's interior.

"Do you think they're serious about that?" said John, gesturing to the sign.

"Definitely not," said Petr, who was lighting a cigarette of his own.

For a few moments they smoked in silence (making paradoxical efforts to catch their breaths and smoke at the same time). Then Petr said, "Care for some tea?"

"Sure," said John. "To tell you the truth, I'd care for a little more than that—I'm pretty hungry. Is there a dining car?"

"No," said Petr, standing up, stretching, opening the door to the corridor. "But there will be someone by before long to sell food. Like at a football game."

"Perfect," said John. Petr, on his tea run, closed the door behind him, and John turned to the window, watching as Moscow began to thin, as the city gave way to forest.

A moment later Petr was back with tea. And for a few moments more, the two men sipped in silence. Then there was a knock on the compartment door.

John started to say "Come in," one of the phrases he'd learned in Russian—but he drew a blank and instead leaned over and opened the door. Outside was a man in a black suit and a peaked cap.

Petr said something to him. The man answered.

"He's asking to see our tickets," said Petr, pulling his out. He handed it over. The man looked at it and handed it back to him, then waved off John's. He said something else in Russian. Petr pulled out the original ticket he'd gotten from the rail station's ticket window. The man waved it away and repeated himself. Petr—with a deep twang of exasperation—answered him. The man answered back. They appeared to have reached an impasse.

"What's going on?" said John.

"He says the tickets we've bought aren't good—the train is under new management, and we have to buy tickets from him."

"Jesus." John pulled out his wallet. "How much this time?"

"A hundred bucks each, he says. American. He must have picked up on your nationality."

"Geez," said John, drawing out ten twenty-dollar bills. "Ask him how many more times we're going to have to do this."

Petr did, and the man gave a vaguely indignant answer.

"He says he is the only legitimate ticket seller on the train and if we have been taken advantage of, it is not his responsibility."

"Great," said John, handing over the money, before adding, with a sardonic smile, "you fucking Cossack."

The man glared at John—evidently he understood at least one word of English—and handed over a third set of tickets. These, at least, were preprinted. "*Spasiba*," said John, and the man withdrew.

Petr laughed and John couldn't help but join him. The original Wild West had probably had a lot of ticket scammers in it too.

A few minutes later, there was another knock on the door. "Hope it's the food this time," said John. "Tell me again how you say 'come in'?"

"*Voydite*," said Petr, loud enough for the knocker to hear him. The door opened.

A man in his early twenties opened the door. He was wearing newish jeans and a heavyish jacket and seemed, curiously, to be pushing a smallish wooden wheelbarrow.

He said something in Russian.

"He's selling books," said Petr.

The man continued.

"And magazines," said Petr. ". . . And comic books . . . And pornography . . ." Petr grimaced. "And German pornography."

"Anything in English?"

Petr translated. The man turned his back and began to look through his wheelbarrow, calling out names for Petr to translate.

"*A Critique of Pure Reason . . . The Metamorphosis . . . Beyond Good and Evil . . . Being and Nothingness . . . Works of Love . . .*"

"Is *Works of Love* a novel?" said John.

"*Works of Love* by Søren Kierkegaard."

"Are you sure it was Søren?" said John. "Not some other Kierkegaard?"

Petr snorted a short laugh and continued to translate.

"*Ethan Frome . . . In the Penal Colony . . . The Amazing Spiderman*, number twenty-eight; featuring Peter Parker's graduation and the first appearance of the Menacing Molten Man."

John laughed.

"*My Man Jeeves . . .*"

"We're getting closer," said John.

"And an en-regard translation of *Dialectical and Historical Materialism*."

"Is that by P. G. Wodehouse too?"

Petr asked. The bookseller answered.

"No," said Petr. "He's says it's by Stalin."

"I'll take *My Man Jeeves*."

Petr said something to the bookseller in Russian; the man shook his head.

"He hasn't got anything in Czech."

Petr asked him another question. The man nodded, searched through his barrow, and retrieved a second book, which he handed to Petr along with *Jeeves*. Petr paid him two dollars, and the man went on his way—knocking, a moment later, on the next door down the corridor.

"You got something in Russian?" said John. "Thanks," he added, accepting his book from Petr.

"Yes," said Petr. "*War and Peace*. I've never read it. But I've heard good things."

John chuckled, and Petr nudged the door closed with an outstretched foot. It had barely closed when there was another knock. This time it was a man selling pipe tobacco and socks.

After him came a cigarette girl. She was dressed in a mildly provocative way, with her cardboard tray of cigarettes slung around her neck, just the way you see in films noir. Petr flirted with her a little—and John had a chance to get in on the chat; she was the first person on the train he'd heard speak English. They both bought a couple packs of Laikas, which was the only brand she had that either recognized.

The next guy spoke English too—he, at last, was selling food. Instant soup mixes to pour into your hot water mug, plus sausage slices, dried fruit, hard cheese, and very hard bread.

It wasn't haute cuisine, but it wasn't bad either. As the two men ate their minimalist smorgasbord, the next few vendors who stopped by were selling trivia. Decks of cards. Postcards. Pencils. Mainly, they were selling themselves. Of the dozen or so girls who formed this succession, only two spoke any English—even so, they had no trouble getting across to John what they had in mind.

"Well, they're a much better deal than the girls in Moscow," said Petr, in between two of them.

"Well, I suppose there's a smaller customer base out here."

"But with all the beds, and a twenty-nine-hour train ride, you'd think demand would be pretty high."

"You want me to go wait in the hall?" said John.

Petr laughed. "No, no. Just an observation on economics."

John smiled and lit a cigarette. "I wonder if this is a Laika-Laika or a Kursk counterfeit Laika."

"How does it taste?"

"Like any cigarette that isn't a Camel."

"Your brand?"

"Yeah, when I can get them. But this . . . I would not walk a mile for this."

Petr opened one of his new Laika packs and lit it, and shrugged. "Tastes like every other Laika I've ever smoked."

"Maybe every other Laika you've ever smoked was a Kursk counterfeit."

"Huh," said Petr. "Now that's a question."

"Why do you lie with your feet toward the door?" said John, who was stretching out on his couch with his head toward the door and his feet toward the window.

"Doesn't everyone? Facing the door is instinct, I think."

"You're missing the view."

"Trees and trees and then big empty fields that stretch to the horizon, and then more trees?"

"So far."

"I've seen it," said Petr.

"At Chekmagush," said John, "how do you think we go about buying vouchers? Just handing out a little money and asking people to spread the word? Tell them anyone who shows up at the station with vouchers can sell them for American hard currency?"

Petr nodded. "Yeah, I think so. Maybe there will be some cab drivers at the station. We can pay them to spread the word, and also give them a commission for any voucher sellers they bring us.

"Good," said John. "Should be a piece of cake."

"Hm," said Petr. "'A piece of cake.' I've never heard that before. Means it should be easy?"

"Yes."

"A piece of cake," repeated Petr. "Hm. Good."

The sun had started to set and the two men began reading their books. When the cabin attendant came to make up their beds, she knocked quietly and got no answer. Deducing they'd fallen asleep, she let them be.

◆

They both slept reasonably soundly for a few hours until an hour or two after midnight, when a rapid knocking snapped John awake. The P. G. Wodehouse book slid off his chest and he reached around for the light switch.

"Please!" said a quiet, urgent voice on the other side of the door. "Please! Open! Please!"

Petr was awake now, too, and John was on his feet, finding the light switch and pulling the door open. It was the cigarette girl, the one who'd been wearing the film noir thing. As soon as the door opened, she slid into the room, pushed the door closed, and locked it.

"Please! Turn out the light." John was still in a semi-stupor and the girl stepped past him and hit the overhead light switch herself. The cabin went dark, except for the dim illumination of a half-moon on a clear night. John's eyes began to adjust. He could just about see the girl's face and the shape of Petr standing by his bed, bracing himself with a hand on the overhead luggage rack.

"What's going—?"

"Shhhhhh," the girl hissed, before adding another plaintive, "Quiet, please."

The words were barely out of her mouth when there was a muffled smash of car four's forward door—the one connecting it to car three—being slammed open. Two men were talking loudly in Russian. John couldn't understand them—he couldn't even make out the words—but he could tell the words were being slurred.

John and Petr's compartment was at the front of the car, closest to the forward door. A few seconds crawled by and then their compartment door began to rattle. Someone was trying to pull it open.

John's eyes had adjusted enough now to see that the cigarette girl's blouse had been torn at the shoulder. The rattling of the door stopped, then resumed at the next compartment. Thirty seconds passed as the Russian voices in the corridor tried each compartment to see if it was unlocked, then seemed to disappear through the door to car five.

"Are you okay?" said John, quietly. "Here, have a sip of this." He handed her what was now a glass of cold tea. She drank it gratefully.

"Sit down," said Petr, gesturing to his own couch-bed. He lit two cigarettes, and handed one to her. "It's safe here; you're fine."

For a moment she stood still, holding the cigarette up to her mouth but otherwise inanimate. Petr sat down on John's bed and the girl sat down on Petr's. John lit a cigarette of his own and sat by Petr. He hoped they didn't look too much like a court of inquiry.

"Would you like us to get someone? The conductor?"

"No," said the girl.

"Would you be more comfortable speaking in Russian?" said John. "My friend here speaks it."

The girl shook her head. "No, it's all right. Thank you."

There was no need to ask her what had happened. For a few minutes they all smoked silently, until John said, "We have some food."

The girl shook her head.

"Why don't you get some rest," said Petr. "Sleep there; I'll take the floor."

"Thank you," said the girl. "I can sleep on the floor."

"No," said Petr, opening a cupboard over the door and removing some bedclothes. "Sleep there. The floor is fine for me." He found an extra pillow and a couple blankets. He handed one to the girl and lay the second on the ground, tossing the pillow at its head, by the window.

"Sorry, John," he said. "Only two."

John nodded and said to the girl, "He's right, get some sleep and we'll see what we can do in the morning."

"Thank you," said the girl, as she wrapped herself in the blanket. She stayed seated upright on Petr's bed. For a moment John and Petr looked at her, then John said, "Okay, break it up everyone. Get some sleep."

"Yes," said Petr. He took his coat off a hook by the door, put it on, and lay down. John lay down too. The girl remained seated upright. But sometime during the night, John rolled over and saw she'd gone to sleep, lying on her side, with her knees pulled up and her back against the wall.

CHAPTER 10

When John woke up, she was sitting at the foot of her bed, by an end table, carefully stirring four mugs of steaming water. John looked at his watch, figured they were probably less than an hour from Chekmagush, and reached down to shake Petr awake.

"We're gonna be there soon," he said. It took Petr a moment to remember where he was. He sat up and looked at the girl and her four mugs of hot water.

"Why four?" he said.

"Two for tea," she said, "and two for kasha."

"Kasha?" said John.

"Porridge," said Petr. "Aren't you going to join us?"

"No," said the girl. "The attendant lady who came to check to see if you needed to return sheets got me the water, and a pin,"—John could see the torn shoulder of her blouse had been fastened with a safety pin, "And told me she would let me out of the train on the side away from the platform. Until then she said I could wait in the lady's lavatory."

"You can wait here," said Petr. "You don't have to wait in a lavatory."

"Thank you, but if you're going to be at your station soon, we're not getting off at the same place."

"We're getting off at Chekmagush," said Petr.

"I'm riding to Ufa," said the girl. "This is the train for Ufa. At Ufa, it stops and then goes back to Moscow."

"Why not get off at Chekmagush and wait for the next train? Don't they come every six hours? That's not so long, and then you won't have to hide."

"I can't afford a second ticket," she said.

"I'll get you a second ticket," said Petr. "It's all right."

"No," she said, "I've already been too much trouble."

"Don't be crazy," said John. "It was no trouble at all, having Petr sleep on the floor."

She smiled. "Thank you, but no."

"Very well," said Petr. "But then let me pay you for breakfast."

"Don't be crazy," she said. Petr shrugged and started to climb off the floor.

"What happened to your cigarette tray?" said John. "Do you want us to get it back for you? Dealing with drunks is a lot easier the morning after."

She turned her back slightly, so neither John nor Petr could see her face.

"They threw it off the train."

Petr swore in Czech, added something in Russian, and then—for John's benefit, added in English, "Fucking cocksucking bastards."

"If you won't let us give you a little money," said John, "at least let us lend you some. You can pay us back whenever you get back on your feet."

"Back on my feet?"

"When you're back to earning money again."

"I'm thankful," she said. "But I don't like to be in debt."

"Do you speak Bashkir?" said Petr. "We're going to be working for a few days in Bashkortostan. My Russian's good but I know some people in the Republics don't speak it."

"I speak Bashkir," she said, turning to look at him. "I speak a lot of the southern federal languages. We studied the Turkic languages at school."

"Come work for us for a few days, as a translator," said Petr. "I promise you we have no, uh . . ." Petr said something to the girl in Russian, and she answered, "ulterior motives."

"Right," said Petr, returning to English, "I promise you we have no ulterior motives."

"My wife's going to have a baby," said John. "If that helps. Even if it doesn't, I really like telling people."

The girl laughed.

"Here," she said. "Your kasha is ready."

As she handed each man a mug of kasha and one of tea, and they tried to figure out what surfaces to place them on, Petr said, "So—will you do it?"

After a moment's hesitation she said, matter-of-factly, "Yes." She gestured to John.

"You are 'John'?"

"Yes," he said.

"And you are Petr,"

"Yes."

"My name is Anna Lydiovna Scherbatskaya. What sort of business are you in?"

CHAPTER 11

John and Petr got off the train at Chekmagush, carrying their duffle bags, with Anna between them, wearing Petr's coat and a babushka given to her by the bed-linen lady.

Per Andrei, Chekmagush was the first town in Bashkortostan that would be large enough to find vouchers in useful quantities. Even so it was small enough that no one else got off at the station. And there were no cabs waiting at the station, which bordered a smallish town square with a statue of Lenin in the center. It wasn't clear if it was the town's main square, or just a square, but it was lined with shops that didn't appear to have many customers.

There were a few old men sitting at stone tables playing chess, and a few old women pushing small metal carts with vegetables and things in them. Everything was gray, except for a few trees that seemed to have pushed through the gaps between the square's heavy cement paving stones.

At the edge of the train platform—which was flush with the ground and also concrete; one giant slab, instead of individual bricks—was a stone table covered with about a half dozen gopniks, Russian teenage boys in Adidas knockoff tracksuits. Petr began to walk toward them, with John and Anna following.

"You speak Russian?" said Petr.

"Of course we speak Russian," translated Anna, for John.

"You know about vouchers? For getting stock in companies."

"Of course."

"You know about Gazneft vouchers?"

The boys were all looking at each other and smiling in the way smug youth do when speaking with an apparently unperceptive adult.

"What do you people want?" Anna translated.

"Gazneft vouchers. We'll pay for them. Five dollars, American, for a voucher, and one dollar to you all, for every person you bring here to sell us vouchers."

"A dollar for each of us?"

"For each person. You share the dollar. Bring us a thousand people and you'll have a thousand dollars to split among yourselves."

The boys conferred for a moment.

"Let us see the money."

"No," said Petr, opening his wallet. "But I'll give you a ten-dollar advance." He produced two five-dollar bills and held them out. "Split among yourselves, as you like. Do we have a deal?"

The boys conferred again, then the leader—or, anyway, the talker—pulled the two fives out of Petr's hand and his little group of crinkling, tracksuited teenagers began to walk away across the square. One of them jogged over to the men playing chess. Another stopped one of the old ladies. As John, Petr, and Anna looked on, the boys split into three groups and disappeared down streets leading away from the square.

"What do we do now?" said Anna.

"Now we wait and see if this works," said John.

◆

It took about forty minutes for people to start to trickle into the square. Long enough that John began to wonder if the kids might have just taken the ten bucks and gone off to have fun with it. Ten bucks American was a lot out here.

While the trio waited, they set up at the stone table that the gopniks had vacated, and John—as discreetly as possible—opened his duffle bag, reached under the clothes piled at the top, and pulled out two of the five hundred wrapped bundles of dollar bills that he and Petr had picked up from Benny before rushing to catch their train.

Each bundle had a hundred singles in it; John and Petr each had two hundred fifty bundles in his duffle bag. Fifty thousand dollars in total. They'd wanted to do a hundred, but then they'd have had to get it in fives to be able to carry it.

John slipped the little paper cuff of off each of the stacks of a hundred, slipped one into his own pocket, and one into Petr's. Petr gave him a thumbs-up and continued his conversation with Anna about why she'd studied Turkic languages. Apparently, it was one of the two options her high school had offered—the other was Slavic languages—and she just thought that the Turkish part of the world was a little more romantic.

Before the Soviet Union had dissolved, she used to dream about going to Sochi and finding a fishing boat in the Black Sea that would take her to Istanbul, where she could become a Russian teacher, maybe, or a nanny or something, and get a little apartment with a view of the Bosporus and the Hagia Sophia.

John asked why she'd learned English too. She said everyone at her school learned English. She wasn't sure if it was in case of war, or in case the Union collapsed, but she did seem a little insulted John's school hadn't made him learn Russian.

When people started showing up, it was mostly housewives, each with four or five or ten vouchers, for herself, her husband, he in-laws, et cetera. The trickle began to thicken into a stream, and soon a line had formed. And then a bus arrived. And then a second bus.

The head gopnik teenager bounded over to explain that his father had purchased the local bus company when it was nationalized and they'd been driving around the edge of town, picking up voucher-holders. Pretending to retrieve cigarettes, John dipped twice more into his duffle-bag money stash.

The bonanza lasted about two hours, and then for about two hours after that, stragglers trickled in. Then the trickle finally stopped and they tallied their totals. For a total of just under five thousand dollars, they'd purchased 944 Gazneft vouchers. Would that be enough? Was it a lot? Was it a little? There was no way of knowing until the auction, but it felt like a good stack. It was early evening now, and aside from a few drunks sitting at the Lenin statue, there was no one left in the square but John, Petr, Anna, and the gopniks waiting to be paid, along with their paterfamilias bus owner. He was hanging around behind the teens, by his buses, one of which he'd driven. He was smoking and chatting with the driver of the other, waiting to see that his kid got paid.

"I think we told you a buck for every person, but we didn't count how many people came, so we'll pay you a buck per voucher," translated Anna, as Petr addressed the gopniks. "And since you did such a good job, we'll round up to an even thousand. Here."

He pulled ten bundles of a hundred out of his bag. There were six gopniks and no easy way to hand out equal money to each, so Petr handed all ten to the leader and told the boys to split it up among themselves. Which they instantly began to do, until the leader's father shooed them away, told them to do it inside somewhere so the money wouldn't blow away. The kids walked quickly toward the edge of the square and disappeared down a street. And then the paterfamilias and his second bus driver approached John, Petr, and Anna, and pulled out a couple of army-issue Makarov pistols.

"Those bags, they're filled with money?" said the father, in English. "We would like to take them. There won't be any violence."

"Do you know who these men are?" said Anna, stepping forward unprompted. "Avtoritets . . ." She switched into Russian, so John kept his face impassive and pretended to understand. After a short, forceful lecture by Anna, the two men nodded, turned, and began to walk away. Anna stopped them and said something else. The two men turned and came back, with downcast faces, holding their pistols out in front of them. Anna took them both and waved the men away.

Once they'd gotten into their buses and driven out of sight, Petr explained what had happened. Anna had told the men that he and John were Avtoritet—Capos—in the Lyuberetskaya Bratva, one of the best-known Moscow Mafia families.

"I told them you were an American from the New York Mafia here to act as an advisor on expanding their operations globally."

"And then," said Petr, "she told them we would take their guns as a show of good faith—no hard feelings toward them from the mob."

Anna handed one of the Makarovs to Petr and held the other out to John. He hesitated a moment, then took it.

"You think this is a good idea?" he said, releasing the magazine so he could pop out the round loaded in the chamber.

"Well," said Petr, "it couldn't hurt. Next time Anna tells someone we're in the Mafia, they might not believe her."

John's first inclination was to laugh but, really, it wasn't that funny. With overcome reluctance, he replaced the magazine and slipped the gun into the pocket of his coat. Then he checked his watch.

"Train should be here in about half an hour," he said. "If it's running on time."

"It should be," said Anna. "They keep their schedule well."

"Power of the free market," said Petr.

CHAPTER 12

On Thursday evening they were back on the train through Bashkortostan. On Friday and Saturday they duplicated their Chekmagush voucher-buying strategy, with considerable success. On Saturday night they left the train for a connecting bus out of Ufa (the capital of the Baskhari Federal Republic) to Baymak, where the first auction would take place at six o'clock Sunday morning.

The bus was an old Soviet war-horse from the fifties. The suspension appeared to use leaf springs off an eighteenth-century oxcart. The ride would take five or six hours. Instead of a bathroom there was a recalcitrant driver who claimed to be eager to keep to his schedule, but for a modest tip would pull over and let out whoever needed to look for a bush. They made stops at nine medium-sized to microscopic towns before finally reaching Baymak.

They arrived at just after three in the morning. No thought was given to finding a hotel room for a couple hours' sleep. Instead, they walked into town, looking for someone to give them directions to the town hall. They found no one—at three in the morning, for some reason, it seemed everyone was asleep. But they did find the town hall, which was inside a pre-Soviet church.

The ex-church was topped, as most Russian churches are, with an onion dome. At the top of the onion dome, where a cross might have stood, there was a shiny metal hammer and sickle. It caught a little bit of very early morning light. It was the middle of summer, around fifty-five degrees north latitude, and by four A.M., dawn was already breaking.

At four, no one had arrived yet to open the town hall. John was pacing up and down, chain-smoking and trying to stay warm. Petr and Anna sat on the entry steps, sharing Petr's heavy coat. Anna was a wisp of a girl, and Petr was pretty skinny himself, so this didn't prove impossible, though it required close contact. At some point between four and five, Anna fell asleep with her head on Petr's shoulder. When John noticed, he caught Petr's eye, and Petr smiled—not a locker-room smile; no smugness. A sort of proud, affectionate smile. John nodded to him and kept pacing.

No one came to open the town hall until five minutes to six. The openers were a trio of men—one who was dressed like a super, and two in expensive suits. John, Petr, and Anna followed them in.

The super—or anyway, the guy who actually had keys to the front door—disappeared into a side room and a moment later the building's lights came on. A small anteroom led into a meeting hall, still filled with church pews.

One of the fancy-suit men took a seat at a dais where an altar had once been, placed a cash-counting machine on it, banged a gavel, and called the meeting to order. Presumably he was someone sent by the IMF to supervise, or maybe chosen by the IMF to supervise.

For some inexplicable reason, the IMF had decided not to trust the auctions to random local officials.

Not a single native Bashkir had showed up. Assuming, that is, that the second fancy-suit guy was the Gazneft buyer. So it looked like it would just be him and them. The real question was, how many vouchers had he brought? Since they were printed by the IMF, there wasn't an unlimited amount. And since Gazneft management didn't expect anyone else to show, they probably hadn't seen much need to risk drawing attention by accumulating too many. Or maybe they hadn't cared. There was really no way to know, until the guy at the dais counted.

This auction was for one-sixth of two-thirds of Gazneft. Or, one-ninth of a company worth roughly twenty billion dollars. Something like two and a quarter of those billions were up for grabs, in this little room in this little town in the middle of a semiautonomous-*stan* that no one had ever heard of.

The man at the dais began speaking, in Russian. Petr translated, "This is an auction to establish the distribution through privatization vouchers of shares in the ownership of the oil and gas company Gazneft. If you have vouchers that you wish to enter for conversion to ownership shares, please step forward."

John and Petr stood up; so did the Gazneft guy. As the three men converged on the dais, the Gazneft man gave John and Petr a look of uncurious malevolence. The man at the dais said something, and Petr gestured politely for the Gazneft man to go first. They were forming a line.

The Gazneft man handed over a manila envelope. John and Petr both craned their necks to see how many vouchers it would hold. The man behind the dais said something in Russian, and Petr said, "He wants us to back up and wait our turn."

He and John took a few steps back and watched as the IMF rep began to feed vouchers into the counting machine. When he was done, he placed them in a second manila envelope—one that he had apparently brought with him, wrote a number on it, wrote a receipt, and handed it to the Gazneft man.

Maybe it was John's imagination running away with him, but he was pretty sure the Gazneft guy had fewer vouchers than they did. In a minute or two, they would know for sure.

The IMF man told the Gazneft man to step to the side and called John and Petr forward. John handed over four rubber-banded bundles of vouchers. The IMF man began to pull off the rubber bands, and the Gazneft man said something to him.

"He wants our vouchers to be checked for forgeries," said Petr.

The IMF man answered.

"He says they are authentic and procedure is being followed."

John exhaled a breath he didn't know he'd been holding.

The IMF man ran their vouchers through the counting machine, put them in a new envelope, wrote a number on it, wrote a second receipt, and handed it to Petr. He produced a ledger from somewhere under the dais—presumably out of the briefcase he'd carried in—and began to enter information.

Because of the special circumstances Gazneft had arranged, the vouchers weren't identified by nine-digit serial numbers like the ones they'd bought in Moscow; instead, they were identified by the towns where they'd been issued, with five-digit numbers, most of them beginning with a zero or two.

John and Petr had spent most of the bus ride filling in the necessary paperwork for official submission, and now the IMF guy asked them to produce it. The Gazneft guy must have had his paperwork in his manila envelope. For a second John thought maybe Gazneft had forgotten it—dare to dream—but the IMF guy checked the sheets against his totals, stamped them, and added them to his official envelopes. He did some arithmetic and entered more data into his ledger, and then began to speak; impassively. This was the moment of truth.

"Of the ownership shares," translated Petr, "being issued and registered here today . . . thirty-eight-point-four percent is issued and registered to the 'Representatives of the Workers of Gazneft' . . . sixty-one-point-six percent is issued to 'Kovac-Mills Fund.'"

The IMF man banged his gavel again and adjourned the meeting, quickly packing up his ledger and counting machine and walking out without a word to anyone.

For a long moment, the Gazneft man glared at Petr and John, then made his own exit also without a word.

Then the room was empty and Petr let out a whoop and John shouted, "Hell fucking yeah," before remembering he was in an ex-church. The two men vigorously high-fived and fist-pumped. Anna walked over to them, tentative if she should join in the celebration. John gave her a big high five and said, "Give us a shout!" As she let go with her own celebratory whoop, Petr picked her up in a bear hug and twirled her around like a poor-man's Fred Astaire. Though no one was feeling poor. They'd just secured 61.6 percent of approximately 2.8 billion dollars' worth of stock. About 1.7 billion dollars of equity. John was up on the dais leading them in the rousing chorus of "We Are the Champions" when all the lights went off.

After a moment of confusion, the super came in and told them to go away.

As they walked out of the ex-church, they debated briefly going to a hotel versus going back to the bus stop and waiting for a ride back to Ufa and its long, long train to Omsk. All told it would be about another twenty-five or thirty hours of travel and, with the return bus (per John's timetable) less than two hours away, they decided if they had to sleep they might as well sleep away some of the travel time.

Even though it wasn't yet seven in the morning, the sun was fully risen and generating a slow mist of melted nighttime frost. The bus stop itself was a small shelter, closed on three sides and decorated with mosaics of Red Army soldiers in various heroic poses from the Great Patriotic War., i.e., World War II.

John and Petr sat down on the bench with Anna between them, once again enfolded in Petr's jacket.

"It's funny," said Petr, to John. "Today everyone acts as if to be a Communist was to be the opposite of a Nazi. They forget that the Communists and Nazis—Stalin and Hitler—were best friends with plans to share Europe between them until Hitler saw the opportunity to take it all and invaded the Soviet half. Till then, your American folk singers like Petr what's his name . . . 'We Shall Overcome' . . ."

"Pete Seeger."

"Yes, like Pete, were singing songs about how America shouldn't get involved in the war against fascism, how Roosevelt shouldn't send them to die for British ideals. Or the Sudetenland."

"Fascist lies," mumbled Anna, who was already drifting off to sleep. "We defeated fascism. America and Britain were in principal spectators to our victory." Without opening her eyes, she snaked a slim arm out of the oversized sleeve in her half of Petr's coat and raised a victorious fist.

Petr smiled but, before he could answer her, a little man jogged into sight and into the bus stop shelter. He took a moment to catch his breath, then said, "John Mills? Petr Kovac?"

"Yeah," said John.

The man began to speak in Russian.

"He's from the hotel," said Petr. "He says our partner from the Hungry Duck has a message for us."

John accepted a folded note and handed back a ten-dollar tip. The man bowed from the waist and began to walk back the way he'd come.

John took a look at the note to confirm it was in Russian, and then handed it over to Petr to read.

"Huh," said Petr. "This is Czech, written phonetically in Cyrillic. I guess our friend didn't want the hotel staff to know what was up."

"Makes sense," said John. "There can't be more than one hotel in this town; the Gazneft guy is probably staying there."

Petr nodded, and began to sound out the message. "Our friend says he, as security chief, has been assaulted with phone calls from, it seems, everyone in the company, trying to figure out who we are and what we were doing there. He says to expect another note at the main station in Omsk to tell us what happens. A news update. He says to look for a policeman holding an envelope on the platform when we get off. I wonder how he knows a policeman in Omsk?"

"More likely he'll just call the police station there and hire someone?"

"Ah, yes, I suppose so. Forgive me, I'm a bit tired."

John chuckled. "We should probably, one of us, be awake to make sure we don't miss the bus. I'll take the first hour."

Petr nodded. "Good, thank you." Anna was asleep now with her head on Petr's shoulder. Petr put his head on hers and inside of two minutes he was asleep. Or at least, he looked asleep. After a few minutes more, with his eyes closed, he said, "John, we made maybe a billion dollars this morning. A good day's work."

"Yes, indeed," said John. Petr didn't say anything else, and John stood up and started to pace, to try to stay awake.

CHAPTER 13

Petr and Anna were sleeping so peacefully, and John was so hopped up on nicotine, he decided to just let them sleep and keep the bus vigil himself. Around nine, the bus arrived. By midafternoon, they were back in Ufa, and by early evening, they were on the train to Omsk.

It was almost identical to the Moscow train—actually, it was the Moscow train, just the through version instead of the return version. It was a little shorter but the cars were identical. John and Petr had decided to shrug off some of their righteous indignation and just buy however many tickets they were asked to buy, figuring it was worth it to make sure they were actually getting the first-class accommodations they were paying for—not so much for the comfort but to make sure they had a locked door between their duffle bags of money and the rest of the train.

They also decided to get Anna her own cabin, and an advance on her salary so she could buy some clothes and her own coat. While she shopped in a Soviet-style folding-table market that ran along the edge of the train platform, John went and found a phone and, after three different exchanges, was connected to Moscow, and through Moscow, managed to place a call to his home in the United States.

The phone rang eight times before being answered—long enough for John to imagine a half dozen catastrophes that could be causing the delay, all of them caused in turn by his failure to be at home with his pregnant wife.

"Sorry—hello?" she said, picking up just before the call went to the answering machine. "I was just coming in with the groceries."

"Should you be carrying groceries? What does the doctor say?"

"John!" she said, and then laughed. "Yes, carrying groceries is fine, I'm a long way from being put on bed rest."

"Is that the Texas cowgirl in you talking?"

"No, that's the doctors talking."

"Texas cowdoctors?"

"You think I've been going to a vet?"

"I don't mean cow-doctors, I mean, like, doctors who are cowboys."

"It was a joke, John."

"But you're really okay?"

"I am, aside from missing you."

"Well, things are moving fast over here. I may be able to come home in triumph sooner than I thought. We're closing in on the Rubicon. I think."

"You're not doing anything dangerous, are you? I mean, I know you said you weren't, but I worry you just don't want me to worry."

"Don't worry, I'm not doing anything dangerous. Right now the biggest danger is to my cholesterol level if I keep eating delicious greasy Slavic food."

There was a sharp whistle—not a train whistle, but a two-fingers-in-the-mouth whistle. John turned around. It was Petr, waving for him to hurry up.

"Honey, I've got to go. I'm totally fine, just promise me you won't go on any cattle drives or anything. Take it easy. Hire a pre-nanny, if that's something that exists."

"Okay, John, I promise. Be careful, okay?"

"Careful is my middle name. I gotta run; give yourself a hug and kiss for me."

"Should I send myself flowers too?"

"Yes. And write something really romantic on the card for me. There's a copy of *Bartlett's* in my office. I'm thinking Keats, Shelley, Wordsworth, something like that."

Petr tugged on his shoulder. Now there was a train whistle. "We'll miss the train, John, come on."

"I love you, Marsha."

"I love you too, John."

John hung up the phone and he and Petr jogged to the train. Anna was standing in the doorway to their train car, keeping a fulminating ticket lady from closing it. John and Petr squeezed past her up onto the train stairs. John held out a ten to mollify the ticket lady, which helped, slightly. As soon as they were out of the way, she slammed the door closed and a moment later the train began to move.

Now they had a good twenty hours to Omsk, for rest and recuperation. The Ufa–Omsk train was strictly an express, so there wouldn't be a chance to get out at the edge of the voucher territory, at an earlier stop, and begin buying vouchers there, moving inward. Instead they'd start in Omsk the city and move outward, spiraling around Omsk the oblast until they reached Tara, where the auction would take place the following Sunday. There really wasn't anything else to be said, planning-wise, at least until the train got to where it was going. So, five minutes after the train began moving, John and Petr were in their compartment, and Anna was in hers, and five minutes after that, they were all asleep.

John slept soundly for the next twelve hours, only waking up twice. The first time was when Petr left the compartment, and John heard their door unlatch, open, and close, then a light knock on Anna's door, followed by it unlatching, opening, and closing. The second time he woke up was when Petr came back. It was dark, but there was enough predawn light in the car that John and Petr briefly made eye contact. Petr shrugged, so did John, and they both went back to sleep.

◆

Sometime in the early morning, still a few hours outside of Omsk, all three members of the voucher traveling party were slept-out and awake. Anna had appointed herself manager of food and had fixed them breakfast and tea in her compartment. As they ate, conversation turned to what the Gazneft execs might do in response to the unexpected competition.

"I'm not really sure what they can do," said Petr, taking a bite of honey-drizzled bread, "if the auctions have already been announced and vouchers have already been distributed."

"And they can't print new ones," said John. "Not without the cooperation of the IMF, which I can't imagine would be forthcoming."

"How much do you think the IMF is involved in this?"

"Hard to guess," said John, with an added "thank you" to Anna as she handed him a fresh mug of tea. "It depends what they're trying to do. On the one hand, they won't want to help Gazneft manager's steal the company. On the other hand, Russia's commissar class—if I can call it that—is already disinclined to turn over any economic power to them. I'd guess they're trying to walk a not-doing-anything-illegal-or-immoral-while-also-not-making-waves tightrope. It can't be easy.

"But if Russia dumps them—tells them to take their financing and shove it—the Russian economy might collapse. And instead of becoming a Westernized, prosperous South Korea, Russia could end up as . . . well, a North Korea. With a new Stalin, no functional markets, and no way to feed itself. And with its only tangible asset being the world's largest nuclear stockpile."

John took a sip of his tea. "If those were the stakes you were dealing with—well, you'd probably turn the other cheek to about anything short of murder, wouldn't you?"

"Do you think what *you're* doing is immoral?" said Anna, who hadn't spoken in a while.

"Carpetbagging, you mean?" said John.

"Carpetbagging?" said Petr.

"It means taking advantage of a postconflict area to buy up undervalued assets. Comes from the American Civil War—or just after it—when Northern speculators were coming down to the Reconstruction-era South and buying stuff up, paying bargain-basement prices for things because they were the only show in town. I mean, underpaying because they were the only ones with money."

"Extreme buyer's market," said Petr. "Carpetbagging. Good to know."

"Yes," said Anna. "That is what I meant. I mean, you are buying things that belong to the Russian people for much less than they're worth."

"Yeah," said John. "That's true. But the reason buyer's markets exist is because people want to sell. And sure, the South got screwed over by carpetbagging, to a certain extent. But, without Northern capital—hard currency, American dollars—they wouldn't have been able to rebuild at all. No one was forcing them to sell. Circumstances were forcing them, sure, but not the people buying from them—they wanted to sell. Willing sellers, willing buyers.

"The people we're buying these vouchers from are selling them because they want our money more than the vouchers. The vouchers are worthless to them, but hard currency is worth a lot. You can barter, maybe, but you can't buy food with the vouchers. And in the end, no matter who owns Gazneft, the jobs will still be in Russia, the gas will still be sold by Russia, it's just a question of where the profits end up. If the managers of the company own it, maybe the money stays in Russia, or maybe it goes to Swiss bank accounts. Either way, the money we're spending into the local economies of these Podunk towns will probably do more good for the people concerned than the Gazneft profits would have.

"And sure, it looks funny, but we're not actually paying less than the vouchers are worth. The vouchers are worth whatever people sell them for. By definition. It seems harsh, but letting markets find their own balance—controlled by an 'invisible hand,' as the first great economist Adam Smith described it—leads to much more prosperity in the end. For everyone."

"Really?" said Anna, skeptically.

"Well," said John. "Look at Japan and India. After the Second World War, they both got new governments. Japan got a free-market system designed by the United States, and India got a protectionist system designed by a British-Colonial transition government.

"India already had industry, whereas Japan's was mostly destroyed. But with free markets—and plenty of carpetbagging—Japan turned into the world's biggest economy, outside the US. And people are saying soon it'll be the biggest.

"Over the same time, India stagnated. The government stopped outsiders from coming in and buying up and modernizing Indian businesses; they wanted to protect traditional stuff like sitting and spinning. As Gandhi put it. And they succeeded, in protecting tradition—but failed in building a prosperous country. No outside investment, no market competition, no invisible hand.

"Based on the size of its population, its natural resources, a culture dedicated to hard work and building for the future of your family, India ought to be the richest country in the world. At least as rich as Japan. But it got the Marx treatment, so most of the country still doesn't have indoor plumbing.

"We'll get rich off this. So will Russia, in the end." John looked at Petr. "At least, that's the theory. Maybe it's just what we tell ourselves so we can sleep at night."

Petr nodded and took a sip of his tea.

"Crossed fingers," he said.

Anna stirred some porridge, pouring boiling water into it as she did.

"Mine will be crossed too."

After breakfast, small talk devolved into all-day naps, which were ended—for John and Petr, anyway—by a train whistle signaling their arrival at Omsk. John and Petr and Anna got off the train into a hectic, surprisingly crowded station. Why it surprised John, he wasn't altogether sure; it was a city with a population of some-thing like a million people. It just seemed so remote from the rest of the world.

Central Asia, on the lonely side of the Himalayas, is a black hole in the minds of most people who don't live there. The only part of the world with fewer people living in it is the Sahara. When people asked Peter the Great about the eastern extent of his empire, he couldn't answer them—it was a hundred years before the United States started existing, and already the west coast of North America was better mapped than the eastern two-thirds of Russia.

Siberia—where Omsk is, where John was for the first time—by itself is one and a half times as large as all of Europe, with one-twentieth the population. John guessed there were more people within a twenty-mile radius of Central Park than in all Siberia. And yet, here was a perfectly normal-looking major city, with people going about their lives as if they were in some normal part of the world. Why shouldn't they? It just felt a little strange.

"There," said Petr, pointing to a policeman holding an enve-lope in front of his chest, like a chauffeur at an airport. The trio walked over to him. Petr said a few words in Russian, the policeman handed over the envelope and walked away without saying anything.

"It's in Czech again," said Petr, having torn the envelope open and slid out a letter. "Huh," he said reading. "Our colonel friend could use some work on his grammar. Of course, Czech is the least Slavic of all the Slavic languages. . . . Let me read to the end. . . ."

Petr sucked his teeth and nodded.

"Good news," said John.

"No," said Petr.

"What does it say?"

"Gazneft has spent the last twenty-four hours panicking about us and trying to figure out who we are. They couldn't change the Omsk auction, which has already been announced for this Sunday in Tara. And the Irkutsk auction has also already been announced and will take place as scheduled next Sunday. But the Jewish Oblast auction and the Magadan Oblast auction had *not* been announced. The locations have been changed, to even tinier and more remote villages. And the dates have been changed. Moved up to this Sunday. So, this Sunday, three simultaneous auctions."

"And the IMF has nothing to say about it."

"The letter doesn't mention the IMF."

"I suppose the argument is that people aren't supposed to be at more than one auction anyway, since theoretically they're supposed to be for locals. So why not have them all at once."

"Yes," said Petr. "So . . . does that mean we're screwed for two of the auctions?"

"Unless we split up," said John.

"True," said Petr. "If we split we can make all of them."

"All but one of them."

Petr looked at him. He looked at Petr. Then he looked at Anna and said, "Would you excuse us for a moment?"

"Of course," she said, looking slightly embarrassed as she walked away to browse a newsstand.

"You don't trust her?"

"With tens of thousands of our money, in cash? No, I don't. Or rather, I'd say, I trust her as much as it's possible to trust anyone you meet as a total stranger on a train who you've known for less than a week."

"I trust her," said Petr.

"Really?"

"Yes. And I think I'm better able to judge."

"Why, because you fucked her?"

Petr narrowed his eyes.

"I'm sorry Petr, I didn't mean that. What I mean is—clearly you like her. I like her too. But neither of us *knows* her."

"We've known her longer than I'd known you when we flew to Russia together."

"That was different."

"Why? Because we met in an expensive hotel instead of on a Soviet train?"

"No—well—yes, actually. I had references. I evaluated you as a businessman. And objectively, I think you're thinking with your dick."

"Fuck you, John."

"Okay, not thinking with your dick—I just didn't want to sound like a teenage girl and say something like you were thinking with your heart. She was a damsel in distress; we rescued her, now you feel protective. It's the oldest story in Western civilization. But that doesn't mean we can hand her a bag of cash. Cash that, by the way, we can't replace. Not out here; there's nothing hard in Siberian banks.

"Your falling for her doesn't mean we can just hand her a bag filled with more money than she has earned, total, in her entire life, and trust her with it. It's not logical. I'm not saying she's a bad person, I'm just saying the only thing we know for sure about her is that she *is* a *person*. A human being. With human flaws, probably."

"She wouldn't take our charity."

"And that's one of the reasons I like her. But let's also consider this: I don't speak Russian. Even if you don't need a translator for Tuvan or Chukchi or something, *I* need one for the lingua franca."

"Flash a five-dollar bill and you'll have fifty translators."

"Translators I can trust?"

"Apparently, you didn't need to trust the one you've been using."

John sighed, closed his eyes, and pushed a finger into the center of his forehead. He was trying to think. He had one of those sleep hangovers you get from sleeping too long and at the wrong time of day.

"Look," said John. "I don't trust her. Not implicitly, anyway. I'm sorry, but I don't. But I do trust *you*. So, if you're sure you want to bet on her . . . then I won't stand in the way."

Petr looked over at Anna. Her back was to them. She was kneeling down in front of a little girl, picking up the girl's fallen scarf, wrapping it around the girl's neck and adjusting it for maximum insulation. It was like the trailer for a heartwarming TV movie. (Thought John.)

"Yes," said Petr. "I'm sure."

"Okay," said John. "Well—let's not waste any more time then."

◆

From there the decisions were easy to make. John, Petr, and Anna would each take a third of their remaining cash on hand. Anna would stay in Omsk and start buying vouchers. John would go to the Jewish Autonomous Oblast and Petr to the Magadan Oblast. All three would spend the week buying as many vouchers as they could.

On Saturday, they'd fill out the voucher paperwork and hire planes, trains, and automobiles to get them on time to the absurd, remote auction sites. Then they'd rendezvous in Irkutsk for the final auction a week after that. Sounded positively simple.

It wasn't until John was in a Lada cab from the train station to the Omsk airport that it occurred to him he should have left Anna the Makarov pistol he'd been carrying. He figured Petr probably would instead—he had stayed behind to give Anna a crash course in the voucher forms she'd have to fill out. Between the two of them—John and Petr, if only one was going to have a gun—Petr would probably be a better choice. Ex-soldier and all that. Of course, John lived in Texas, so maybe it was a wash.

Back at the station, it took Petr an hour or so to teach Anna the ins and outs of the absurdly tedious number-transfer voucher-form procedure. John was already in the air by the time he finished. He and Anna parted at the taxi stand. She was going stay behind and check for vouchers in the train station bric-a-brac market; he was following John to the airport to find a flight of his own. He pulled the Makarov out of his pocket and tried to slip it into hers. She put her hand on his and stopped him.

"I hate guns." She kissed him on the cheek, he kissed her on the mouth, and for a moment they embraced. As Petr held her, he couldn't help but wonder at his getting wrapped up in this kind of flighty, stranger-in-a-strange-land holiday romance. Of course it wouldn't last. In a few weeks, she'd go home to her family a very wealthy woman; he'd go back to Prague a very, very, very wealthy man, and they would almost certainly never see each other again. Right?

If he hadn't known all that, and known that this kind of exciting adventure brought people together in strange ways, he might have said he was feeling . . . pangs of love for her. But what can you do? He wasn't naive. Neither was she.

Their embrace broke and they parted. She looked back at him several times before she disappeared into the market. A minute after that he was in a taxi to the airport, idly running his hand over the pistol in his pocket, wondering if he'd be able to take it on the plane.

CHAPTER 14

As it happens, he *was* able to take it on the plane. There were no Omsk–Magadan commercial flights, so he had to charter something. And the sturdiest-looking plane with the range to get him to Magadan was not the small single- or maybe double-engine job he'd had in mind. It was a retired, privatized—privately owned and operated—Tupolev Tu-4. Which is to say, it was the Soviet copy of the American B-29, the Superfortress bomber that dropped Little Boy and Fat Man on Hiroshima and Nagasaki.

Strange plane on its own. During the War, the Soviets had repeatedly asked for B-29s to be included in Lend-Lease and had been repeatedly rebuffed. But three B-29s were forced to make emergency landings in the Soviet far east after bombing raids on Japan.

The Americans requested they be returned, and were rebuffed. Instead, the B-29s were flown to Moscow, to the Tupolev design bureau. Reverse engineering them became a sort of Manhattan

Project with nearly a thousand different Soviet factories being used to produce individual duplicate parts.

Because Soviet tooling was all metric, the B-29's thin aluminum skin had to be thickened to the nearest metric unit, making the Tupolev copy substantially heavier. The Soviets had to suss out the chemical formulas of the superstrong, super-lightweight metal alloys used in the B-29's construction, which they did with surprising alacrity. Or perhaps it was unsurprising alacrity, as Russia had produced a gigantic proportion of the world's greatest scientists and mathematicians and had been forced into reverse engineering not by a lack of brains but by an overabundance of Communism.

Other than its relative heftiness, the Tu-4 was a perfect copy, from the computer-controlled gun system to the automatic wing deicers. The only major changes were the engines—which were copied from a different American radial engine design—and the radios, which were cribbed not from the B-29, but the B-25s Russia *had* been given in Lend-Lease.

Even with an industrial maximum effort, the reverse-engineering program didn't finish in time for World War II. Instead, the planes were debuted in 1947 in highly dramatic fashion. Americans were invited to attend a Russian military parade. Three Tu-4s were flown over. The implication was that these were the three captured B-29s. Then a fourth flew over, on its own, and the Americans knew that the Russians now had a strategic bomber that could drop a nuke on any American city from Chicago to LA.

Petr learned all of this in a lengthy and rather frank lecture from his pilot, the Tu-4's only crewman. No copilot or flight engineer or any of the other members of the standard crew of eleven. Though, the pilot explained, they were mainly unnecessary, since it's not like he needed gunners or a bombardier, and he was his own navigator.

Petr sat in the copilot's seat, with the big hemisphere of glass that constituted the front of the plane wrapping around him, making him think of the Millennium Falcon. He mentioned this to the pilot, who asked if it was true that Czechoslovakia had split because *Stars Wars* had been released with subtitles in Czech but not Slovak.

Then the pilot made a joke about the plane being a piece of junk, and never telling him the odds. When Petr asked if he'd ever crashed a plane, the pilot said, "Not this plane."

After that, they didn't talk for a few hours, until Petr asked if the plane had a toilet, and was instructed on the lavatorial use of the bomb bay. Petr was actually a little disappointed when the pilot told him he was only kidding, and yes, there was a regular toilet. (Though in its own way, he said, it was still a bomb bay.)

When they landed, late in the evening, they did a shot together of deicing fluid—which was, to Petr's amusement, high-octane vodka. Apparently, it was perfect for the job. Then Petr said his goodbyes and climbed out of the plane, and walked across the (unseasonably?) icy and very windy tarmac to the small Soviet terminal, where a lone attendant said she would be unable to call him a cab but advised him that the hotel was only a short walk up the road.

Three hours later and chilled to his bone marrow, Petr checked into the Hotel Revolution Engels Marx. He asked another lone attendant, a middle-aged, reasonably attractive lady at the hotel's desk, if she could find him a rental car for the morning and for about a week's use after that. She said no. He asked if she could find him a car to buy. She said she would try. She handed him his room key and asked if he would like a space heater for the room or a prostitute. He said a space heater would be adequate, even though—as she pointed out—the price was the same.

The next morning, only mildly regretting his choice re room heating, he walked the ten paces from his room to the tiny lobby, where a tiny table was set up with black bread and some sort of schmaltz to spread on it, and a tea samovar. The same woman was still on duty, and told him she had found him a car, which he could purchase for a thousand dollars American. He asked what it was. She said a 1967 ZAZ Zaporozhets.

Petr countered with an offer of fifty dollars American. She said the price was a thousand dollars because it was the only car available for sale. Petr countered that for a thousand dollars, every car in Magadan was for sale. They settled on two hundred for the car and a fifty-dollar finder's fee, plus Petr's promise to return the car to her when he didn't need it anymore. He handed over the money, she handed over the keys, and he walked out into the cold June morning. Still in the low forties, Fahrenheit, likely to rise to a high of around fifty.

Still, things were not so bad. An advantage of Magadan is that it is so remote and so empty that virtually the entire population of the Magadan Oblast lived in Magadan city, so the voucher buying wouldn't be too great an obstacle.

No, the obstacle would be getting to the Bering Sea fishing town where the actual auction was being held. But he had a few days still before he had to worry about that.

He climbed into his new '67 ZAZ, and—after flipping the fuel pump switch—pressed the red starter button in the center of the dashboard and held it for about thirty seconds until the engine turned over. He had just wrestled off the hand brake when there was a tapping at the window. It was the lady from the front desk. The window didn't seem to roll down, so Petr opened the door and leaned out.

She pointed to the passenger-side footwell.

"There is a flap there, in the floor. You can open it so you can ice fish without having to leave the car."

Petr gave her a second to continue. When she didn't, he said, "Thank you very much," and drove away, wondering how fatalist one had to be to drive a ZAZ onto a frozen lake.

CHAPTER 15

John's flight was somewhat less dramatic—no B-29 copy for him, though in a way, not so far off. His flight to the Yevreyskaya Avtonomnaya Oblast, the bizarre historical relic, the Jewish Autonomous Oblast, was in a Lisunov Li-2—a copy of the American DC-3, the legendarily indestructible prewar passenger plane. It wasn't a reverse engineer job; it was actually produced under license from its American designer. Despite having the same metric-conversion problems—the heavier skin and so forth—it seemed to be an unflappably solid plane and was surprisingly comfortable.

Unlike Petr's Tu-4 charter, this was an actual scheduled airline flight—and not only did there seem to be no Jewish passengers (perhaps unsurprisingly), there were no Caucasian passengers, other than John, anyway. The passengers were all East Asian. Probably this flight, to the JAO's capital Birobidzhan, was the closest thing to a flight to extreme northeast China. The Chinese border was only a few miles away. Maybe there was a connecting flight into Chinese territory. Either way, John landed in the only territory in the world whose official language was Yiddish listening to Mandarin and Korean and what he assumed was Manchu.

There were cabs waiting outside of the miniterminal but no one needed one but John, as the entire contingent of Chinese and Korean passengers got aboard a bus and disappeared. The cab driver spoke no English and, apparently, no Yiddish, as John tried speaking to him in German. But John had picked up enough Russian to ask for a hotel, which is where he ended up.

There was a man at the hotel's front desk. John crossed his fingers and asked if the man spoke English.

"But of course, sir."

"Do you really? Ha," said John, with considerable relief.

"I do really, sir. May I get you a room for the night?"

"You may," said John, tickled by the formality. "May I ask where you learned English?"

"Israel," said the man.

"Oh, are you Jewish?"

The man laughed. "No, of course not, sir—no Jews live here. But there was an exchange program to try to promote Jewish remigration to Soviet territory."

"Did it work?"

"It did not, sir."

"Do you speak Hebrew?"

"I do not, sir."

"Huh. Anyway—yes, I'd like a room and, if you could manage it, a rental car and a translator for the morning."

"I believe I can arrange a hire car. A translator may be difficult."

"Were you the only exchange student?"

"No, sir. But I'm the only one who came back."

John laughed. The man continued: "Still, there are a few other people who speak English but they're mainly Chinese, concerned with cross-border trade. Not likely to accept outside work without permission, which would likely be difficult to obtain."

"How about you?"

"I own this hotel, sir."

"Do you have any other guests?"

"Yes, sir. Business is good."

"They're Chinese?"

"Yes, sir. And Russians doing business with the Chinese."

"Do you have someone—an assistant—who could take your place for a few days?"

"It's possible, sir, but I am reluctant."

"Do you own a car?"

"I do, sir. A very fine car. A Subaru." The man was obviously very proud—and hell, why not. John had nothing but respect for Subarus.

"The hotel must be doing well."

"Yes, sir."

"Pardon my intrusion on your personal business."

"Not at all, sir."

"How much to hire you and your car for a week?"

The man hesitated.

"I'm happy to include salary for your replacement."

The man continued to hesitate.

"How about a thousand dollars American? Half now, half when I leave, on Sunday or Monday."

The man nodded. "Yes, sir, I could do that." He turned and pulled a key off a hook.

"You will be in room four. I will have my car here at seven tomorrow morning. Will that be satisfactory?"

"Perfectly," said John. "Thank you."

"Thank you, sir. Have a pleasant evening."

CHAPTER 16

Petr had been standing in Magadan square, buying vouchers and looking for the right kids to hire to spread the word around town—the standard operating procedure he and John and Anna had worked out—when a car pulled up directly beside him. A black Mercedes. A tall, blond, suit-wearing Russian got out, straightened his shiny necktie, and approached. Petr felt suddenly relieved to have the Makarov in his pocket.

"You," said the man, addressing Petr. "You cannot do business here without permission."

"Permission from who?" said Petr.

"The Boss," said the man.

"Do you know who I am?"

"No," said the man.

"An Avtoritet in the Lyuberetskaya Bratva." He was pretty sure that was the Mafia name Anna had used.

The man paused, ruminated, and went on: "We were not informed of your arrival."

"You should have been. I'll have a word with my secretary when I get back."

"I noticed you are not Russian," said the man.

"I am one of the new European market men."

The tall man in the suit nodded. "The Boss will want to greet you personally. He is very particular about such things."

Petr nodded. "Of course. When would be convenient for him?"

"We will have you to him very quickly."

Petr felt the water closing over his head. He checked his watch.

"Sir," said the man, opening the back door of the Mercedes and gesturing for Petr to climb inside. Petr wondered momentarily if he shouldn't make a run for it. But then what? A shoot out?

"Very well. But I'm short of time."

"Of course, sir," said the tall man, closing Petr's door and getting in beside him, from the other side.

"We're going to see the Boss," the tall man said to the driver. And without turning or answering, the driver began to drive.

◆

Petr expected to be delivered to a dacha. Instead, he was taken back to the airport, to a derelict Soviet hangar. The tall, blond guy got out of the Mercedes and went into the hangar through a side door. A moment later the hangar's main doors opened. There was a Learjet inside.

The waters over Petr's head had closed. He climbed out of the car. The tall man was lowering the Learjet's fold-away staircase.

"Where is the Boss?"

"On the Caspian, sir. It will be a short flight."

"Splendid," said Petr. He looked back at the Mercedes, sighed, and climbed aboard. The tall man followed him up, pulled in the ladder, closed the door, and five minutes later they were in the air.

◆

So, less than twelve hours after an eight-hour flight east, Petr was back on a plane for an eight-hour flight west. And he had no idea what waited for him at the other end. A charade where he continued to play the mafioso? Would he be playing *to* a mafioso? A friendly mafioso? A competing mafioso? Would he be found out and killed? Would he pull it off and be killed for infringing on someone else's territory?

Beside the tall, blond, shiny-suit-wearing man who had brought him to the plane, there were two other tracksuit-wearing young mafia types on the plane, and two pilots. Were mafia pilots in the Mafia or were they outside contractors? Assuming he would leave the pilots alone—after all, without the pilots, what would the point be?—there were three bad guys on the plane Petr would have to deal with . . . if he wanted to hijack the jet, say, and have it fly him somewhere safe. He had a pistol with eight rounds in it. He was an ex-soldier. He thought there was a fair chance he could kill the three mafiosos before they knew what was happening.

However, he had no idea if the Makarov was in working order. It might not fire; if it did fire, it might not cycle. He had no way of knowing if the bad guys Anna had taken it from were using it as a gun or as a prop.

Add to that: *Goldfinger.* The James Bond movie. According to Bond's chat with Pussy Galore aboard Goldfinger's private jet, a

stray bullet would cause a pressurized plane cabin—like the Learjet's—to instantly vent into the thin outside air, sucking everything
and everyone in the plane along with it. Petr had absolutely no idea
if this were true but it sounded plausible. And, add to that, he could
feel his hands shaking, slightly.

Add to that the fundamental insanity of his hijacking a plane.

No, he'd just have to let this play out. Better to take his chances
with whatever he'd got himself into than commit accidental suicide.

"Would you like a drink?" said the tall man, cutting into Petr's
mental image of himself being sucked out a cabin window like
Gert Fröbe.

"Yes," said Petr.

"We're bringing supplies to the Boss," said the man. "He would
want me to make you comfortable." He stood up and walked
toward the back of the plane, where wooden crates were held down
by a series of twine nets.

"Whiskey? Gin? Champagne? A cocktail, perhaps?"

"Champagne, why not," said Petr. The tall man laughed and
walked back to Petr's seat near the front. He held a bottle of vodka
out for Petr to inspect.

"Is the year okay? Would you like to smell the cork?"

Petr smiled. Big joke. The tall man retrieved six glasses from a
cupboard and began to pour.

"It is from his vineyard in France," said the tall man. "Only
the finest grapes are grown there." One of the men in tracksuits laughed and the other laughed with him. The tall man
handed Petr a glass, handed one to each of the tracksuit guys,
then walked forward to the cockpit carrying two more. When
he returned a moment later, empty handed, Petr asked, "They
drink and fly?"

"It would be rude not to offer it to them. And it would be rude for them to say no. Am I correct?" This time he laughed and Petr did his best to laugh along. He must not have been very persuasive.

"Do not worry, friend, they are both MiG pilots. You are in safe hands. What do you say in Czechoslovakia, when you drink?"

"*Na zdraví.*"

"*Na zdraví!*" said the tall man, and then the two guys in tracksuits. Petr nodded his head and they all drank.

"What's in your duffle bag?" said the tall man. Petr opened the bag of money, so the tall man could see the clothes on top.

"What?" the tall man continued, "They don't give you money for luggage, when you come to work for the Bratva?"

"I use a cheap bag so no one tries to steal this off me," said Petr. The man nodded, and began to pour a second round.

◆

Petr woke up when the Learjet's wheels hit the landing strip. His head throbbed. Around him, the three mafiosos had also been woken up and were gradually collecting themselves. Petr lit a cigarette and offered his pack, one by one, to the three other men. They each accepted and lit up with their own lighters. Three or four empty bottles rolled lackadaisically around the cabin. Through the fog in his head, Petr was vaguely surprised they hadn't broken when the plane landed. It was a truly awful landing.

No one said anything as the plane came to a halt. One of the pilots opened the door and let the ladder down. As Petr and his three drinking companions filed off the plane into the brisk evening air, they all began to take deep breaths and come back to life.

"Where are we?" said Petr.

"Astrakhan," said the blond man. There was a Mercedes waiting for them, along with a big Gaz jeep. The two men in tracksuits and several more out of the Gaz began to unload crates of vodka from the plane and reload them into the Gaz. The tall blond man directed Petr into the Mercedes and told the driver to drive.

◆

Petr wasn't sure how much more time passed before he woke up again—this time with a truly miserable hangover. It was night, anyway; the sky was black, but illuminated by flashing blue lights, on the roofs of what seemed like a million police cars. Were they being arrested? Would that be good or bad?

"Come on," said the tall, blond man, shaking Petr's shoulder. "The Boss will be waiting."

"What's with all the cops?" said Petr.

"Security."

"Security?"

"I don't know the Czech word. Like, protection."

"I know what security means—" They were speaking Russian— "Why are you getting it from the cops?"

"It's cheaper than paying for full-time, bringing everyone from Magadan. The Boss is just on vacation, after all."

Petr nodded. He could hear water sloshing and smell salt. Once his eyes adjusted to the flashing lights, he could see a yacht tied up just beyond the cars. And he could hear music. It was in English, over distorted guitars. Something about someone destroying the singer's sweater by pulling a thread as he walked away.

Petr hadn't grasped that the flashing blue police lights weren't being used for policing—they were being used as disco balls for a party on the yacht—a yacht that was almost disconcertingly elegant. A long, sleek, wooden sailing yacht, about a hundred feet long that looked like it had had its mast (or masts) removed and its elegant stern covered with four gigantic outboard motors. Between the motors, Petr could see bits of Farsi. Presumably this was a Persian yacht from the Caspian's southern edge that had gone missing and ended up in Astrakhan.

The tall man led Petr aboard and over to a large man built like a wrestler who was sitting on a rear-facing bench with his feet up on a table near the boat's bow. Also on the table, and around it, and around the man, and around several other mafiosos—some seated and some on their feet—were girls, holding drinks and dancing, with their very long legs barely concealed by their very short skirts. They were swaying seductively to the somewhat melancholy sweater song. Just as the tall man and Petr arrived at the Boss's side, the music switched to an aggressively upbeat, distorted-guitar number about some guys "dissing" the singer's girl.

"Do you like the music?" said the Boss to the tall man and Petr. "It's new. I just had it flown in from Alaska two days ago. Big hit in America. It's called *Weezer*."

"Is 'Weezer' like 'Grunge' and 'Disco'?" said Petr, accepting the seat he was pointed to, at the Boss's left elbow.

"No, it's the name. Of the album. And the band. And maybe the style, too, who knows. But I like it."

The music started to say something about Buddy Holly, and the tall man cut in: "This guy showed up in Magadan yesterday and started trying to buy vouchers. He says he's with the Lyubeetskaya Bratva. An Avtoritet. He's Czech."

"I can tell he's Czech," said the Boss. "And I don't give a shit about vouchers."

"But Boss—"

"Did you hear what I said? I don't give a shit about vouchers." He grabbed an empty vodka bottle from the couch and threw it at the tall man's head. The tall man ducked, so did two girls behind him, and the bottle sailed off into the Volga River. The tall man said nothing.

"Did you fucking hear me?" said the Boss.

"Yes, Boss."

"I didn't come here to talk about business. I came here to get drunk and fuck and fish. Every day of the year my hands are full of business. For three days they're going to be empty. I—don't—give—a—shit—about—VOUCHERS." ·

The dancing had all stopped. The music continued. The singer began to vamp as the song came to an end. For a moment there was silence, before the next song began with a virtuoso distorted-guitar solo. "Now fuck off!" said the Boss. "And the rest of you—" he said, softening his tone dramatically, "dance. Everybody do a shot!" There was a general cheer from the two- or three-dozen partyers—who Petr now saw included a number of in-uniform policemen.

"Well," said Petr. "I should go. I'm sorry to have wasted your time."

"No," said the Boss. He pointed to the tall man. "He should go. You stay. Have a drink."

He handed Petr an unopened bottle of vodka as Petr watched the tall man scuttle away into the crowd.

"He's an idiot," said the Boss.

"Someone's nephew?"

"No," said the Boss. "Someone's son. Mine."

"Your son calls you 'Boss'?"

"Oh, he doesn't know it. His bitch whore of a mother dropped him on me when he was already a teenager and fucked off to Japan to be a nanny or some stupid shit."

Petr shrugged and opened his bottle of vodka. "Salut," he said, and took a long sip.

"Salut," said the Boss. "He's an idiot but he is right, you need my permission to do business in Magadan."

"Forgive me. May I have it?"

"And if you were with the Bratva you'd know that. So I assume you're another European banker with American money who thinks he can get rich in Russia. But let me tell you—those vouchers aren't worth shit. They'll never be worth shit. If Russians could trust their government, we'd be the richest country in the world. Fucking comedy-tragedy—see? The only things those vouchers are good for is wiping your ass with them."

Petr nodded. "You may be right. But I don't run the show, I just do a job, and I get paid whether they're used for profit or ass-wiping."

"Good man," said the Boss. "Stay and go fishing with me tomorrow. We'll be out on the Caspian at first light."

"Thank you," said Petr. "You're very kind but I should really get back."

"If you leave without me you'll have to walk back."

"Can your son drive me to the airport? Astrakhan has one, I presume."

"Sure. But I'll tell you what—if you spot a bigger fish than me, I'll let you buy vouchers in my city."

"Ah," said Petr. "Spot a fish? What is this, a nature club?"

The Boss laughed. "I'll explain in the morning. For now, drink up and find a couple girls to fuck. They all graduated from high school last week. I'm here to help them celebrate."

Petr took another long swig of his vodka. Somewhere, a giant stereo was blasting a song about taking a holiday. And Petr took another long swig of his vodka.

◆

Petr woke up in a state room, somewhere in the boat's mahogany interior. There were three girls scattered around the bed, at various acute angles. His head throbbed. Above him, somewhere, the giant stereo was still playing Weezer . . . some song he'd heard eighty times the night before, as the album played over and over and over, and everyone was much too drunk to care.

Petr pawed a bedside table looking for his watch; it wasn't there. After a short search of the room, he discovered one of the sleeping girls was wearing it as an anklet. He held up her leg to check the time. It was the middle of the afternoon. He dropped the leg back onto the bed and went to his en suite bathroom in search of a razor, didn't find one, and settled instead for washing his face with brain-shocking splashes of cold water.

Which is when he spun around and dashed back into the bedroom, looking for his duffle bag. A short, panicked search and he found it safely tucked under the bed, its contents undisturbed. He pushed it back under the bed, woke each girl with a smack to her bottom, left them stirring, and exited the room to head on deck.

The sailboat turned motor-yacht was puttering gracefully down the Volga; the open sea of the Caspian was already visible ahead.

The Boss was sitting just where Petr last remembered seeing him, on his backward-facing couch near the boat's rear. He saw Petr and smiled—and held up a bottle of vodka he had apparently just opened.

"Good morning, Petya! How did you sleep?"

"Well, thanks."

"I bet you did. Some of the men are annoyed that you monopolized the girls. My idiot son had to sleep alone."

"Sorry to hear that," said Petr, picking up a pack of cigarettes off a table. Finding it empty, he picked up another one, and pulled out a square. As he lit it, the Boss asked, "How many did you have?"

"Three," said Petr. "When I woke up."

The Boss laughed. "Good! Good, I knew I judged you well. I like Czechs; they're men. They have good Hun blood. Not like these fucking Volga peasants."

He whistled a few bars of the "Song of the Volga Boatmen," and threw the freshly opened bottle of vodka to Petr.

"Drink," he said. "To Good King Wenceslas."

Petr shrugged—hair of the dog, and all that—and took a long swig, before tossing the bottle back and plopping himself down on an adjacent couch.

"So, what are we fishing?"

"Are you joking?"

"No. Do I look like a fisherman? Czechoslovakia was landlocked."

"We're fishing dinosaurs."

"What?"

"Sturgeon! Two meters long. True dinosaurs, unchanged from the late Cretaceous epoch of the Mesozoic."

Petr's head hurt a bit. "What?"

"Didn't you study dinosaurs at school?"

"Not fucking . . . caviar fish dinosaurs."

"Prague must have had shit schools."

"And where did you go to primary school. The Sorbonne?"

"No, but there are many good fossil sites in Eastern Siberia; Magadan has a fine museum of bones."

"Huh," said Petr, turning to throw his down-to-the-filter cigarette overboard, then back to the table to find another. "So, these dinosaur fish are big enough to spot at a distance? Do they have fins?"

The Boss laughed again. "No, no. That's not quite how it works. When we're out on the water, you'll see."

"Can we change this goddamn music?" said Petr. "And can I get some of that coffee?" Nearer the front of the ship, some hungover cops were sharing a large thermos.

"Bring that back here," shouted the Boss, and one of the cops instantly began to walk sternward with a steaming cup. "What's the matter, you don't like this Weezer?"

"I liked it the first fifty thousand times I heard it. If I hear this guy say he's got a Dungeon Master's Guide one more time, I'm going to slit my fucking wrists."

The cop was holding out the coffee for the Boss. "Give it to him," said the Boss. Petr accepted the cup and discovered it was tea. Fucking Russians.

"You don't like tea?" said the Boss, reading Petr's face and laughing at his irritation.

"I like it fine but I'd give my left kidney for a cup of coffee."

The Boss laughed again: "You shouldn't say things like that in Russia. Someone will take you up on it," and turning from Petr to the front of the boat, he bellowed, "Coffee."

"Thanks," said Petr.

"So, who is the dumb shit you're working for to buy vouchers? Since it's clearly not the Bratva."

"Why shouldn't it be the Bratva? Aside from my forgetting to get your permission."

"'Cause they know, like I know, that there's no money in it. You might as well buy bonds in the government of Austria-Hungary."

Petr shrugged. "You may be right but, anyway, I'm just the middleman."

"For who?" The Boss had gotten up and was looking through a drawer in a sort of wet bar. He pulled out a CD, then opened another cabinet, and turned off Weezer. Petr meanwhile struggled to think of someone sufficiently scary that it could end the conversation. But who were Russian mobsters frightened of? He could say Cosa Nostra or Camorra or 'Ndrangheta or something Italian, but that might just start a turf war. He could say the CIA but then he ran the chance of the mob guy getting all patriotic on him.

"Mossad," said Petr. The Boss laughed. He was a surprisingly jovial guy.

"No shit," he said. "Trying to get the refuseniks' money back in Russia? Good. Those fucking Jews taking all our shit with them."

"I thought they weren't allowed to take anything with them."

"They weren't, but they were Jews. Rabinovich knows how to take care of himself."

The boat began to heave about a bit as they moved into the Caspian. It was a calm day but not river-calm.

"So how far out do we go before we start fishing?"

"Depends," said the Boss. "Grab those binoculars," he said, pointing to a pair among the scatterings of cigarette packs and butts and glasses and panties on the table in front of him.

"What do I do with them?"

"Start looking for a fishing boat."

"You don't frown on stealing someone's fishing spot?"

"We're not stealing anyone's fishing spot," said the Boss, then raising his voice to talk to the cops near the front of the boat, "Bring the fishing rods, I want to show Petya."

Petr's brewed-to-order coffee arrived at the same time as the "fishing rods," which came in three wooden crates—two so big and heavy that it took two men each to carry, and one small and heavy that also took two men to carry. They had police markings on them. The Boss stood up as the carriers began to pry up the boxes' nailed-down tops. Petr followed.

The first box told the whole story. The Boss reached into it and pulled out a newish police AK-74. About half the box held 74s, packed upright; most of the other half were AK-47s, and what looked like some SKSs left over from World War II. The other big box was filled with ammunition cans.

"You shoot the fish?" said Petr. The top of the third box came off and Petr looked inside. Hand grenades.

"Hand grenades?"

The Boss pulled the empty magazine from the 74 he was holding and tossed it to one of the cops, who began to load it from an ammo can.

"Do we shoot the fish?" he repeated for the benefit of the amused policemen. They all shared a good laugh at Petr's expense. "Do we shoot the fish? No, Petya, we don't shoot the fish. We take the guns, we find a fishing boat, and we take the fish."

"You're joking."

The Boss switched momentarily to heavily accented English: "I never joke about my work." Then he laughed.

Petr continued in Russian: "What if they have guns too?"

"They will," said the Boss. "Most likely."

"So, are we going to have a shootout over fish? That's insane."

The Boss laughed again. "Petya, Petya, what d'you think—that we're savages?" He shook his head and clicked his tongue. "No, of course we're not going to have a shootout. There are rules."

"Rules?"

"Yes. We go to a fishing boat. We put all our guns on the deck. They put all their guns on the deck. Whoever has more gets the fish." The cops laughed.

Petr nodded. He wasn't sure if the Boss was pulling his leg about that last part. He sipped his coffee. It was terrible. The Boss had returned to the stereo system and was starting a new album. It was *Waterloo* by ABBA.

CHAPTER 17

In the Jewish Autonomous Oblast, with his maître d' translator, and his maître d's Subaru, buying up vouchers had been a breeze. The bag stuffed with tens of thousands of dollars was now stuffed with tens of thousands of vouchers. John had exhausted the JAO's rubber-band supply, and—having given up on trying to slide vouchers into the emptied paper cuffs the bank had fastened around the cash—was now tying hundred-voucher bundles with twine. On Saturday, the maître d' took him to the bush plane—so called—that he'd arranged to take John to Kyzyl-Syr, a microscopic town on the Vilyui River, twenty or so miles from a Gazneft refinery at the edge of a gas field.

The refinery had its own small town that had sprung up around it, and a small municipal airport—and, the maître d' assured John, as the airport was served by a twice weekly scheduled airline from Yakutsk, it would be able to provide him with transportation into town. The maître d' offered to call ahead to ensure that a car would be waiting for him, but John firmly declined. He already wasn't thrilled about flying into what was essentially a Gazneft airport.

At a minimum, he didn't want to give them advance notice of his arrival.

He and the maître d' parted at the airport with a firm handshake and mutual best wishes. A few minutes later John was in the air, in the right-hand seat of some little Russian Cessna knock-off. He didn't want to get ahead of himself, or fall victim to hubris, but things seemed to be going well.

The flight took John over the corner of the Gazneft gas field. The summer sun was very low. It had set and risen again during the flight, leaving about four, maybe five, hours of darkness in between. It was about half past three in the morning now and the shadows of the spindly gas towers were gigantic, stretching on almost as far as the eye could see, making the snowy ground look like a giant piece of college-ruled paper. The airport was a single strip of cement blocks, next to a refinery of some sort. Funny to think that he already owned a large piece of all this.

The landing was smooth, though there was a bit of a skid toward the end; some of the landing strip was glazed with ice. No harm done but just a few degrees north and many, many fewer degrees Fahrenheit and John seemed to have gone from tourist-Siberia to gulag-Siberia, where a nice summer day meant a high of 33°.

John cinched his collar a little tighter, hoisted his duffle onto his back, and set off toward a tiny booth that seemed to be all the airport had by way of a terminal. There was no control tower or, actually, any other buildings around at all.

There were some low tower blocks, very Soviet, near the refinery. John thought he could just make out a playground. It was the only thing he could see that wasn't some shade of gray. A red and green plastic play tower was backlit by the sun, making it translucent. There were faint twinkling lights on the refinery itself, none in the tower blocks—but one in the little terminal booth, which made John hopeful he'd find someone there to call him a cab. If not, he'd have to walk to the refinery or one of the apartment buildings and hope they didn't know who he was.

The booth was a little larger than John had realized; the weird shadows had obscured its depth. It was about the size of a shipping container. There was no one inside but there was a courtesy phone and a number tacked up on a bulletin board. The number came along with a caption in Russian, which John couldn't read, but there was a little drawing of a car under it so he figured there was a better than middling chance it was the number to call a cab.

He dialed and a sleepy voice on the other end answered. John said, "Machina?" which he'd picked up as the Russian word for car, and, "Taxi cab?" and then, "Aeroport."

The voice on the other end said "Da" and hung up. John checked his watch. It was close to four in the morning. The only source of heat in the booth-office was the ceiling lamp, so John stood under it and waited. It was damned cold but at least he was out of the wind.

After about ten minutes, he began to pace, flapping his arms occasionally to keep the blood circulating. It took another forty, forty-five minutes for the cab to arrive. John was thinking again about plan Bs—what to do if it never arrived—when it pulled up outside the terminal booth. John went out to meet it with only a moment's hesitation before braving the elements again. He climbed into the back, arranged his bag on his lap for a little insulation, and said, "Kyzyl-Syr?"

The cab driver nodded, and set off. John checked his watch and the direction of the shadows to make sure they were going in roughly the right direction and then began to relax a little.

"English?" he said.

"Little," said the man. "Little English."

"Did you come from Kyzyl-Syr?"

"*Ya ne ponimayu*," said the driver. This was the Russian phrase John was most practiced in. "I don't understand."

"You . . . house? In Kyzyl-Syr?"

The man shook his head. "No. By aeroport."

Well, it certainly took you long enough to get going, thought John. In fairness, it was still before five A.M. and fucking freezing.

"You work for Gazneft?"

"*Net*," said the man. "No Gazneft. Driver."

John nodded. "Do a lot of people arrive at the aeroport needing a driver?"

"Sometimes," said the man.

For a moment, they lapsed into silence.

"How far to Kyzyl-Syr?" said John.

"*Dvadtsat' minuta*," said the driver.

"*Dvadtsat'*?" said John, with a shake of his head to show he didn't understand.

The man held up five fingers, then closed his hand, then five fingers again. He repeated this twice more.

"Twenty," said John.

"Yes," said the driver. "*Dvadtsat' minuta*."

Ten minutes later, the driver rolled to a gradual halt, while John tried to figure out what they were looking at. There was a tank straddling the road. An honest to God tank. With treads and armor plating and a giant cannon and everything. The cannon, at least, was pointed forward, relative to the tank, and not at the taxi. Small favors.

For maybe a full minute, John and the driver stared at it.

"Can you go around?" said John.

"*Ya ne ponimayu*," said the driver.

There was frost on the inside of the car's windows; John leaned forward and drew a rough diagram on the passenger-side frost with his index finger. A small tank (he hoped it looked enough like a tank) straddling a straight line that stood for the road. Then a semicircular arrow around it.

"*Net*," said the driver. "Mud. Car, stop. Die."

John wasn't sure if he meant the car would die or that he and John would die, but either way, John could see his point. Either side of the road, where the dirt hadn't been compacted, was a swamp of half-frozen, mushy-looking ground. The giant track marks laid down by the tank looked like they were about two feet deep, with mud slowly oozing into them, filling them back in. Of course, a tank weighed a damned sight more than the car but it also had power enough to pull itself out of a sticky situation. The Lada taxi clearly did not.

John had little doubt that Gazneft had arranged this. His main question now was whether his driver was in on it. The good thing was he hadn't paid his fare yet. The bad thing was that he'd been so successful buying vouchers that he was actually starting to run out of American currency—he was down to his last two hundred dollars with no prospect of replenishing the supply until he could get back to a major city. He was in the uncomfortable position of knowing that Gazneft could outbribe him.

If John got out of the cab to negotiate with the tank and the cab drove away he would probably freeze to death. If he offered too much to the cab driver, he wouldn't have anything left to offer the tank driver—assuming there *was* a tank driver, and this wasn't simply an immovable object. But the tank tracks looked fresh so there was a hope.

He did some math in his head, and figured a hundred dollars—which had to be about a year's salary out here—ought to be enough to get the cabbie to stay. He said a little prayer, and counted out twenty-five dollar bills. He held them up, and said, "You wait?"

The man nodded.

"I wait."

The man reached out his hand.

"After," said John. "After? I . . . talk. To the tank." John pointed to himself and then to the tank. "I talk. You wait. *Da?*"

"*Da,*" said the man.

John climbed out of the Lada. He took the duffle with him and slipped it onto his shoulder. There were about ten yards separating the cab and the tank. John approached slowly, trying to figure out how to get the attention of someone inside. The tank's tracks came up to his chest. He tossed the duffle up onto the tank's deck and hoisted himself up after it, using one of the track wheels as a step, hoping the tank didn't choose that instant to drive forward and tear off one of his legs.

As he got to his feet on the tank's deck, steadying himself against the turret, he heard the taxi shift into gear. He turned and watched as it did a five-point turn and scurried off the way it had come.

"*Fuck,*" said John. Was the driver working for Gazneft or was he just a little chicken-shit son-of-a-bitch bastard asshole? It didn't really matter now, did it? John could walk forward to Kyzyl-Syr, or back to the airport, and either way he would probably freeze to death if another car didn't happen by. And the odds of that seemed slim, especially with the tank here. The cab had driven him, what, halfway? So, he'd have to walk ten miles in subzero weather, in either direction? He didn't like the odds. He wished he had boots. And a heavier coat. Several heavier coats. He banged on the top of the tank's hatch.

"Hello? *Zdravstvuyte?*"

"Hello," came a voice from inside, speaking accented but understandable English. "Who is it?"

"Boris Yeltsin," said John.

For a moment there was silence, then the silence was broken by the sound of badly oiled wheels and gears turning. And then the hatch opened.

"Mister President, how can I help you?"

"Yeah. Can I ask why you happen to be parked right here, in this particular spot?"

"I was hired to come and park here. In this particular spot. More or less."

"By who?"

The man shrugged.

"Do you not know or do you not want to tell me?"

"It would be indiscreet."

"Your English is very good."

"Thank you. I learned it from John le Carré."

"I'm surprised they let John le Carré novels in Russia."

"Why not? They are very morally relativistic, you know."

"Yes, I know."

"Anyway, they are smuggled in from Pakistan. During Soviet Union times."

"Can I come in?" said John, pointing down into the tank. "I'm freezing my nuts off."

"If you like."

"Is there anyone else in there?"

"No, just me."

The man descended back down the hatch. John climbed up onto the tank's turret and swung his legs into the hatch to follow.

"No, no, go in the other one."

"What?"

"The other hatch. There's only room for one on this side. Commander's seat. Go in the gunner's hatch. Here, let me open it."

"Ah," said John, as the tank man reached over and, after a moment of unscrewing, opened a second hatch in the tank's turret. John crawled over to it, stuck his legs in, and descended, pulling his duffle behind him.

Once he was inside, he wasn't sure anymore exactly what he had expected but the descent from the hatch dropped him directly into an uncomfortably narrow metal seat. Directly ahead of him was the rubber eyepiece of a periscope. Ahead and down a little was a small open space with another seat in it and what looked like a wine-rack for magnum champagne bottles. Probably for tank shells, he figured.

To his right was the tank guy in his own seat, slightly roomier, and to the tank guy's right there was a small hot plate with a tea kettle on it.

"Chai?" said the man.

"Sure," said John. "Thanks."

The man poured a cup while John tried to take in his circumstance—inside a metal lattice of tubes and handles and switches—inside a Soviet tank—in Siberia. Being offered tea.

"Thanks," said John, accepting a cup. "It's not very roomy in here, is it?"

"You are welcome to wait outside if you prefer."

"Wait for what?" said John, taking a sip of tea. "This is good, thank you."

"Wait for . . ." the tank guy checked his watch. "Wait for another nine hours. Approximate."

So until the auction was over, thought John to himself.

"How much are you being paid?" said John.

"I'm not sure I should say."

"I'll triple it," said John.

"Direct to triple, ey?" said the tank guy. "But more-than-enough multiplied three times is still just more-than-enough, you know? And I wouldn't want to damage possible long-term business relationship."

"With Gazneft?"

"With private business partner."

"I don't want to seem . . . vulgar?" said John.

The man nodded his head to indicate he understood.

"I don't want to seem vulgar, but I presume there must be some amount of money that could induce you to move this thing."

"If I move it, what, you will walk to Kyzyl-Syr?"

"One problem at a time," said John. The tank man shrugged.

"How much money you got?"

"A lot," said John. "Again, not wanting to be vulgar about it."

"Show me," said the tank man.

"I don't have it with me," said John.

"Ah, well, you see," said the tank man, "I cannot work on credit."

"Two hundred dollars?" said John. The tank man laughed. John continued: "No. I didn't think so. So what happens in nine hours? Approximately."

"I get down into the driver's compartment and drive back to base."

"You're an army officer?"

"Yes."

"They don't mind if you borrow tanks?"

"Depends how you ask," said the tank man. John nodded.

They lapsed into silence. John sighed deeply.

"If you are now thinking how far you could walk in this weather, I wouldn't," said the man.

"Will you stop me?"

"Oh, no, of course not. I am like India; not ideologically aligned with you or other side. But you will freeze to death long time before you reach Kyzyl-Syr."

"So," said John. "We just sit here."

"Yes," said the tank guy. "Just sit here. Can also listen to the radio, or read. Would you care to look in my library?"

John exhaled slowly and shrugged. "Sure, why not?"

The tank man nodded, twisted around in his seat, and from some hidden storage compartment, produced a stack of glossy magazines. He held them out to John. John took them. They were all *Playboy*s, the last year or so, up to the most recent issue. John laughed.

"No le Carré, eh?"

"He hasn't published anything new in a while."

John flipped through the magazines with his thumb, the way you would with a deck of cards.

"Huh," he said to himself. Then to the tank guy: "That radio is two ways, right?"

"Yes."

"What's the range?"

"About ten kilometers. Why?"

"Do you have ham radio in Russia?"

"Ham radio?" the tank man shook his head.

"Amateur radio."

"Ah. Yes. Not during the Soviet Union, of course, but now we have the Soyuz Radiolyubitelei Rossiya."

"What would that be in English?"

"Union of Russia Amateur Radios."

"Can you tune into their frequency?"

"I could. But you must explain yourself."

"I know there's a radio repeating network in the Arctic. If you could connect to an amateur network that would repeat a signal north through Siberia, we could get a signal through Alaska down the West Coast, to Los Angeles."

"Yes," said the tank guy. "I do not follow. We have a repeating network in Siberia that can transmit from me to the Bering Sea."

"Perfect."

"Why should I connect to Los Angeles?"

"Wouldn't you like to talk to Hollywood?"

"I suppose. I had never really thought about it."

"Let me ask you, which one of these girls is your favorite?" John held up the *Playboys*.

"Oh, Miss Nina Bowyer. Cover girl, October 1992."

John thumbed through the magazines, looking for Nina Bowyer. He found her in a purple corset-type thing with a built-in pair of hands to hold up her breasts. It was hard to disagree with the tank man's selection.

"You have fine taste, friend," said John, holding up the magazine to make sure he'd found the right one. The tank guy nodded, and John continued: "How'd you like to meet her?"

"I would like very much to meet her. But to talk to her on the radio?"

"No, to actually meet her. In person. Maybe take her to dinner?"

"You want to trade the *ochi chornyye*, Nina Bowyer, to me, for dinner, to move my tank?"

"Yes."

"How can you guarantee this? Do you know her?"

"I can't, and I don't, but if you're game I'm willing to give it a shot."

"You are joking with me?"

"Radio Alaska."

The tank guy paused and pondered. And then he reached above him to a radio tuner, and began searching for the right frequency, tuning up and down the amateur bands to find a ham in Alaska he could reach by repeater. It took two or three minutes of crackling and the tank guy repeating his call sign before a voice crackled through from the other end.

"Uniform-One-Mike-India-Romeo: I got you. This is November–Alpha-One-Sierra-Sierra. What's up?"

John waved for the tank guy to hand him the radio handset.

"November Alpha, mind if I ask your location?"

"Sure, I'm in Dutch Harbor, Alaska. How about you?"

"I'm in a Russian tank in Siberia and I'm trying to get a message through to Los Angeles. Have you got a phone?"

"Sure."

"A speakerphone?"

"Yeah."

"Could you place a collect call for me and key your mic into the conversation? I don't want to be a nuisance, but I'm in kind of a jam here. And you might get some fun Hollywood gossip out of it."

November-Alpha-One-Sierra-Sierra laughed.

"No problem, man. What's the number?"

"323-xxx-9199."

"Okay . . . I'm gonna key through and dial. Who should I say is calling?"

"John Mills."

"Okay. Here goes."

John and the tank guy listened as a speakerphone in Alaska beeped a telephone number. A recording answered. "This is one-eight-hundred-collect. Our rates are twenty-nine-ninety-nine for the first five minutes and two-ninety-nine for every minute after that. If you wish to continue, press 1."

There was another beep.

"Speaking clearly, please say your name."

"John Mills," said November-Alpha.

"Your name is—" here the phone inserted November-Alpha's voice snippet: "'John Mills.' If that is correct, press 1."

Another beep.

"Thank you. At the tone, please enter the ten-digit number of the party you wish to speak to."

A dial tone, then ten more beeps, then a long busy signal. And then a scratchy rendition of Donny Dietrich's voice came over the line, "John? Is that you? What's going on, brother?"

"Hi," said November-Alpha. "This is actually a ham radio operator in Alaska, I'm patching John Mills in from a tank in Siberia."

"Uh—what? Did you say John's in a tank in Siberia?"

"So he tells me. If you're willing, I'm going to key through his mic now so he can talk. Both of you say 'over' when you're done talking and you want me to key out in the other direction, okay?"

"Um, okay," said Donny. "Over."

"Okay, keying over to John. Over."

"Donny? This is John. Can you hear me? Over."

"Yeah, John, I can hear you. What the hell is going on? . . . Over."

"I'm in a Soviet tank in Siberia and I need to know if you know Nina Bowyer. Over."

"Are you drunk? Over."

"No, just having a strange day. Over."

"Evidently. Over."

"Nina Bowyer, Donny. Do you know her? Over."

"Yeah, Nina Bowyer, she's in this new film-festival flick, *Cold Modesty*. Over."

"I mean do you know her personally. Over."

"No. Over."

"Who does? Over."

"Umm . . . I remember she did a movie with Michael Keaton. I know his agent. You want me to conference him in? Over."

John couldn't help but laugh. "Yes, please. Over."

"What am I asking him for? Her phone number? Over."

"Yeah. Over."

"And what do you want to ask *her.* Over."

"If she'll go out to dinner with a Russian Army officer. He's clean cut, polite, and very well-spoken."

"Okay, before I do anything else—If you're jerking me around, John, now is the time to say so. Or there's going to be some shit. Over."

"I'm deadly serious, Donny. It's for the fund. And can you get this guy a round trip flight from, um, Novosibirsk to LA? I'm good for it. Over."

"Um, yeah, well, why the heck not? Okay, John. Give me a sec. Should I try for sometime next week? Over."

John looked at the tank commander, who wore a big smile and flashed John an aggressive thumbs-up.

"Next week is good. Over."

There was a brief silence, then another ten beeps, and then a new, even scratchier voice at the other end:

"Lisa Vogel."

"Lisa—it's Donny Dietrich."

"Donny, hey, what can I do for you?"

"Out of the blue question: do you know Nina Bowyer?"

"Yeah, she's with my agency. Her guy's in the next office. You want me to get him?"

"If you could, that'd be awesome."

"No problem—hold on a sec."

For about thirty seconds, elevator music played. Then Lisa Vogel was back on the line.

"Donny Dietrich, I'm here with Stu Watanabe, Nina Bowyer's agent."

"Mr. Dietrich, what can I do for you?"

"Stu, this is going to sound crazy, but could I possibly arrange a dinner meeting between Nina and a friend of a friend? For some-time next week, maybe? Whenever's good for her."

"I'd have to ask her. Who's the friend of the friend?"

"A very polite Russian who's . . . sort of a business partner of mine. It's fan service, but I'll owe her one. Big time."

"Okay, hold on, let me call her. Can I use the other phone?"

"Sure," said Lisa. There were another ten beeps. Stu's voice resumed.

"Hi, Nina? It's Stu. Could I set you up on a dinner meeting with a friend of Donny Dietrich's sometime next week? It's not work related, but it'll be the basis for a great connection with Donny."

There was a pause.

"Yeah, it's with a fan. A very polite one. A businessman from Russia."

Another pause.

"Hold on, I'll ask. Mr. Dietrich. She's a little wary of meeting a stranger for dinner, since the *Playboy* cover. Could your friend do lunch? Next Tuesday at Spago?"

"Lemme check . . . John, how's lunch? Over."

John looked at the tank guy, who gave another very eager thumbs-up.

"Lunch works. Over."

"You get that, Stu?" said Donny.

"Uh . . . yeah."

"If you're wondering about the 'over' thing, it's a long story, which I would be happy to tell you sometime."

"That'd be great, Mr. Dietrich. Hold on one sec."

Another pause.

"Okay, Nina says we're good for Spago at one next Tuesday. I'll make the reservation myself."

"Awesome, Stu. Lisa, Stu, you guys are lifesavers. I'll be in touch."

There was a chorus of goodbyes and then Donny's voice alone: "John, you get all that? Over."

"Roger-roger, Donny. You're a guardian angel, my friend. Over."

"I'll make the flight for next Saturday? From Novo-what?"

"Yeah, Saturday, from Novosibirsk."

"Under whose name?"

John looked at the tank guy and held out the mic for him to speak into it.

"Vladimir Nikolayevich Piatagorsky."

"Over," added John.

"Piatagorsky like the cellist? Over."

"Sure," said John. "Why not. Over."

"Okay. And you're going to give me an explanation for all this as soon as its physically possible?"

"That's a big ten-four, Donny. And I promise you'll approve. Over."

"Okay, John. Over and out, I guess."

There was a brief dial tone, and November-Alpha came back on the line.

"Well, that was gosh-darn hilarious. Is that all you needed, Uniform-One?"

"That's all November-Alpha. If you'll give me your physical address, I'd like to send you a thank-you-something. I owe you big time."

"Not necessary, Uniform-One."

"I'd like to anyway, November-Alpha."

"Well, if you insist—it's Twelve Dungeness Circle, Dutch Harbor, Unalaska, Alaska, USA."

"Dungeness, like the crab?"

"Like the crab," said November-Alpha.

"Awesome. Thanks again. Uniform-whatever, over and out." John released the talk button and handed the handset back to Piatagorsky.

"So, are we all set?" said John.

An hour later John rolled into Kyzyl-Syr on the back of a T-54 Soviet main battle tank. The few people who saw the tank arrive didn't give it a second glance.

CHAPTER 18

After a successful haul of someone else's sturgeon—and the discovery that fresh caviar is actually terrible, that the salt isn't just a preservative—Petr had been delivered graciously back to Magadan with best wishes from the Boss to do just as he liked with vouchers. To this permission he added a Russian proverb, "The elbow is close but you can't bite it," which Petr assumed meant something like the Czech proverb, "Not all that glitters is gold." Petr's unexpressed response to this was that it was very lucky the Russian Mafia had decided that stock markets et al. were fool's gold. It was probably Russia's best hope for a free market and competent management.

With the paid help of some of the Boss's boys, gathering the vouchers of Magadan took no time at all. Even with the bizarre two-day loss to the Caspian, Petr was in the air in a bush plane by early Saturday morning, flying the nine hundred miles to Chukotka in about twelve hours, with four fuel stops along the way. The final destination was Anadyr, the tiny town which served as

Chukotka's capital, and held about a quarter of its hundred thousand inhabitants.

Doing some back-of-the-envelope calculations, Petr figured Chukotka was about twice as large as its close neighbor Japan, with about eight hundredths of 1 percent of the population.

The remoteness of the auction did, though, provide Petr an unexpected fringe benefit. Chukotka, being in Russia's extreme northeast—so far north and east that Alaska is actually visible from some of its outlying islands—when Petr landed in Anadyr, it would be his first time setting foot in the Western Hemisphere. Until now, the closest he'd come was Dublin.

The last of the four fuel stops had been only about a hundred miles southwest of Anadyr, at an ex–Soviet airbase that was covered with slowly disintegrating Korean War–era MiG jets. There seemed to be only one person there, an elderly man who approached the little bush plane with a Korean-era Soviet rifle, warning Petr and the pilot to stay close while he fueled the plane, because the local bear population had taken to huffing the fumes out of long-abandoned jet-fuel drums. Petr asked if that made them especially dangerous, and the man said no, it actually made them very friendly and playful. But they'd punctured and huffed every empty fuel drum on the base, and now the bears were going through withdrawal. And *that* made them especially dangerous.

Back in the air, it was about an hour more to Anadyr, and its single, lonely airstrip. Circling above it, Petr got his own look at an old Soviet tank, which was parked directly in the center of the single, lonely airstrip. The pilot had no idea what was going on, but Petr could guess. And when the pilot said they'd have to turn around and fly back to the rehabbing bears, Petr asked him if there was anywhere else he could put the plane down, anywhere within a few hours travel of Anadyr. The pilot said there wasn't so much as a shtetl in a hundred-mile radius of Anadyr.

Petr asked the pilot if he could land the plane in a field. The pilot said no—but he could land it on a large pond or a lake. Petr said, "Perfect; how do we find one?" The pilot consulted a map, then turned a few degrees, and began to follow a silvery strip through the tundra, a frozen stream reflecting the remains of the day, that the map told him would lead to a lake.

There was actually a lake just beside the airport, but—the pilot explained—it would be brackish, perhaps not entirely frozen, being inside the tidal plane of Anadyr, a coastal city on the Bering Sea. The lake the pilot had in mind was three or four miles southwest of Anadyr.

Petr was dressed very warmly, with good army boots he'd picked up at a street market in Magadan. He figured, with the summer sun keeping the snow thin on the ground, he could walk it without too much difficulty. According to the map, the lake had no name, but as they approached, a little way back from the lakeshore, Petr could see a small patch of land dotted with small fires.

"Boy scouts?" said Petr. The pilot shook his head.

"Chukchi. Nomads. Chukotka Autonomous Okrug is named for them."

"They're caribou herders?"

"Yes," said the pilot.

"Are they welcoming to guests?"

"Very. They are a kind, innocent people."

Petr wasn't sure if the pilot meant "innocent" as an indictment of Russia, or Russians, or what. Maybe he just liked these Chukchi. Petr had guessed the pilot was Tuvan or Mongolian, based on his somewhat East Asian features.

"Do you speak Chukchi?" said Petr.

"No," said the pilot. "But they all speak Russian. Lenin had their caribou herds collectivized and made them all learn Russian and Cyrillic."

"Are you Chukchi?" said Petr.

"No," said the pilot. "Tatar."

It was a glassy smooth landing on the surface of the lake. Coming to a stop, though, led to a long skid, like a car on an icy highway. This didn't seem to surprise the pilot, and Petr supposed it probably shouldn't have surprised him either.

Petr asked the pilot to wait. The pilot said he would. Petr considered dropping the name of the Magadan Boss, by way of an implicit threat, but the pilot seemed to be the sort of proud, serious man with whom an implicit threat would do more harm than good.

Anyway, after they landed, the pilot accompanied Petr across the lake—blown clean of snow by the tundra winds—to the Chukchi settlement. The pilot had given Petr a map and a compass, but suggested the Chukchi might have a faster way into town. They might have sled dogs to spare. Petr asked how one would go about bartering for sled dogs—or, at least, for a short-term sled-dog lease. The pilot said money would do fine—they were nomads, but they went to town occasionally too. Mostly for medical care and rubberized clothing.

The Chukchi camp was made up of about two dozen huts. Tents? It looked like they were wood frames wrapped in tanned animal hides, easily taken down, moved, and put up again as the caribou migrated. The caribou herd itself was a looming background presence, a herd of lumpy shadows beyond the fires, from which low snorts and wheezes could be heard. Petr hadn't realized it at first, but the sun had set—it had still been visible from the air, but from ground level it was already behind the horizon. Petr had gone back and forth through so many time zones over the last few days—and combine that with the absurd behavior of the midnight sun—that his internal clock had simply switched off. He asked the pilot what time it was.

"Two-thirty," said the pilot. Petr nodded.

The Chukchi camp was neither asleep nor awake. Herdsmen, at least a dozen, manned the herd and the fires. Petr observed to the pilot that there didn't seem to be any dogs.

"They sleep inside the homes," said the pilot. "Where it's warm."

"Warm?" said Petr.

"Warmer," said the pilot.

They reached the shore and began to crunch through the snow.

"It must be a very hard life," said Petr, after a while.

"Yes," said the pilot.

The camp was about a hundred yards back from the frozen lake. Petr wondered how cold the water was that the Chukchi drank and washed with, here where it was frozen in the middle of summer.

As they approached, a man turned to face them, raising a rifle to his shoulder. If it had been a movie, there would have been a sound of a bolt being closed and locked, but since this was a guy watching for wolves, he already had the gun ready to fire. When he saw that the shapes looming out of the darkness were men, he lowered the gun and said, in Russian, "You came with the plane, friends?"

"Yes, friend," said the pilot.

"Welcome," said the man. "Are you well? Have you had a problem?"

"No problem. We are well, thank you," said the pilot. "We're looking for transportation for my friend here into Anadyr."

"We have a snowmobile, friend, but we are waiting for a new track for it; now it doesn't run."

"Perhaps my friend could help you pay for it," said the pilot, "in exchange for the loan of some dogs to take him to town?"

"That would be very generous of him. Speak to Rul-Tyne—he is there at that fire, with the cup in his hands."

"Thank you, friend," said the pilot.

"Thank you," added Petr, as they walked past the man toward the man indicated.

"How much money do you want to give them?" said the pilot.

"How much will they want?"

"They'll take whatever you offer. They're not greedy and they like to help people."

"How much should I give them? I have no idea how much it costs to fix a snowmobile."

"For them, twenty American would be a lot."

Petr nodded. "Okay." They reached the fire, and the pilot spoke for him, addressing the Chukchi indicated, Rul-Tyne.

"Friend, we are told your snowmobile needs repair. Could my friend give you twenty dollars for its repair, in exchange for the loan of a dog team to take him to Anadyr?"

The Chukcha stood up and led them to one of the tents. "Can your friend drive dogs?"

"No," said Petr.

"Friend, it is very simple. Say 'go' and they will go. 'Stop' and they stop. Say 'right' and the leader will turn right, and they will all follow. Say 'left' and they will turn left. But also, say 'Anadyr' and they will know where to go, and say 'home' and they will know where to go. How long will you need them?"

"Not more than half a day," said Petr.

"Good," said the Chukchi. He ducked into the tent and, a moment later, there was barking. And a little yelping. A deeply fluffy puppy hopped out of the tent and began to play among Petr's and the pilot's feet. The pilot picked him up.

"They are good hand warmers. But they make your face cold." Petr was going to ask how when the pilot allowed the squirming puppy to do what it wanted, which was to lick his face, vigorously. Petr laughed.

While he was laughing, a parade of six dogs, two by two, emerged from the tent, wearing nylon harnesses and fastened together by nylon ropes. Rul-Tyne followed them out and led them to a one-man sled. He tied them on and then addressed Petr.

"Friend, put your feet here," he indicated the runners, "and your hands here," he indicated the wheelbarrow-like handles.

Petr was suddenly apprehensive. Both about being able to control the dogs and being responsible for them. He imagined the man had probably raised these dogs, and trained them, from the time they were puppies. Petr had had a deep emotional attachment to his first car. Imagine the attachment if it had been six cars that all liked to lick your face. He pulled out his wallet and counted out twelve five-dollar bills. He held them out to Rul-Tyne.

"Twenty for the dogs, and twenty for the sled, and twenty to apologize for waking your family."

Rul-Tyne took the money and, without counting it, stuck it somewhere inside his heavy, fur-lined jacket. "Thank you, friend," he said. "I will see you in half a day?"

"Yes," said Petr. "My friend, I think, will wait in your camp?" he turned to the pilot.

"If you will have me, friend?"

"Of course, friend," said Rul-Tyne.

"Could you point me to Anadyr?"

"It's that way. There is a rig road that the dogs will follow, that is only a short way back from the camp. You will see."

"Thank you, Rul-Tyne." Petr turned to the pilot, with whom, under these strange circumstances, he now felt a strong kinship. As a stranger in a strange land. "Wish me luck."

"Good luck," said the pilot.

"Good luck," said Rul-Tyne.

Petr addressed the sled, stepped onto the runners, gripped the handles. The dogs were lined up and poised, eager to begin. Petr said, "Go. To Anadyr." The dogs jolted forward, and Petr only just managed to hang on.

Two minutes later, the dim light of the campfires had dwindled to nothing and the only thing lighting the desolate, unfriendly tundra was the glow of moonlight on the snow.

CHAPTER 19

It took Petr most of an hour to get into Anadyr. For most of the last mile, he was pelted miserably by sleet that, as he reached town, turned—to Petr's great relief—into snow. The dogs seemed totally unconcerned by the changing weather. If anything, they seemed to enjoy it.

Anadyr was slightly larger than Petr had expected but, after a few minutes of sledding awkwardly through streets that seemed to radiate from the town center, he spotted a large, onion-domed building which he took to be the town hall. It was, and after tying up the dogs in a covered bicycle garage (basically a pill box with one open side), he headed to the town hall's entrance.

At its doorway, he stopped, checked the time, and then jogged across the street to a bus depot which had its lights on. Maybe it was the last stop on some trans-Siberian bus odyssey. (What else could it be? Anadyr was, in essence, the end of Russia.) As he'd hoped, there was an all-night cafeteria there. After surveying the meat options, he settled on some long "Siberian style" slices of boiled venison, which he brought to the dogs. He ate one himself and, thinking it actually wasn't half-bad, he walked back to the threshold of the town hall, this time going inside.

It was another pine-paneled former church, and Petr was—despite everything—several hours early. At least, unlike Baymak, he wouldn't have to wait outside. He took a seat in a pew near the front of the ex-chapel and tried to get comfortable. He thought he might doze awhile, but when he couldn't, he got up and looked for something to read.

He found a stack of Bibles. Perhaps this was an ex-ex-church-cum-town hall? He took one, returned to his spot in the pews, and began to read. Petr had been raised a pure Marxist and had no familiarity with any of the basic Bible stories that even atheist Western children know vaguely.

He opened up the book at random and found himself reading about Joseph being taken as a slave from Israel to Egypt, how he turned down the advances of the wife of his master, was falsely accused of attempted rape, ended up in a dungeon from which he extricated himself by correctly interpreting the dreams of other prisoners, who recommended him to Pharaoh. A real rags-to-riches story.

He found it quite engrossing and didn't notice the IMF man beginning to set up at a folding table placed where the altar had once been until someone's shadow fell over the page he was reading. He looked up. A man whom Petr didn't recognized loomed over him. Petr may not have recognized him but he was pretty sure he could guess the man's reason for looming.

"Were you at Baymak last week?" said the man.

"What is it to you?" said Petr, standing.

"Just a friendly warning not to involve yourself in the business of others."

Petr's hand rested on the Makarov automatic in his pocket. "Was the tank on the runway a warning too?"

"It was. Pity you ignored it."

"Pity for whom?" said Petr. The man ignored him and walked up the aisle away from the altar, toward the street. After a moment of seeing if anyone else had anything to say to him, Petr sat down again.

The IMF man who was laying out ledgers and a counting machine *was* the same guy who'd been in Baymak. A few minutes later, a man Petr assumed was a Gazneft rep—not the one who'd threatened him, and not the one who'd been at Baymak, took a seat near the front of the pews, across the aisle from Petr. He looked at Petr briefly but kept his face expressionless and said nothing. After a few minutes more—perhaps to give the imaginary other people who might arrive a chance to arrive?—the voucher counting commenced.

When it was finished, the Kovac-Mills investment group had secured just over 40 percent of the stock on offer—42.6 percent of 2.8 billion dollars' worth of stock. Another triumph, but Petr didn't let himself gloat for more than a moment. He had no idea if Gazneft had any more dirty tricks in mind—why should they bother, now that the deal had already been closed?—but all the same, he didn't intend to stick around longer than he had to.

Briefly shaking the IMF guy's hand—to the IMF guy's total and complete indifference—he walked up the aisle and back outside, into what was now a driving snowstorm. Whipped by the tundra wind into a thick swirling mass, even though the sun had risen while Petr was waiting in the church, the storm made it dark as night.

Leaning into the wind, Petr walked down the town hall steps, and rounded the corner to where the dogs were waiting for him. What he found made him spin around and vomit onto the snow.

Each of the six dogs had been shot—repeatedly. Bursts of fire from a light machine gun. Petr wondered how he hadn't heard the gunfire from inside the church. It must have been drowned out by the wind. Maybe the gun had been silenced. Blood splattered the concrete floor and walls. The ceiling too. Where snow had blown in through the hutch's open front, it was spattered red and pink.

Petr heard a whimper from one of the dogs. He walked over to it with tears in his eyes. He couldn't believe it was still alive; its limbs and torso had a dozen bullet-gouges in them. The dog's eyes were closed and it—he—was taking rapid, shallow breaths. Petr was certain he was in incredible pain. Petr knelt beside him and put his hand on the dog's muzzle, hoping to give it a little comfort. He wasn't sure the dog could even tell he was there. Petr took the Makarov out of his pocket, racked the slide to load a bullet into the chamber, put it on the dog's head, looked away, and pulled the trigger. The sound of the shot made his ears rings. He stood up, staggered back out to the snowy street, and vomited again.

What kind of animals was he dealing with?

Pulling himself together, be walked toward the bus terminal on the far side of the street. He had blood on his pants and hands. He left bloody prints in the snow as he went. He pulled the door open and stepped inside. His hand was on the Makarov he'd returned to his pocket. If he'd seen the man who threatened him in the church, Petr felt certain he'd have killed him.

But the handful of people waiting in the terminal were strangers he'd never seen before, and mostly they were asleep. The one or two who looked up at Petr let their eyes widen at the sight of him soaked in blood, before looking away, not wanting to get involved with whatever was going on.

He walked over to a ticket window, from behind which the ticket lady promptly disappeared. There was a large, double-wide door to the right of the window, leading (per its sign) to the boarding area. Inside he found a lot of empty space and a single old Soviet bus with big, chunky mud wheels. And, in one corner, near a small heater, a man at a table drinking and playing solitaire.

"I need a ride," said Petr, walking toward the man. "Are you a driver?"

"I am," said the man, looking up at him, looking at the blood, and then looking back down at his cards. Total indifference. Whether it was sincere or an act, Petr couldn't tell. The driver continued: "You are Petr Kovac?"

"I am," said Petr.

"I have been asked not to drive you," said the man.

"Why is that?" said Petr. "Black nine on the red ten."

"Thank you," said the man. "I don't know why not to drive you but I have been paid. It is an end to it. Find someone else."

"Who else is there?" said Petr. The man shrugged.

Petr pulled out the Makarov. "Okay," he said. "I can take your keys and drive myself but look at the blood I'm covered in and look at the gun. I took a life two minutes ago. Get on that bus and drive or I'll kill you too. It won't make any difference. Except maybe to whoever's job it is to clean brains off the walls of the bus terminal."

Without another word, the man stood and walked toward the bus. Petr followed him.

CHAPTER 20

During John's appearance at his auction, in another ex-church, in Kyzyl-Syr, he received a similar threat from a similarly anonymous Gazneft man. And, like Petr, he had rested his hand on his Makarov and wondered if he'd have to use it.

But, fortunately for John, he had asked tank commander Piatagorsky to wait and drive him back to the airstrip. The man who threatened him sat across the street from the town-hall auction site in a Mercedes-Benz 600sl. He made no effort to disguise himself, or the fact that he was staring at John. John figured his plan was to follow John back to airstrip and then, what—kill him? Shoot him in a kneecap? Who knew? Fortunately, parked on the near side of the street was Piatagorsky's T-54 main battle tank. The Mercedes could try to follow if it wanted, but slow and steady wins the race.

John climbed aboard and let himself down through the gunner's hatch. Piatagorsky had pinned up Nina Bowyer's cover on some of the metal work above the hot plate where he was brewing fresh tea.

"Vladimir Nikolayevich," said John, lowering himself into his seat. "Do mafia types ever mess around with the Russian army?"

Vladimir Nikolayevich Piatagorsky laughed. "Of course not. Not if they don't want to end up in the basement of the Lubyanka."

"Great," said John. "Could you drive over someone's car for me?"

"Of course," said Piatagorsky. "But why?"

"I'm pretty sure he's going to follow me back to the airstrip and kill me."

"Oh," said Piatagorsky. "Well, sure, I could run over his car, but I think we can handle it more cleanly than that. But let's wait till we're on the road. Are you ready to go?"

"I am," said John.

"Your auction went well?" asked Piatagorsky as he began to slide himself forward out of his chair, past the loader's station, down into the driver's seat, in a deep well beneath the level of the turret at the front of the tank's interior compartment.

"It did," said John. "Very well, indeed, Vladimir Nikolayevich."

"Good, I am glad to hear it. Put on again those headphones hanging next to your head, so you can hear me while we're driving. This time, you get to help run the tank. How exciting!"

John laughed to himself. Piatagorsky was wasted on the tank corps—what he needed was his own daytime talk show.

The engine cranked back to life. Everything inside the tank began to vibrate, as did everything inside John, who briefly thought his lungs would shake loose. Piatagorsky dropped the clutch and the tank jolted forward and started to roll through the wide, muddy streets of Kyzyl-Syr. Using the gunner's periscope, John looked back and saw the Mercedes was, indeed, following them—at the tank's slow, turtle-ish pace of about twenty miles an hour—and making no effort to hide it.

It took about fifteen minutes for John, Piatagorsky, and the tank to get out of sight of Kyzyl-Syr. And then Piatagorsky's voice crackled over the headphones.

"Is he still there?"

"Yes, he is," said John.

"Good. So, now, do what I tell you. First, flip the red switch on the left side of the periscope. This brings up the gunsight and locks the view to the direction of the gun. Okay?"

"Yes," said John. "Flipped, and locked."

"Good," said Piatagorsky. "Now: there are two handles—tillers—on either side of your seat. Do you see them?"

"Yes," said John.

"The one on the right rotates the turret. Pull back to turn right, push forward to turn left. The tiller on the left raises and lowers the cannon. Pull back to raise it, push forward to lower it. Got it?"

"Yup," said John.

"Okay," said Piatagorsky. "I'm going to stop the tank a moment."

"Okay," said John. The tank slowed to a stop. In neutral, the engine was even louder than it had been in gear. It was sort of like sitting on top of a washing machine during an earthquake.

"Now, aim the cannon at the Mercedes."

Even having realized where this was going, John couldn't help but laugh. He pushed the right-hand tiller forward and the turret circled—surprisingly quickly—to the left. Then he pushed the left-hand tiller forward and the giant barrel of the giant cannon lowered, along with the view from the periscope. He put the periscope reticle—the circle and crosshair gunsight—directly over the face of the guy who'd threatened him in the church. Through the crystal-clear lenses of the periscope, John watched the man's confusion turn to panic, throw the car into reverse, and back away at top speed. When he was fifty or a hundred yards back, he did a J turn, then gunned it, and a moment after that he'd disappeared from view.

"Is he still there?" said Piatagorsky.

"Nope," said John.

"Good," said Piatagorsky. "Shall we continue?"

"Yes," said John. "Let's."

CHAPTER 21

In Omsk, Anna had an almost entirely uneventful week—only a few hours after she arrived, she discovered that, like Moscow—albeit on a much smaller scale—Omsk had its own voucher market already set up. It lacked the organization of the table-rings, and ran much more like a flea market, but it meant that Anna didn't have go looking for vouchers, they came to her, looking for money.

And along with size and organization, Omsk's voucher market lacked something else available in Moscow—hard, American currency.

Some of the Siberians arriving to trade accepted rubles, but most didn't and instead used vouchers to pay directly for foodstuff. Mostly grains to be milled, or flours that had been milled already, and vodka. The presence of actual, solid money made Anna the instant favorite buyer of the auction. It also made her table, which she'd bought from another vendor, an intense buyer's market. And Anna—being Russian and therefore feeling no notion of carpet-bagging or taking advantage of a recovering post-Communist people—used her advantage on the supply side of supply and demand to drive very hard bargains.

She bargained on cigarette prices all day, every day that she worked the Moscow–Volga trains, and she was good at it. It was a good thing to be good at because, being a basically honest person, she didn't like to cheat people, and in the Soviet and post-Soviet economies, the only ways to get ahead were being either sharp or crooked. Being a cigarette girl on a train and a part-time prostitute might not have seemed like the height of ambition and entrepreneurship—but it was, when you compared it to her other options.

Most other girls as young and pretty as she was were "kept." A few by rich men, but most of them either by pimps or in brothels. She was her own boss, more or less, and slowly but surely she'd been earning the money she needed to get out of Russia and teach in Istanbul—maybe even Western Europe or the United States, with the cash windfall she was getting from this whole voucher thing.

Anyway—the short version was, she drove a hard bargain and bought every Gazneft voucher that appeared in Omsk. She guessed—based on the way they poured in and kept pouring in, like taxis into the taxi lane at a big train station—she had most of them, a lion's share of all the Omsk-Gazneft vouchers on the market.

The only small bump in the otherwise smooth road—the only memorable event in an uneventful week—was contending with a man in a suit who approached her table looking not at all like a Siberian peasant, and with no vouchers. Uninvited, he walked around the table to her side, leaned close to her face and, in a low tone, asked her why she was buying Gazneft vouchers.

"What is it to you?" she said, with the blank, uninterested coldness that Russians do so well.

"It is my business, too, Gazneft vouchers. You are Russian?"

Both a question and not a question, as clearly he knew she was.

"Of course. Do I seem like anything else? Am I wearing blue jeans? Dooooooo Iyyyyyyy sooouuuuuunnd liiiiiiiike aaaaan Eeeeestooooooniiiiiiaaaaaan?" Russians' have fixed notions of—among other peoples—Americans and Estonians, with the former wearing nothing but denim, the latter speaking very slowly, with very drawn-out vowel sounds. Anna could tell when a man was hostile and she'd found ethnic humor was the most effective way to diffuse such situations. If the Estonia joke didn't work, she had a great one about Ukrainians in her back pocket.

The man smiled, shallowly, and in an unfriendly way.

"No. I only wondered at a Russian helping foreigners steal the wealth of this country."

"Oh, is that what you wonder about? Well, then you will be relieved to hear that I am doing no such thing."

"You are," said the man. "But as a Russian girl, I will do you the courtesy of letting you remove yourself from the situation gracefully. And even to turn a profit."

"And how is that?" said Anna, crossing her arms.

"Sell me the vouchers you've gathered. I will give you a fair price. Take the money, and whatever money you have left over from the foreigners, and leave."

For a moment Anna looked at him. Thinking. Weighing things in her mind.

"No," she said, at length. "No, thank you; I am not at liberty to do that."

"You are," said the man. Anna just looked at him, her arms still crossed. He continued, "I will give you a day or two to think it over. I have faith you will decide wisely. Good day. I will be back."

"Good day," said Anna, acidly. When he was gone, she packed up her table and walked to the nearest police station, where she hired two cops to work as her security. They were standing at either end of her table when the threatening man came back, two days later. This was Friday morning, two days before the Omsk Oblast auction.

"Have you thought about what I said?" said the man, this time standing directly in front of Anna, on the opposite side of the table. Either because of the cops, or because he was no longer interested in attracting attention, Anna wasn't sure.

"I have," said Anna. "My answer has not changed."

"Do you know anything about South America?" said the man. "No, of course you don't," he said, without waiting for an answer. "Why would a cheap whore from the Moscow–Kazan line know something about South America? How foolish of me. Well, in South America, there are a lot of drug dealers. Unpleasant people, you know. They have this expression—*plata o plomo*—do you know what that means? Of course you don't. It's Spanish. It means silver or lead. And do you understand what that means? Maybe you do, being a cheap whore from the Moscow–Kazan line. It means, if someone is determined to make a deal with you, it's a better idea to take the money—the silver—than it is to take a bullet—the lead. You see? Do you understand me?"

Anna stared at him a moment, and then turned her head, left, then right, to her police escort. "Would you please ask this man to leave?" she said.

"No need," said the threatening man. "I have my answer now. But it's a shame. That such a smart girl should be so stupid."

He turned and walked out and Anna was left feeling frightened as she tried to persuade herself that the man's game was to frighten her into doing what he wanted rather than actually to hurt her to get what he wanted. It's much easier to make a threat than to carry it out. And it's not like Gazneft was Baader-Meinhof. It was one of the largest companies in the world, and—if she understood Petr correctly—it was a company that wished, ultimately, to attract foreign business and foreign investment. Surely their business model didn't include murder. She hoped.

CHAPTER 22

On Saturday, the day before the auction, Anna didn't have to worry about finding a plane to take her to some unbelievably remote auction site. Having been announced prior to John and Petr's arrival on the scene, the site of the Omsk Oblast auction had been set for Tara and, per the IMF, couldn't (or anyway, hadn't) been moved. All Anna had to do was take a simple six-hour car ride in a less-uncomfortable-than-it-looked police car. A chauffeured ride for which she had paid her two security cops handsomely.

They left Omsk in the morning and, for the first couple hours, neither the cops nor Anna said anything. This wasn't unusual. Russians are not exactly known for making small talk. Not when they're sober, anyway. Still, Anna was nervous and the longer the silence lasted, the more she felt like talking. Finally, she did.

"Did you ever hear about the three Finns driving from Omsk to Tara?"

Neither cop answered, for a good thirty seconds. Finally, the one in the front passenger seat turned around to Anna—who was by herself in the back—and said, "Well?"

"For the first hour," said Anna, "they drove in silence." The Russian stereotypes of Finns are that they talk and move and think in a very sluggish way. Sort of like Estonians, but colder and less talkative.

"Then after the second hour, an animal ran out of the woods and across the road ahead of them. An hour after that, one of the three Finns said, 'Iyyyyy thiiiiiiiiiiiink iiiiit waaaaaaaas aaaaaaaa Fooooooooooox.' Another hour of silence passes, and the second Finn says, 'Iyyyyyy thiiiiiink aaaaaactuuuuaaaalyyyyy, iiiiiit waaaaaaas aaaaaa woooooooolf.' Another hour of silence passes, and the third Finn says, 'Foooooor goooooooood's saaaaaaaake, wooooould youuuuuuu twoooooo pleeeeeeease stoooooooop fiiiiightiiiiiing?'"

The Russian cops laughed. The one in the passenger seat said, "Very good," and then everyone lapsed back into silence for another minute or so. Then the cop driving said, with a quick glance over his shoulder,

"Have you heard about the two Finns fishing together?"

"Well?" said Anna.

"Tarmo and Tarvo are in a rowboat on a lake. After an hour it begins to rain. An hour after that, Tarmo holds out his hand and says, 'Raaaaaaaiiiiin.' An hour after that they go home, and Tarvo says to his wife, 'Iyyyyyy wooooooon't fiiiiiiish with Taaaaaaarmoooooo aaaaaaaannyyyyyymoooooooooore. Heeeee's tooooooo chaaaaaaaaaattyyyyyy.'"

Anna laughed. Now the cop in the passenger seat chimed in.

"Did you hear about the Finn going to Helsinki?"

"Well?" said Anna.

"He was pulling a heavy cart, and says to another Finn at the side of the road, 'Aaaaaam Iyyyyyy faaaaaaaar froooooooooom

Heeeeeelsiiiiiiinkiiiiii?' And the Finn at the side of the road says, 'Nooooooo. Cooooooome, Iyyyyy wiiiiill heeeeeeelp puuuuuull yooooooour caaaaaaart.' An hour after that, the Finn from the side of the road turns to the first and says, '*Nooooooooow* yooooouuuu aaaaaare faaaaaar frooooom Heeeeeelsiiiiiiinkiiiiii.'"

Anna and the driver laughed.

It took them about an hour to go through all the ethnic jokes they knew. Then they moved on to Soviet jokes.

An hour after that, the driver was saying, "Do you know what the greatest success of Communist industry was?"

"Well?" said Anna.

"Chernobyl! It met its five-year quota for energy production in four milliseconds!"

"Hey," said the cop in the passenger seat, pointing at the road ahead. "What's that?"

They were driving north along the Irtysh River and more or less directly toward the low sun, which made it hard to see the road ahead.

"Slow down," said the cop in the passenger seat.

The cop driving laughed—not in amusement but in surprise. "I think it's a tank."

He stopped the car and for a moment they lapsed back into silence, staring at the giant, metal, heavily armed, heavily armored roadblock.

The cop in the driver seat honked his horn.

"What are you doing?" said the passenger-cop, sardonically. "You stay with her. I'll see what's going on."

"Okay," said the driver-cop. The passenger-cop climbed out of the passenger seat and walked toward the tank. Anna saw him unfasten the snap that held his pistol in its holster.

The police car had stopped about fifty feet short of the tank. When the passenger-cop was about ten feet away, the tank's hatch opened. Anna couldn't hear what they were saying, only that the guy in the tank and her policeman were talking. Then the policeman—the passenger-cop—turned around and walked back to the car. He climbed back into the passenger seat and said to the driver, "He says someone paid him to park there and block the road."

"What?" said the driver. "That's crazy."

Anna said nothing.

The passenger-cop picked up the handset for the car's radio. He radioed his station and asked them to look up the personal details of one Captain Dmitri Gregoryvich Gryshenko. Then they waited in silence for about ten minutes before the radio crackled on again. Some policeman back in Omsk told the passenger-cop that Captain Gryshenko was married, lived with his wife and parents, and had an adult daughter studying at the Omsk State Medical University.

"Good," said the passenger-cop. "Let's see if he'd like his parents, wife, and daughter to be arrested for conspiracy to misappropriate state defense assets, threatening the national security of the Russian Federation." The passenger-cop climbed out again and walked back to the tank. There was another short conversation between the cop and the guy in the tank, and then the tank guy ducked back into the tank and closed the hatch behind him. A moment later the tank's gigantically loud engine came on, and backed the tank out of the road. The passenger-cop was just climbing back into the car.

"Good," he said. "Drive on."

CHAPTER 23

When Anna and her cops arrived at Tara, it was nearly midnight Saturday; six hours still to go to the voucher auction. The two cops escorted her into Tara's only hotel and, after she checked into her room, they took turns standing guard outside it. Using her surplus voucher-buying money, Anna was paying them extremely well—almost as well as she was being paid by Petr and John—but still, she felt a sort of kinship had formed between them; something of a fraternal nature, and that they actually seemed to be concerned with her safety. Anyway, she felt a lot better with them keeping watch over her than she would have without them.

Even so, she slept badly. At four the next morning, with only an hour or two of sleep managed, she woke and dressed, and found that her hands were shaking too badly to put on her makeup. Maybe from nerves, maybe from exhaustion? It didn't matter.

She gathered up the vouchers and the paperwork, and stepped out of her room, where she found one of the policemen—the one who'd talked to the tank driver—on guard and reasonably alert. They exchanged good mornings and descended a flight of stairs to the lobby and a few steps more to the parking lot, where the other cop was asleep in the back seat of the police car. The on-duty cop woke him up. He smoothed his rumpled self out a bit, got into the driver's seat, and drove them all to Tara's town hall.

Anna and the driver-cop waited a moment while the passenger-cop went into the town hall—another ex-church—and checked that it was safe. Then he came out and got Anna. He would wait with her inside till the auction was over; his partner would keep a watch on the entrance, from the police car.

It was now approaching five. The auction would be held at six. There was an hour more to wait. Anna looked around the auction room, saw no one was there yet; no one from Gazneft, no one from the IMF. The cold Siberian summer morning had stopped her hands from shaking, more or less. Maybe the fresh air relaxed her, or maybe it was just the cold slowing her heart down a little. She told the cop escorting her that she was going to the ladies' room. He nodded and walked ahead of her. He checked the bathroom was empty, then stepped back into the hall, turning his back to the bathroom door and waiting outside as she stepped in.

She put her voluminous purse on the sink and began to take out her makeup. As she began to put it on, it was just about five in the morning in her time zone. Tara was in GMT+7. John was in GMT+10; his auction had already been over for two hours. In Anadyr—GMT+13—Petr's auction had already been over for six hours. It hadn't occurred to either John or Petr—or to Anna—that this might create a problem.

By the time it was five A.M. Anna's time, Gazneft already knew that moving the auctions around, rescheduling them, arranging roadblocks, closing airports, had not dissuaded their rival syndicate from showing up at the IMF auctions and acquiring big chunks of

Gazneft equity. Probably Anna or Petr or John should have suspected that if neither threats nor obstacles worked, Gazneft might
be prepared to try something more drastic. At five A.M. Anna's
time, Gazneft had had five hours to come up with something worse
than killing dogs.

None of that popped into Anna's head when she heard shots.
They were muffled and far away, but still, unmistakably gun-
shots. She spun away from the mirror and heard her escort-cop
say—loudly enough to be heard through the door but no louder—
"Stay in there and lock the door." Doing as she was told, she was
standing at the door locking it when she heard two more shots,
then the sound of her escort-cop shouting in pain, then the sound
of his body crumpling onto the floor.

Anna ran to the window and tried to pry it open. It was painted
closed. She grabbed her purse and used it to break the glass. Behind
her someone was trying to kick the door in. The windowsill was at
the height of her chest, and she had to pull and kick to get herself
through it. She felt a leftover jag of glass cut her as she pulled and
then pushed her way out the opening, falling onto the frost-covered
ground beneath her.

She got up and started to run—away from the street, toward
the forest. It was twenty or thirty yards away, behind the town
hall. She kicked off her heels to run faster. Better to lose a toe to
frostbite than lose everything to a bullet.

A bullet whizzed past her head just as she passed into the
trees.

It was a birch forest. The jumble of white trunks and long
shadows had a dazzling, confusing effect. She tried to watch the
ground ahead of her, trying to avoid roots and rocks. Up ahead she
could see a wheat field. She made it her goal. In a wheat field she

could hide among the head-high stalks. She could hide as long as she had to. Forever, if she had to—no one would be able to find her there, not until harvest time.

At the same time, she could hear running footsteps behind her. She forced herself not to look—forced herself to keep running. She was getting close. And she was running downhill now, picking up speed. The ground was slick with deadfall and frost. She fell, and rolled, banging elbows and knees and arriving at the bottom of the hill in a tangle, in a small runoff gulch, still fifty yards short of the wheat. But now she could hear the running footsteps very close.

There was a small hollow where the gully had washed away the soil around the roots of a tree and she crawled into it, pushing herself into the freezing mud as far as she could go, pulling her knees up to her chest. Most of her fit inside. She was completely in shadow now, where it was bitterly cold, but maybe it would make her harder to see. She prayed it would. She kept praying.

The running footsteps were coming down the hill now. There were at least two pairs of feet. Anna could see the legs of two men step over the gully and walk—quietly now—toward the wheat field. They were looking for her. And she was so close. She forced herself not to shiver. One of them stopped, looking left and right. She twisted her face away from the men, into her little hollow, hoping the back of her head would be harder to see than the front. She held her breath.

And then suddenly she felt a hand grabbing onto the back of her collar, pulling her roughly out of her hiding place. Dragging her out of the gully, then throwing her face first onto the ground. She lay still, waiting for one of the men to say something to her. And she kept praying.

CHAPTER 24

Irkutsk is an unusual city. It's nicknamed the Paris of Siberia, and not ironically.

It got the nickname after the Decembrist Revolt of 1825. The Decembrists were several hundred prominent Russians—members of the aristocracy, the military, writers and poets, and so forth. They all were subscribers to the new enlightenment philosophy of the rights of man and the necessity for self-governance who sought to overthrow the Czarist system and replaced it with a federal constitutional monarchy. They planned to keep the czar as head of state, as in England, but to devolve most of his power to a congress.

The proposed new constitution, and the bill of rights it contained, were modeled closely on the American constitution, a document then not forty years old, but already—by any measure—a great success. Under different circumstances, its author, Nikita Mikhailovich Muravyov, might have gone down in history as Russia's Thomas Jefferson, with his face carved into a cliff in the

Ural Mountains. Imagine what Russia, and the world, would be like today if they had succeeded!

They didn't. The planned revolution—staged during the succession crisis after the death of Czar Alexander the First—failed. Many of the conspirators were executed, but many were simply too well-known, or too well-liked, by the elite of St. Petersburg for execution to be practical. So their sentences were commuted to exile and they were sent to Siberia. Principally, to Irkutsk.

This was an act of mercy in more ways than one. Relative to most of Siberia, the weather in Irkutsk is lovely. Lake Baikal—far and away the world's largest lake, by volume, containing a quarter of the planet's fresh water—forms a giant crescent just east of Irkutsk and creates a natural barrier against the worst of Siberia's storms and chills. Consequently, Irkutsk's climate is more comparable to Wyoming's than Alaska's.

So, when suddenly in the 1820s an already niceish town had a lot of wealthy and freedom-minded Decembrists suddenly dumped into it, the town's economy and art scene thrived. And because these were Jeffersonian-style revolutionaries instead of Robespierrists, the town remained fundamentally patriotic. So the central government left it more or less alone until, in 1920, it became the site of the last stand of anti-Bolshevism.

John had a chance to absorb all this in the two days he spent in Irkutsk by himself, awaiting the arrival of Petr and Anna. Late Wednesday—his second day in Irkutsk—he began to worry. Petr arrived on Thursday, a relief to John, but anxiety for Petr, who'd assumed he'd be the last to show. Privately John began to wonder if Anna had simply taken the money and run or had made some sort of deal with Gazneft.

Personally, he liked her. He had frankly believed she would show up with a big chunk of stock for them. But by Thursday her absence provoked the obvious suspicion that he'd been wrong. He didn't mention this to Petr, who probably had the same suspicions and was taking the whole thing much harder than John was.

Behind both the facade of hoping Anna was just delayed in arriving—clearly Gazneft was good at delaying people—and the unspoken worry that she'd been unfaithful to them, there was a much more serious concern: that something bad had happened to her. Something very bad. Petr had told John about the slaughtered sled dogs. His late arrival to Irkutsk was the result of trying to make things right with Rul-Tyne and the Chukchi. (Not because they demanded it, but because his conscience did.)

John had been gathering vouchers since he arrived; Petr had joined the effort since arriving himself. The hope that this might distract from the Anna situation was futile (and, really, had been unrealistic to begin with).

On Friday Anna still hadn't arrived, but Petr had finally managed to persuade a succession of telephone operators to connect him to the Kovac-Mills office in Moscow. When the phone on the other end began ringing, Petr handed the phone to John. Partly because Andrei, who was running the office, saw John, who had hired him, as his true boss—with Petr as a sort of deputy-pretender—and partly because Petr needed a moment to collect his temper. Long distance Russian telephoning could easily drive a man insane. Watching Petr attempt it had been like watching one of those monks who sticks his hand in boiling water to test himself.

The phone rang. Andrei answered and John asked him if there was any news.

"That guy Menshikov won't stop calling and coming by. I tell him I don't know from shit about voucher business but the guy will not stop it."

"Menshikov? The *Forbes* reporter?" said John. He was holding the phone slightly away from his ear so Petr could listen in.

"Yeah, George Menshikov. American *Forbes* reporter with Russian names."

"Tell him to fuck off or you'll have him assassinated," said Petr.

"You want me to actually tell him that?"

"No," said Petr. "It was a joke," he explained, switching to Russian, then mouthing the English translation for John.

"Forget Menshikov," said John. "Tell us about the business."

"Business is good, keeping everyone working very hard, buying lots of vouchers from Petr's list, getting them registered with help from Benny's people. Steak at Uncle Guilly's is better than the rest of the food in Moscow combined. Life has been worse and probably will be again soon."

"Don't give up on your chickens before they die, Andrei," said John.

"I assume this is a droll American idiom," said Andrei.

"Sort of," said John. "Anything else we should know about?"

"A colonel named Krylenko has come by twice. He was very friendly, wanted to know about voucher operation, said you and Petr were doing work for him in Siberia. I told him I couldn't give him any private business data. He became less friendly and I told him to screw. If I am assassinated, please tell my family I never loved them."

". . . Um," said John.

"That was a joke," said Andrei. "What, only Kovac is allowed to make jokes?"

"Right," said John. "Well, it's true we're working with Krylenko but it's also good not to give him any of our info. He can ask us about it when we see him. We should be back next week."

"Good," said Andrei. "Let me know so I can pick you up with the car."

"Thanks Andrei—honestly don't know what we'd do without you."

"I don't know either," said Andrei.

"We'll be in touch," said John. *"Do svidaniya."*

"Buh-bye," said Andrei. John dropped the phone onto its receiver and looked at Petr.

"What now?"

They were in the lobby of a hotel on the edge of the Angara River, near Irkutsk's city center. It had become their de facto headquarters, the place where the gopniks brought vouchers and got paid. Petr had a distracted, nervous look on his face.

"I don't know." For a moment they stood facing each other over the lobby courtesy phone. ("Courtesy" not in the sense that it was free—it wasn't—but it was available to use and the only public phone in the hotel.)

"I'm going to go check again for messages," said Petr, at length. He walked off, and John, with a mental shrug (how many times could he check?) headed for the bar. It was a room with a curious mix of quality wood paneling and linoleum. Half executive dining room, half high school cafeteria. John went to the bar's bar and ordered a couple beers. By the time Petr finally joined him, he'd finished the first, given up waiting, and started the second.

"Sorry," he said as Petr walked over, looking not so much concerned as absent-minded. "I'm drinking your beer."

"No messages," said Petr. "And I had them call around to the other hotels in Irkutsk for me and nothing from any of them either."

"Look," said John, "she's a tough girl, I'm sure she'll—"

"I called Krylenko," said Petr. "I asked if he had any contacts in Omsk."

When Petr didn't go on, John prompted him. "And does he?"

"Yes," said Petr. "Yes, he says he knows people in Omsk. He's going to make inquiries. He said he'd get back to me as soon as he heard something."

John nodded. Petr lapsed into silence again. John finished the second beer and looked at the wall clock. Like Petr's, John's internal clock had given up a long time ago. Mostly this problem was obviated by Russia's use of twenty-four-hour time, but this particular bar had an old fashioned, bourgeois hand clock. It read quarter to twelve. John was genuinely unsure if that meant quarter to noon or quarter to midnight. He checked his watch. It had the same twelve-hour problem but at least he could check to see if the date was about to tick over to Saturday. He squinted at the little date number and realized his eyes were blurry.

"You should get some sleep," he said, feeling that whatever time it actually was, it was good advice. "Why don't you sack down for a while? I'll keep an eye on the gopniks. You can take over when you've gotten some rest."

"No," said Petr, shaking his head slowly. "No, I think I'll wait down here. He may call. Why don't you take the first sleep shift and come down when you're ready?"

John nodded. He wasn't going to argue. He was damned tired. And though he was more than a little worried about Anna himself, resting first was probably good manners. A recognition of Petr's having priority in the emotional-attachment hierarchy. Romantic trumps fraternal. Being honest with himself, John hoped—he really hoped—she'd just taken the money. No question that that was the best outcome now, for all of them.

"Okay," said John, pushing back from the bar and standing up. "Come get me if you need a break."

"I will," said Petr, holding up one of John's empty beer bottles to signal the barmaid that he'd like one for himself.

CHAPTER 25

Loud knocking on his hotel-room door woke John up. He picked up the watch by his bed. It was about six, on Saturday. He wondered if he'd slept six hours or eighteen. "Next time I come to Siberia in a race against corrupt management to buy an ex-Soviet gas company, I'm getting a digital watch," he told himself, rolling out of bed, smiling at his own little joke and walking to the door.

He opened the door. Petr was there. His face was full-on Communist-raised Slavic blankness. No emotion; total concealment.

"Hey," said John. "How long have I been asleep? You want me to take over?"

"Yes," said Petr. "I should sleep for a while. I heard back from Krylenko. Anna's gone—so's our money, so are our vouchers."

"Jesus."

"I'm sorry, John."

"Better than having her blood on our hands, I suppose."

"Yeah."

John wanted to buck Petr up, but wasn't sure how. Before he could think of anything to say, Petr said, "I misjudged her."

"It happens," said John. "When this is done we're gonna have all the money in the world anyway. Losing one auction doesn't really make any difference."

"Yeah," said Petr. He turned and walked up the hall to his room.

"Just forget about it, Petr," said John.

"Wake me when you get tired," said Petr. He wasn't looking at John; he was unlocking his hotel-room door.

"I will," said John. "Get some sleep."

"I will," said Petr, closing the door behind him.

CHAPTER 26

After Petr had gone to sleep, John went back on gopnik duty after a quick stop at the main desk to find out if it was A.M. or P.M. As it turned out, it was six in the morning Saturday. Twenty-four hours till the final auction, in Tayshet.

He and Petr had already made plans for transportation; they'd bought a Lada Niva, one of the few Soviet cars known to actually work well, according to Petr. It was a little four-wheel drive off-roader, the Russians' answer to Jeep and Land Rover.

No telling what Gazneft might try to put in the way this time. This way, they wouldn't have to worry about roadblocks et al.— either on roads or airstrips. They'd filled the Niva's trunk with gas-filled jerricans; enough extra gas to get them there and back twice. If they had to, they'd simply turn off the road and drive cross country, according to Petr. John didn't doubt that Petr was right. After all, the Communists knew their tractors, and the Niva was basically just a tractor with a car's body and a more reasonable gear ratio.

John was just expecting the worst. The report of Anna's betrayal had landed him in a bit of a funk. Morale was temporarily low. It would be an eight-hour drive. They wouldn't be going to a hotel at the other end—they'd head straight for the auction. In and out as fast as possible. Even so, they'd settled on leaving sixteen hours for the eight-hour drive, just in case something came up. So they'd leave in eight hours. (John found the base-twelve roundness of the numbers appealing.) That gave Petr eight hours to sleep before they left, and John eight hours to accumulate any late-arrival vouchers to add to the thousands they already had.

Even writing off Anna's work in Omsk, John estimated they now owned close to a quarter of Gazneft. It meant simply holding on to the shares until the stock became negotiable on the brand-new Russian stock market. It was already functioning at the Moscow Interbank Currency Exchange, which had, in Soviet times, been the central authority at which one could buy and sell rubles. Holding the shares until Gazneft went public on the MICEX would net them billions of dollars. Literally billions of dollars.

Still, morale was low. The whole Anna thing left John feeling stung by betrayal. Petr, though, looked like he'd taken a real body blow. Could Petr actually have fallen in love with her?

During their eight-hour drive to Tayshet, they spoke about almost nothing. Petr found a radio station playing Western pop hits and Bach. *Why Bach?* was one of their few conversations. Petr explained that while not officially banned, classical music had simply gone extinct in the period of Socialist Realism—a style intentionally devoid of complexity or subtext, where everything had to be acceptable to the scrutiny of the secret police and very obviously intended to praise the Soviet socialist system.

Then in 1957, the legendary pianist Glenn Gould became the first Westerner to tour Russia since the Revolution. His program varied, but the core of every concert was Gould's specialty, Bach. It was pure, divine, soul-tingling music of a sort no Russian had heard in forty years. Young people had never heard it at all. People clung to rafters, climbed on to one another's shoulders, pushed their ears to windows, to get a chance to hear Gould play Bach. "Since then," said Petr, "it's been an important part of the counterculture."

John nodded. The radio finished the Fourth English Suite, and began to play "Back in the USSR."

◆

When Petr took his first shift driving, John fell asleep and slept soundly until Petr reached over and shook him awake.

"Hey, John, wake up," his voice sounded urgent. "Wake up."

"I'm up—I'm here, what's wrong?"

"Look," said Petr, pointing out the windshield. "What the fuck is that?"

Petr hadn't slowed down yet—there was still a long way to go on a long flat road before they encountered the obstacle ahead . . . which appeared to be a bonfire.

"A fire?"

"I know it's a fucking fire," said Petr. "What do we do?"

"Go around it?" said John. "That's the point of this car, right?"

"Yes, but if I wanted to shoot someone I'd get them to slow with an obstacle they could drive around and then shoot them."

"How much would we have to slow down?"

"No idea," said Petr. "How fast do you drive a Jeep through mud?"

"Faster than you drive a Jeep through fire. We'll fucking melt."

"What if we just blow through it really fast?"

"What if there's a tank behind it that we slam into?"

"I think it's a pile of burning tires."

"Well unless they're see-through tires, you don't know what's on the other side."

"So you think I should go around?"

"Yes—yes—go around."

"Shit," said Petr. They were only a hundred yards or so away from the fire now. "Okay." He slowed down and turned off the road. The tundra was frozen solid. Petr had to saw at the wheel a little but soon he was speeding up again. The bonfire flew by on the right—John got a good look at it.

"You were right," he said. "Burning tires."

"And nothing behind them?"

"Nothing behind them."

"So we could have driven through."

"Yeah, maybe," said John. "Pretty glad we didn't, though."

"I didn't hear any shots," said Petr.

"No," said John. "Me neither."

"Good. I'll go another hundred meters and get back on the road."

John gave Petr a thumbs-up and let out a long sigh of relief. As Petr turned them back onto the road, John said, "Do you think we're being too paranoid?"

Petr swung his head over and looked at John hard before looking back to the road.

"Right," said John. "Of fucking course we aren't."

CHAPTER 27

The actual auction was a rather somber affair. The vouchers and paperwork were submitted, John and Petr's investment fund racked up 30 percent of the Irkutsk share issuance. The Gazneft bidder came in at the last moment and left the moment the vouchers had been submitted. Petr shouted at him as he left, trying to get him to stop and talk to them, but the man simply walked faster, out of the town hall and into a black Mercedes, which sped away.

John suggested they spend the night in Tayshet rather than driving the eight hours back right away—but Petr said he'd slept enough on the drive up and he wanted to get on with it—get back on the road, get back to Irkutsk, back to Moscow, cash out, and get back to Prague. John didn't want to argue. Petr said he'd take the first driving shift. John napped in the passenger seat. Petr didn't bother waking him up for a turn at the wheel. He parked the Niva back at the hotel, where he woke John with a gentle shake of his shoulder and suggested he pack while Petr called the airport and found when the first flight to Moscow was. John nodded groggily and followed Petr inside. He left Petr at the courtesy phone and went up to stuff his clothes into his duffle. Now empty of both money and vouchers, it was less like a soldier's rucksack and more like a hobo's bindle. With the difficulty in doing laundry over the last two weeks, John was tempted just to throw it out and buy new stuff in Moscow. But who knew if he'd be able to find something in Moscow that wasn't chrome-shiny silk or a tracksuit? He was bundling the duffle tight, trussing it up with its drawstrings, when someone knocked on his door.

"Come in."

It was Petr.

"I called the airport and got us on a nonstop flight back to Moscow. On a real-life jet airliner."

"Great," said John. "I don't think I could take another crazy, bouncy bush ride. And I sure as shit didn't want to take a week-long train ride."

"Yeah," said Petr. "It's good. It leaves in about six hours. We're only a few minutes from the airport; we can leave when you're ready."

"I'm ready," said John.

"Good," said Petr. "Let me get my bag and we can get going."

John nodded.

Petr started to walk up the hall to his own room.

"Also, I talked Krylenko," he said, unlocking his door. "He left a message at the desk, asking us to call. To let him know when we'll be back. I told him how it went and he said he'd meet us at the airport."

"Good," said John. "It'll save Andrei the drive, anyway."

Petr smiled, slightly. "Sure."

At the airport, they checked in with the airline and then went to the cafeteria to get some tea and wait for their flight to board. The café actually had some coffee—an almost forgotten luxury, to John's mind—and it perked up their moods a bit. After his second cup, Petr said, "What the hell is wrong with me? When we cash out this stock, I could buy every hooker in Europe. I don't think this particular one should be such a big deal."

"Eh. The heart wants what it wants. But you'll get over it. People get brought together by stress and adventure. It wouldn't have worked out anyway. You'd always have wondered if she was just with you for the money. Which, it turns out, she probably would have been."

Petr laughed for the first time in a week.

"Do you ever worry if your wife is with you for your money?" said Petr.

"Nope," said John. "When we got married, I was already making seven figures but so was she."

"She was a banker too?"

"Nope, her father was an early investor in bubble wrap."

"Bubble wrap?"

"Yeah. Those little plastic air bubbles they use to ship fragile stuff."

"Ah. That's good. An equal footing for marriage."

"Yeah," said John.

"Like in Jane Austen."

"Um. Yeah, sort of."

They drank on in silence for a while, until Petr finally said, "Shit, we should be celebrating. What's our final number? I've got us at about a third of the issued stock."

"So . . . ," said John. "Fourteen billion total over five auctions. Two-point-eight billion per auction. We got sixty-one-point-six percent at Baymak, and thirty-four-point-one percent at Tayshet. I got forty-five-point-nine percent at Kyzyl-Syr. You got . . ."

"Forty-two-point-six."

"Forty-two-point-six percent at Anadyr. That gives us an average of thirty-six-point-eight four percent, over all five auctions. Thirty-six-point-eight four percent of fourteen billion . . ."

John pulled out a pen to finish off the math on a napkin.

"Five billion, one hundred and fifty-seven million, six hundred thousand dollars of Gazneft stock. At Krylenko's twenty billion valuation."

Petr whistled.

"Well, that's a pretty good month's work."

John nodded, and went on. "Half of that goes to Krylenko, our investors get half of what's left, and we each get half of what's left after that."

Now Petr was doing some mental arithmetic.

"So that's . . . six hundred forty-four million, seven hundred thousand dollars for each of us?"

John smiled. "Yeah. That's the number I'm getting."

"Before taxes," said Petr.

John laughed.

◆

The plane—an Ilyushin Il-62—was about half-full. Aside from unusually thick, shaggy carpeting, there was nothing to tell it apart from a Boeing or an Airbus. Which is to say it was just as plasticky and cramped and generally unpleasant as any other modern airliner.

John and Petr took their seats near the back of the first-class compartment—John wondering, as he had on the train, how it was ex-Soviet planes had first-class compartments. After about ten minutes in a taxi line, the plane took off. A few minutes after it took off, a stewardess came over, carrying an envelope.

"Are you Petr Kovac and John Mills?" she said, in Russian.

"Yes," said Petr.

"We were asked to bring this from Moscow to give to you. We were asked to say that, once you've looked at it, a satellite phone has been placed in the forward crew compartment for you to use."

"What's going on?" said Petr.

"That's all I know, sir," said the stewardess, holding the envelope out.

"Thank you," said Petr, accepting it and quickly translating the exchange for John. "The envelope says it's from Krylenko."

As the stewardess walked away, Petr tore the envelope open.

There was a short contract inside, with copies in Russian and English, and a cover note that said, "Call me," with a phone number, signed Krylenko.

"What the fuck is this?" Petr handed John the English language version. They both started to read.

"This is an agreement," said John, "to transfer all our shares in the Kovac-Mills Fund . . . to Colonel Semyon Sergeyevich Krylenko. Outright."

"What the fuck is this?" repeated Petr.

They got up and headed to the front of the cabin, where the stewardess showed them to a small nook just behind the cockpit with a three-level bunkbed for the crew to rest in. She handed over a chunky yellow satellite phone and left them alone.

Petr dialed and held the phone so he and John could both hear.

A woman's voice answered, "Golokova."

Petr cranked the volume nob as high as it would go so they could hear over the sound of the jet and said, "I have a note here from Colonel Krylenko to call this number."

"Yes," said the woman.

"You speak English?"

"Yes," said the woman—this time in English.

"Who am I speaking to?"

"Irina Fydorovna Golokova, chief financial officer of the Gazneft."

"Where's Krylenko?" said John.

"Colonel Krylenko is no longer with us."

"No longer with you?" said John. "What does that mean? Did you fire him or is he dead?"

"He attempted to register a large share of Omsk Oblast stock in his own name. So now he is no longer with us."

"Anna's stock," mouthed Petr. John nodded.

"Okay," said Petr, "so what does that have to do with us?"

"Like him, you have illegally attempted to register a large share of Gazneft stock."

"No, not like him," said John. "Because it wasn't illegal, and we didn't *try* to register it—we registered it. It's on the books with the International Monetary Fund."

"That is immaterial. You will return the stock to us immediately, upon your landing in Moscow. Contracts will be ready for you to sign. I've seen the draft of what Krylenko sent you. It will be mostly the same; his name replaced with Representatives of the Workers of Gazneft."

"How do you know where we are?" said Petr.

"Does it matter? Krylenko told us before he was terminated."

"Terminated," said John. "Hah."

"Did he tell you how he got our Omsk stock?" said Petr.

"He said it was acquired from a young lady in Tara."

"Did he tell you where she is now?" said Petr.

"Istanbul," said Golokova. Petr shook his head. "We would have liked to speak with her, but ultimately it will not be necessary. What is necessary is this: you will sign over your stock immediately upon your plane landing in Moscow."

"Or else what?" said John. "You'll have us terminated?"

"No," said Golokova. "I'll have you killed."

". . . Oh," said John.

"Your 'partner' Krylenko made these arrangements; we are simply taking over his private investment plan. It would seem, from the beginning, this was the inevitable outcome. Resign yourself to it. I will meet you at the airport to countersign in the presence of a notary."

The line went dead.

"How long is this flight?" said John.

"Five hours," said Petr.

John nodded. "I think we might be fucked."

CHAPTER 28

"There must be some way to beat them on this."

"I don't know," said John. "What counteroffer can you make to someone who says she's going to kill you? 'How about you just cripple us and we split it fifty-fifty?'"

"What if we offered fifty-fifty, like the deal we had with Krylenko?"

"Why would they take it?"

"So they don't have to kill us?"

"Well, even if we assume that would be inconvenient for them—and frankly, I'm not sure that's true—but even if they would prefer *not* to kill us, they know we know we think they're capable of it. Which means they know that, with guns to our heads, we're going to sign, and they won't have to kill us. So it's sort of a moot point."

"But if they do kill us," said Petr, "it's a lose-lose. The stock won't revert to them if we're dead—it'll still be the property of the Kovac-Mills Fund. It just means the money bypasses us and goes on to our investors and heirs and assignees. Maybe we can persuade them we'd rather die and leave the money to our kids as a legacy than live with the humiliating failure."

"You don't have kids, do you?"

"No," said Petr. "None that I know of, anyway. But your wife is pregnant."

"Yeah," said John. "Which I think is a good reason not to get killed. And I think they'll think I'll be thinking that."

"Unless you tell them that providing for your child is more important than living to see him."

"But I'm kind of rich already and they know it."

Petr took a beat to think. "Yes," he said. "You're right."

They fell back into silence.

Petr had his head leaned back. He was looking vacantly at a plastic light fixture on the ceiling. "We must have some kind of leverage. We own the stock. They're not even disputing it."

"Yeah," said John. "But it's a very aggressive buyer's market."

"Yes," said Petr.

"We can't sell the stock outside Russia, because of the IMF arrangement."

"Correct," said Petr.

"And we can't sell the stock inside Russia, because anyone who bought it would get the same your-stock-or-life treatment we are. Gazneft still gets the stock and we still get killed."

"Also correct."

More silence.

"What if we threatened to just give it away," said John. "Make it someone else's problem."

"That's the same as threatening to want to leave it for your kids," said Petr. "Besides, who would take it?"

"Yeah," said John. "I guess so."

More silence.

"Who could we offer it to," said John, "who wouldn't be afraid of Gazneft?"

Petr scratched his forehead. "Kursk Tobacco?"

John laughed.

More silence.

"Wait," said John. "That could actually work."

"What, giving the stock to the Russian Mafia? That would actually not work. We'd not only end up dead, but heavily invested in the worst people in the world."

"No," said John. "But what if we did give it to someone who Gazneft could be scared of?"

"What would Gazneft be scared of outside of people like the Mafia threatening to kill them for not playing ball?"

"The IMF. The IMF could revoke the tender for a foreign stock issuance. Without foreign money, from the US and Europe and Japan, Gazneft's stock is going to end up being worth exactly zero dollars, pounds, francs, whatever, of hard currency. If the company can't do a public offering outside Russia, Gazneft is fucked. It'd be like oil in Libya. Something's only valuable if you can sell it."

"There are two problems, though," said Petr. "First, we can't transfer the stock to the IMF because they aren't incorporated in Russia, and this is Russia-only stock. Second, if the IMF were willing to get involved, they wouldn't have looked the other way when Gazneft tried to fix the auctions."

After a pregnant pause, John said, "Right." And then, "Yeah, I guess not." The two men lapsed into silence.

The first-class stewardess began to serve tea, in extremely unappetizing orange-brown plastic saucers that looked as if they'd been swiped from a hospital cafeteria. John and Petr drank in silence, until Petr said, "So that's it? We've lost?"

John took a sip of tea and nodded his head. "Yeah. I guess so."

There was nothing more to say. The stewardess announced that a movie would be shown, and about two minutes later, that a movie would not be shown. There was no explanation, but John assumed a projector bulb had burned out and there was no spare. John and Petr finished their tea and after a while, each of the exhausted, defeated men drifted off to sleep.

◆

"Petr, wake up." John was nudging the sleeping Czech in the shoulder. "Wake up."

"What?" said Petr, with irritation very plain in his voice.

"The IMF can threaten Gazneft, but the IMF won't do anything, and Gazneft knows it. But what if Gazneft knew that we could force the IMF's hand? What if we tell Gazneft we're going to give the stock to George Menshikov? He's a Russian citizen. And they can't just kill him—they can't take the risk. Him working for Forbes? As a reporter reporting on nationalization vouchers? Gazneft couldn't keep that quiet. Forbes has major pull—they could blow the IMF deal out of the water, push for sanctions."

"And he'd get a fantastic story out of it," said Petr. "What an ending! 'American and Czech businessmen murdered on runway at Moscow Airport.'"

"No, but—"

"No, I'm with you," said Petr. "It's mutually assured destruction—either they make a deal with us, or no one gets the stock. It's perfect."

"We need to call Andrei. We need to talk to Menshikov."

CHAPTER 29

George Menshikov's phone rang, in a small office in the semi-renovated, soon-to-be very chic *Forbes* Russia HQ.

"Menshikov," he said, picking it up.

"George Menshikov? This is John Mills."

"John! Thanks for calling me."

"Would you still be interested in picking my brain, and Petr Kovac's, about vouchers and so on, if Gazneft were off-limits?"

"I thought Gazneft wasn't doing a voucher issuance."

"Right. So, are you on board?"

"You guys are into Kursk Tobacco and Babayev Chocolate, right? Those are two of my main targets right now. Research targets."

John moved the satellite phone away from his mouth for a second, and asked Petr, "What's Babayev Chocolate?"

"One of the biggest candy companies in the world."

"And we're in on it?"

"Yes. Assuming Andrei got the vouchers in."

"Yeah," said John, talking again to Menshikov. "We're in Babayev and we were in Kursk."

"Awesome. Yes, I would love to pick your brains—but why the change of heart?"

"We need something from you."

"Sure. What?"

"We need to give you a big scoop that you can't use unless we get killed."

"What?"

"And we need to threaten to give you five billion dollars of Gazneft stock."

There was long pause.

"What?"

"And it could definitely be dangerous."

"Kursk Tobacco is run by the Russian mob, right?" said Menshikov.

"Yeah," said John.

"How much more dangerous could it be?"

"Well," said John. "Let me tell you a story."

CHAPTER 30

George agreed to John's plan. John and Petr each took a turn emphasizing the potential danger but George shrugged it off. John asked how long it would take him to have contracts drawn up. They needed two sets—one offering Gazneft a 50-50 split on new terms, and the other, the threat-contract, signing all the stock over to George. George said he could get the contracts written and get to the airport in two hours. Petr flagged down a stewardess and asked how long till they landed.

"About half an hour," she said.

"Please ask the pilots how much it would cost to keep us in the air an extra ninety minutes."

"But—" she started to say.

"Just ask them," said Petr, pulling a couple fives out of his pocket and handing them to her. "Please."

She came back a few minutes later. "The pilots say they only have enough gas to stay in the air for an additional hour. To delay landing will cost one thousand dollars American."

"George," said John into the phone. "Could you have everything at the airport in ninety minutes? That's our deadline."

"Yes," said George, after a moment's thought. "I think so. I'll meet you on the tarmac?"

"Yeah," said John. "With my fingers crossed."

◆

When John and Petr's plane landed in Moscow, they waited in their seats until the plane was empty and the pilots told them they had to leave. When they stepped onto the deplaning stairs and scanned the ground below them, there was a large, menacing, black-suit-wearing man standing next to a stretch limo. But no sign of Menshikov.

They walked down, slowly. The big suit-wearing man approached.

"There he is!" said Petr, pointing to a figure jogging out of the terminal. He was holding a sheath of paper above his head. "I think that's him."

"It's him," said John. More in hope than certainty.

At the bottom of the deplaning stairs the big guy in the black suit stepped in front of them and waved them left toward the stretch limo.

But they could see the face of the guy holding up the papers now and goddamned if it wasn't George Menshikov. He continued to jog toward the plane. Petr waved to him, and he veered slightly, heading straight for the trio of Petr, John, and the big guy instead.

The big guy ushering John and Petr to the limo tried to intervene.

"He's with us," said Petr. "He's part of the Golokova deal." The big guy in the suit hesitated a moment, then shrugged and stood aside. And George, breathing a little hard, fell in with Petr and John.

"Are those the contracts?" said Petr.

"Yup," said Menshikov. He handed copies to John and Petr. They were written in Russian, so they didn't mean anything to John, but Petr gave him a thumbs-up. And then added, "It's a Linc-mo."

"A what?"

"A Lincoln limousine," he said, pointing to the car they were walking toward.

"Do people actually call it that?"

"Yes," said Petr. "Everyone."

John wasn't sure if he was being serious or just very dry. The man in the suit reached around them, opened the Linc-mo's door, and waved them inside. He hadn't said a word. Probably part of his schtick.

As George turned to get out of the way of the opening door, John saw he had a large, deep purple bruise on his left cheek and a stitched-up cut under his left eye.

"What happened to you?"

"Babayev Chocolate," said George.

John nodded and climbed into car, followed by Petr, then George.

The three spread themselves out on the curved back seat of the stretched Lincoln.

Irina Fydorovna Golokova was seated at the far end of the limo, with a man beside her who John assumed was a notary or a lawyer. She was a woman in her sixties, thin and somewhat gaunt. She had clearly been pretty in her youth but looked as if she hadn't smiled since the Cuban Missile Crisis. She was drinking either water or vodka from a crystal glass and smoking a cigarette. She didn't say anything. Probably part of *her* schtick. Waiting for them to go first. So John did.

"Golokova, I presume?"

She nodded, then made a little gesture with her hand, which prompted the man sitting next to her to awkwardly slide down the limo's side bench and hand John a set of contracts.

"Thanks," said John. "And here's our counteroffer."

"I'm not interested, Mr. Mills, in your counteroffer," said Golokova, speaking for the first time. "I've told you what your options are. Sign or accept the consequences."

"Do you know who this is?" said John pointing to Menshikov.

"I do not."

"That's George Menshikov. *Forbes* magazine—you know *Forbes*?"

She nodded, curtly, to show the question annoyed her.

"*Forbes* magazine sent him over here to write about corruption in the issuance of privatization vouchers. *Forbes*—as you know—being one of the top financial publications in the world. This contract," said John, holding it up—

Petr shook his head. Wrong contract. John would have to remember to learn Russian.

"This contract," said John, holding up the other one, "transfers all our interest in Kovac-Mills investments to Mr. Menshikov. Outright. Mr. Menshikov would defend his claim in court and, if necessary, with the IMF, with the backing of, and the protection of, the Forbes group. If anything were to happen to Mr. Menshikov, it would attract—via Forbes—a great deal of international attention."

Golokova said nothing. She took a drag of her cigarette and kept her face blank.

"This contract," said John, holding up the other one, "will transfer to your management fund—the 'Representatives of the

Workers of Gazneft'?—one hundred percent of the stock currently registered to the Kovac-Mills Fund. In exchange, Gazneft will transfer to Kovac-Mills shares in Gazneft equal to fifty percent of the shares being transferred to you—with these new shares to be internationally negotiable. So that we can get out of your hair, and out of Russia, before anyone else tries to murder us."

Golokova took another long drag on her cigarette.

"Give them to the attorney," she said, finally. "He will look at them."

John handed them over, then looked at Petr, who nodded and gestured that they should wait outside. John nodded.

"We'll give you an opportunity to discuss in private," said Petr, reaching over George to open the door. George climbed back out of the Linc-mo; Petr and John followed.

Outside, they all lit cigarettes and waited.

"Are you sure you don't want us to cut you in on the final deal?" said John, to George.

"I'm sure. I can't take money from a subject on which I'm reporting."

"You know," said Petr. "We give you just a few percent of this, you'll never have to report on anything ever again."

George smiled and exhaled a puff of blue smoke. "Thanks, Kovac, but I don't do this job for the money. Either you have honest reporters and democracy or you have dishonest reporters and tyranny." He flicked away the butt of his cigarette. "That's how I see it, anyway."

Petr nodded, gravely. Among the three of them, there was now the awkward discomfort men feel when expressing admiration for one another. John finally got it over with by saying, "You're a good man, George. Call me if I can ever help out with that."

"And me," said Petr.

"Thanks," said George, and they all tried to think of a new subject of conversation.

Using his cigarette to point at George's cheek, Petr said, "What the fuck happened to your face?"

"Babayev Chocolate. I got beat up by a masked candy man."

Petr chuckled and shook his head.

One of the Linc-mo's doors opened and Golokova's attorney climbed out. "She wants you," he said, briefly.

Back inside, Golokova looked as impassive as ever. She made eye contact with each of them in turn and, after a pregnant pause, said, "I will have to discuss this further with my fellow directors. In the meantime, we will be watching you. Do not leave Moscow."

"Okay," said Petr.

"Do leave my car," said Golokova.

"Sure thing," said John.

Petr opened the door and climbed out with George just behind him. John followed, with a quick glance over his shoulder, looking for a final glimpse of Irina Fydorovna Golokova. He was looking for a hint on her face of how angry she was. Her face remained totally inexpressive. John shut the door behind him and a moment later the Linc-mo drove away.

For a long few beats, John watched it go. He took a deep breath.

"Well," he said, beginning a thought, then stopping. He took another deep breath. "Holy shit."

"Yeah," said Petr.

"Live to fight another day, right?" said John.

"Yeah," said Petr.

"So, what's more exciting," asked George. "Not losing a gigantic fortune or not getting killed?"

John cocked his head. It was a good question. "Not getting killed?" he said, looking at Petr. "By a nose?"

Petr nodded. "It's close," he said. "Very close. What does 'by a nose' mean?"

"Horse racing expression. When a horse wins a race by just his nose being in front of the next closest horse."

"Useful expression," said Petr. He turned to George. "John's from Texas."

George chuckled.

Petr scratched the back of his neck. "What now?" he said.

"Do you think they'll actually take the deal?" said George.

"I don't know," said John. "Should we just get out of town now and play it safe?"

"I wouldn't," said George. "When they say they're watching you, they're definitely watching you."

"I think he's right," said Petr. "I think the best thing to do now is go back to the hotel and wait."

"Okay," said John. "Geez. My heart's pounding."

"Perhaps, then," said Petr, "the best thing to do now is go back to the hotel and drink."

John laughed, in spite of himself.

"You two owe me an interview," said George.

"Tomorrow morning?" said John.

"Bright and early," said George.

John stuck out his hand. "Thanks, George. I mean it. You came through for us in a big way. No matter how this turns out, I'm indebted to you."

"And me too," said Petr, shaking George's hand in turn. "We might not be leaving the airport alive if it weren't for you."

George shrugged in an *aw shucks* sort of way. "Anytime. Can I give you a lift back into town?"

George Menshikov dropped John and Petr back at the Hotel Metropol, where they decided to forgo a nightcap and begin catching up on sleep. Petr disappeared into his side of the hotel suite, and John called Marsha. He told her he'd made it back to Moscow and everything seemed to be, for the moment, okay. He didn't bother telling her about the death threat hanging over his head. What would be the point? He'd cross that bridge when he came to it. In the meantime, he just told her he loved her and expected to be back stateside soon. She said she loved him, too, and to hurry home. He asked how she was feeling, how things were going, what was new in Texas. She said she was feeling great, everything was going great, and that he'd been asked after by Jim Schultz, whom she'd run into at a small get-together hosted by a friend who was a Schultz in-law. They'd talked a little about the fund and he'd invited them for dinner—an open invitation for whenever John happened to be back in the West and Jim was in Texas rather than DC. Which seemed to be more and more these days, he'd told her, in a gratified sort of way.

"That's nice of him," said John. "Like I said, I hope I'll be back soon."

"Wonderful," said Marsha, adding a repeated, "I love you. Sleep tight."

"I love you too," said John.

After that, John turned in, and slept peacefully, until about two in the morning. There was a loud banging. Maybe Petr had been sleeping restlessly because this time he beat John out of his bedroom and was the first to the source of the noise—their suite's front door.

Petr opened it. There was a large, muscle-bound man standing outside, in a dark gray overcoat cinched at the waist. John couldn't help thinking he looked a lot like a stereotypical gestapo man.

"Your offer has been rejected," said the man, holding out a hand and dumping small, torn-up pieces of the Menshikov-deal contract onto the floor at Petr's feet. "Here is Gazneft's counteroffer. It is identical to the original. You have one hour to sign it. I will wait for you out here."

Petr looked at John, who was looking at Petr, who turned back to the gestapo man, who had backed away slightly. Petr closed the door.

"I guess they decided they're not afraid of Forbes," said Petr after a few long beats.

John had sat down on one of the suite's chaises longues. Petr nudged the pile of torn-up contract with his feet.

"We could try and run for it," he said.

"With that Gazneft gorilla at the door?" said John. "If we got past him, what chance would we have?"

Petr thought for a moment, and answered: "Zero. I'm not sure we would even make it through the lobby."

He sat down in an imperial-style gilt armchair and sighed.

"So that's the end," he said. John shook his head.

"There's one more card we could try playing," he said.

"Oh yeah?" said Petr, not looking at John, keeping his eyes downcast. He sounded deeply skeptical.

"We can try telling on them."

"Telling on them? What does that mean?"

"I mean, reporting them to a higher authority. Making a complaint."

Petr snorted contemptuously. "Making a complaint to who?" he said. "Our desires next to theirs are worth precisely nothing."

"True," said John, leaning toward a phone on the coffee table, "but let me try making a call."

◆

For the second time that night, John called Texas. In his home near Dallas, Jim Schultz answered.

"Schultz," he said, in the regular curt way of a man who's right in the middle of something.

"Jim, it's John Mills. Am I getting you during dinner?"

"No, not yet. John Mills. It's good to hear from you. I just talked to Marsha the other day, asked you two over to the ranch."

"Yeah, she told me. But that's not what I'm calling about," said John. "There's a little problem with the Russia-voucher fund."

"What do you mean, 'a little problem'?" said Schultz. "What kind of little problem?"

"We've secured a Gazneft ownership stake. When we monetize it, it will put us—the fund that is—several billion dollars in the black."

"Billion." said Schultz. "With a *b*. That's good work, Mills. Very good work. Not that I ever doubted you for a second," he said, briefly emphasizing his Texas twang. "So, what's the problem?"

"Gazneft is going to murder me and Petr Kovac in one hour unless we give it back to them."

"Ah," said Schultz. "Yes. I would say that qualifies as a problem. Of unspecified littleness."

"Can you help us?" said John. "You know the Russian government better than anyone. And, well, Yeltsin probably owes you a favor, right? From the whole tank thing? The coup d'etat?"

"No," said Schultz. "Boris Yeltsin does not owe me a favor. And if you're asking me to call the president of Russia at—what is it there? Two A.M.?—to ask him to intervene in a private business deal? It's just not possible, John. The man's got a big country to run."

"Sure, sure. It's just that there's a guy waiting outside my hotel room to kill me if I don't do what Gazneft wants."

"Ah, shit," said Schultz. "Did you try making a counteroffer?"

"It was rejected," said John, looking at the pile of torn contract on the floor. "We offered them half. Or specifically, we offered to trade our stock for half its value in stuff we could trade internationally. And then we could get the hell out of Russia and leave them in peace."

"Geez," said Schultz. "Is there a deadline for this?"

"One hour," said John.

"Jesus Christ." There was a long silence and then Schultz said. "Hold tight. Let me see what I can do. Give me the number I can reach you at." John dictated and Schultz jotted the number down. "Okay. Stay by the phone." He hung up without waiting for John to respond.

◆

Jim Schultz was not the sort of man who sat around bemoaning unfortunate events. In Washington, DC, people had already started leaving work for the day. He wanted to catch the State Department guys he knew best before the night shift came on. And it's not always easy to get someone at Foggy Bottom on a direct line, so he called his office. Or technically, the office of his number two, a guy named Rob Landau.

"Rob, this is time sensitive so I'm going to cut to the chase. Get someone to check the files and see if I'm right in thinking that the new Russian prime minister, Chernomyrdin, used to be Minister of Energy. Get me a quick career summary. While that's drawn up, call some of our friends at the State Department and ask how I can get Chernomyrdin on the telephone. I need this inside of twenty minutes. Ten would be better."

"I'm on it," said Landau. Schultz heard the line go dead. He put his own phone down and waited for it to ring.

◆

Viktor Chernomyrdin was standing outside his apartment while his security man unlocked it. Not carrying keys was one of the perks of being prime minister, but he was also a good boss to his security detail, which meant that, sometimes, at the end of the night, hand-eye coordination suffered.

Finally, with an eye roll, he said, "Give it to me, you drunken Cossack. Go take an ice bath." The security guard mumbled his apologies and handed Chernomyrdin his key. He waited till his boss was inside before slinking away down the hall.

The apartment had recently belonged to the Deputy Security of the Communist Party of Russia. It had been a perk of that job and was now another perk of Chernomyrdin's. Lavish was not the right word for it—it didn't compare in gaudiness to the new apartment buildings springing up all over Moscow—but it was very comfortably appointed. Everything was wood and leather, dating from a time when most Muscovites would have considered fiberboard and Naugahyde a luxury. In the daytime, there was a splendid view of St. Basil's. As it was nighttime, Chernomyrdin poured himself a drink and prepared to spend a few hours watching American TV on videotape. It may have been late, but he had no compulsory work hours, and there was no one to tell him not to nap in his office if he felt like it.

Before the first episode of *I Love Lucy* began, his phone rang.

"Yes," he said, in a demonstrably irritated tone.

"There is a call, sir, from the American State Department. Deputy Secretary Bowles. He stresses that the matter is urgent but in no way official and wonders if you would do him the honor of speaking to him."

"Very well," grumbled Chernomyrdin, who actually thought that sounded rather interesting. He waited a moment for a rat's maze of telephone exchanges to connect, and then Mr. Bowles began rattling out American-accented Russian to apologize for calling him at such an ungodly hour.

"It's fine, it's fine," Chernomyrdin repeated several times. "Come to the point, if you would."

"Mr. Prime Minister, the point is that a good friend of both the American government and the Russian government, Mr. James Schultz, has an emergency—of, I repeat, an unofficial nature—but wonders if he might have a few minutes of your time. I have him on the other line, ready to connect."

"Schultz, Schultz, why didn't he call me himself? Of course, put him on, put him on."

"Thank you, sir, thank you very much."

"Yes, yes," said Chernomyrdin. He waited a moment and then Jim Schultz's voice came on the line.

"Mr. Prime Minister," said Schultz. "It's very kind of you to speak to me. I apologize for the late hour."

"Never mind, never mind. It has been a long time, Jim. I think I have not seen you since *Georgi* Bush was still your president."

"Yes, I think you're right, Mr. Prime Minister," said Schultz.

"It's too late for titles, Jim. Save time and call me Viktor."

"Thank you, sir. Viktor. I have a favor to ask. When you were Minister for Energy, and before, I assume you worked with Gazneft."

"Of course," said Chernomyrdin. "Gazneft, Rosneft, Gazprom, Northgaz, Lukoil. All of them. Why?"

"Some friends of mine have bought shares in Gazneft. Quite a few shares, actually."

"How? Are they Russian?"

"Their business is Russian," said Schultz. "But Gazneft's directors want to, uh, recover those shares."

Chernomyrdin laughed. "I'm not surprised. Greedy bastards."

"My friends have offered to give them all their shares in exchange for a fifty-percent equivalent in shares that are internationally negotiable."

"Okay," said Chernomyrdin. "And the Gaz-niks said 'no'?"

"Correct," said Schultz. "They would prefer to have all the stock in exchange for not murdering my friends."

Chernomyrdin laughed hard, from the belly. "Yes, yes, that sounds like them. And you would rather your friends not be murdered, is that correct?"

"That's correct," said Schultz. "I should add—I am invested in their business. So, it's a personal favor I'm asking, and not strictly altruistic. Just so you have all the facts."

"Of course you are," said Chernomyrdin. "Of course you are. Well, well, let me call Voroshilov, their CEO. I'll let him know that he is fucking with the investment of a friend of the Federation. Maybe we can work something out."

"Thank you, Viktor. Thank you. If I could just add: Gazneft gave them an hour to sign, and that was about forty minutes ago. So . . . you know . . ."

Chernomyrdin started to belly laugh again. He was still laughing when he tapped the phone's receiver to end the call. He redialed and the phone rang in the office of his night secretary.

"Wake up Voroshilov and get him on the phone," said Chernomyrdin.

"Yes, sir, right away."

"*Right* away," repeated Chernomyrdin. "I expect to be speaking to him before five minutes have passed."

Chernomyrdin hung up the phone and started a *Lucy* episode.

◆

"I guess our hour is up," said Petr, when the Gazneft gestapo guy began banging on their door again.

"I guess so," said John. The two men were seated on their respective imperial Metropol couches. At one point Petr had mumbled something about dying with his pants on and had decamped to his room, returning a few minutes later in slacks and a sports coat. John had followed suit. Now they were chain-smoking and waiting for something to happen.

Of course, they fully intended to sign over their stock, if that's what it took. In a *your money or your life situation*, you give up the money. Of course. But after that—would they get shot anyway? Hard to say. But even if the cost were only losing a very hard-won, gigantic, life-changing cash windfall—defeat snatched from the jaws of victory—that was enough to blacken their moods. Better than dying but, still, pretty darned bad.

The pounding on the door, which had stopped, started again.

"Maybe it's just room service," said Petr.

"We could barricade the door," said John. "Or pretend we're not home."

But gallows humor wasn't making either of them any more optimistic. The banging continued; finally, John got up to answer the door.

"What's a really good Russian insult?" he said to Petr, as he approached the threshold.

"*Kozel*," said Petr.

"What does it mean?"

"A goat who is incompetent in his job of being a farm animal."

"Really?"

"Yes."

"Useful word," said John, opening the door. "Fuck you, *kozel*," said John.

The Gazneft man ignored him, looked at Petr, then back at John, and said, "Good, you're already dressed. You will come with me."

"Yes?" said Petr.

"Yes," said the man. "It is in your interest not to complicate the situation."

"Where are we going?" said John.

"A meeting with Gazneft."

John looked at Petr. Petr shrugged and cocked his head. *Could it make things worse?*

John shook his head. *Probably not.* Then shrugged and raised his eyebrows. *Unless they're taking us out to kill us.*

Petr shook his head. *They're not going to kill us before we sign.*

John hoped he was right.

◆

Five minutes later they were sitting in the back seat of another Linc-mo, driving toward the outskirts of Moscow. Twenty minutes after that, it was clear they were leaving the city behind them. The Gazneft guy who'd collected them at the hotel had led them to the car and shut the door behind them. The privacy shield between the passenger compartment and the driver was up. When they tried to lower it, the driver raised it back up again. So now they were just waiting to see where they ended up.

Where they ended up was a dacha deep in the forest.

The driver pulled up outside the front door. He didn't say anything to them. He just pulled up and waited. After a few beats, John and Petr climbed out and walked slowly up onto the dacha's porch.

There was music coming from inside. Slow, thumping music. John knocked, hard and loud. He was about to knock again when the door was opened by a hooker. At least, she looked like a hooker. And she did not look pleased to see them.

"You're here," she said, icily. Petr translated for John's benefit. She walked away from the door without saying anything else. John and Petr stepped inside.

The hooker was walking toward an open door into a kitchen. John could see bags of European snack food piled on a counter beside bottles of vodka.

"Where do we go?" said Petr.

"End of the hall," she said.

"Will you show us?" said Petr.

"Fuck no," said the hooker. "He's furious."

Petr translated and he and John made their way down the hall, following the sound of the music, which was growing louder. At the end of the hall was a doorway that led, apparently, to the master bedroom. The door was open and they could see a man dressed only in sweat pants pacing furiously. On the bed, a couple more working girls were perched, looking vaguely disgusted.

The disgust was very clearly aimed at John and Petr. Then the pacing man saw them. He was shirtless, fat but clearly very strong. Very hairy chest and stomach. If he'd had facial hair, he'd have looked a lot like a bear. Though, really, he looked a lot like a bear anyway.

"You're here," he said, in English. He slapped the top of a boom box, shutting the music off.

"Where is here?" said John.

"Shut up—just shut the fuck up, I'm not interested in speaking with you. Chernomyrdin says we must compromise, that we must accept your compromise. Here are the papers. They are signed. You sign them. Polina will notarize." He pointed with his thumb to one of the scantily clad girls on the bed, who nodded her agreement. "And then you will get the fuck out and never, ever, attempt to fuck with my business again. Or your big-shot friends will be unable to help you."

Petr started to say something and the man cut him off. "Sign. Now."

The contracts were in Russian. Petr read through them quickly, confirming they were the stock-for-half-that-amount-in-international-stock agreement George Menshikov had brought to the airport. They'd been signed already by the CEO of Gazneft— who they assumed was the guy they were talking to but they chose not to inquire further.

After they signed, one of the working girls actually produced, from her purse, a pair of glasses and a notary stamp. She signed both copies, stamped them, and handed both to the large man.

He looked at them, then held out one copy in John and Petr's direction.

"One of you take this," he said. "And get the fuck out of here."

He was speaking Russian again. Petr translated for John and accepted the contract. And that was that. The man turned the music back on and John and Petr backed out of the room before turning to walk back to the front of the house. In the hallway, they passed the girl who'd answered the door, who now appeared to be carrying an armful of milk-chocolate bars, with a bottle of vodka balanced on top. She was holding it in place with her chin. She walked past them as if they weren't there. John and Petr let themselves out and were glad to find the Linc-mo still waiting for them. They climbed back in. The celebration in the car was muted. Neither wanted to tempt fate until they were back at the Metropol, safe and sound.

CHAPTER 31

I t took about a week to get everything sorted out with the stock transfer. In the meantime, John and Petr had given George the complete rundown of the Kovac-Mills operation. Really though, with their focus on Gazneft, it was Andrei who had taken the reigns of the Kovac-Mills day-to-day. Though reluctant at first to talk to a reporter—probably a holdover from a Soviet childhood and probably the reason no one else mass-buying vouchers in Moscow would talk to Menshikov—Andrei agreed to walk George through the whole process. In particular, how it could be gamed and who seemed to be gaming it—on the buying side, on the selling side, and on the government side.

Though his experience with the voucher business had only started two months earlier, Andrei had proved (like someone who could learn English from radio broadcasts of *Cheers*) to be an extremely quick study.

At the end of the week, when everything had been said and done, John cashed out. The first Gazneft stock in Europe fetched a pretty penny in private offerings John made via contacts at various European investment banks and brokerages.

Of the new Gazneft owners, though, only John sold his holdings. Petr and Jim Schultz and Donny Deitrich and Soichiro Yamamura (and Andrei) all opted to stay in and let their investments continue to appreciate. John agreed that, in all probability, they *would* appreciate—but he wanted out. He wanted to get back home to Texas, to his wife, his pregnant wife, raise his kids, and, if he was ever inclined to get back into business, do it strictly with his own money.

Back at the Hotel Metropol, after what had seemed like an eternity of trans-Siberian adventuring, John was finally able to call his wife and find out how her pregnancy was going. "Perfectly," as it turned out. John told her he'd be home in a few days. She asked if there was anything special she could cook for him. He said he'd think about it. He was intentionally cagey about how the business deals had concluded—only because they hadn't officially concluded yet. Mostly they just talked about the banalities of Texas home life and being a semiretired tourist in Moscow.

Petr had already bought out John's share of Kovac-Mills, paying him in Gazneft stock, and they parted very amicably—almost like brothers after only knowing each other a couple months. Those are the kind of friendships that were forged by the wild, wild east. They promised to meet up soon—as soon as Petr was ready to turn over the running of the fund to Andrei full-time and go home to Prague, and once John had done his bit changing diapers. At the time, neither knew they wouldn't see each other again for almost twenty-five years.

On his way out of town, John dropped by the Hungry Duck to thank Doug Steele. Doug asked if John knew what had happened to Krylenko, and John told him.

"Guess it's back to staying indoors until I find a new security guy," said Doug.

"Sorry about that," said John. Doug shrugged.

"C'est la vie. Look me up next time you want to go nuts."

John smiled and promised he would. They shook hands and John sent his best to the masseuses and Asdrubal. Doug told John that Asdrubal had left the country the day after the fight with the Chechens. John didn't know what to say to that so they left it there.

❖

The last guy John saw in Moscow was Benny Sheldon, to thank him, too, and to check on the final financial disposition of his cashing out.

"Everything's in your designated accounts—including the cash-out of Petr's buying your share of the voucher fund. Everything's stamped and delivered. Thanks for not cashing out here or you might have caused a run on the bank. But I think you're good to go."

John smiled. "Well, then, I'm gonna go. With everything finalized—how much am I gonna clear on this deal?"

Benny consulted some papers on his desk.

"Five hundred and twenty-two million, four hundred and forty-four thousand, six hundred and nineteen dollars. And twelve cents."

John nodded. That was a pretty decent paycheck.

"Don't blow it all at once," said Benny, standing up and shaking John's hand. John laughed, and Benny laughed, and then an hour later, John was on a nonstop flight from Moscow to Texas.

CHAPTER 32

Sixteen hours after boarding in Moscow, John's flight landed at Dallas Fort Worth. And twenty-five years after that, things were still going pretty well.

John had taken his five hundred million and multiplied it several times. His first kid was about to turn twenty-five, and he had two others. A daughter and another son. The daughter had just been married and now his first grandkid was on the way. He still lived in Texas in the same house with the same circle of friends. His wine cellar was a little more richly stocked than it had been in his pre-Gazneft days, but that was one of his only indulgent concessions to nigh on unfathomable wealth. The others were a smart vacation house in the Bahamas, and a medium-sized private jet to carry friends and family back and forth.

The Bahamas place was tucked in a gated community called Lyford Cay, on the northwest shoulder of Nassau Island, of James Bond fame. In fact, he was just up the road from the *Thunderball* shark pool, and only a few blocks over from local Scottish evangelist Sean Connery. John lived on the beach. Sean lived on the golf course.

When they were in the Bahamas and Marsha didn't feel like tennis, John tended to play a few holes in the early morning, when the air was crisp and there was no one around but the occasional wandering flock of migratory birds. On this particular winter morning ("winter" only in the technical sense), John played through some indifferent ducks, made par, and began a half-mile walk back to his house from the green of the ninth hole. He was about halfway home when he ran into the wife of Lyford Cay's other James Bond—Robin Shand, whose better half was a veteran of the British SAS.

Robin and John were longtime friends whose bond was astounding levels of success in the petrochemical business. Before she'd switched to charity work, Robin had been one of the most successful oil traders in the world—essentially cornering the Iraqi market, via Russia, on behalf of a Dutch energy company.

Like Marsha, she was annoyingly ageless. She looked forty, which would have meant that she'd reached the peak of the oil world when she was a toddler, which seemed unlikely. Walking back from the golf course, John didn't see her coming—she tootled up behind him in an (ironically, electric) little open-topped, open-sided car and said, "Hello stranger, need a lift?"

"Hi," said John turning around. "Man, that thing is *quiet.*"

"I know," said Robin. "It's terrible—I run over children constantly."

John laughed, slung his clubs over the back seat, and climbed aboard.

"Any grandbaby news? Has Marsha set up an advent calendar counting down the days?"

"She was on the phone with Marguerite when I left, dispensing pregnancy advice, so I guess we'll see."

Robin pulled up at John's crushed-seashell driveway. "Tell her to come over for a cup of tea if she wants to chat about it."

"Come in for a cup now," said John, retrieving his clubs. "She always wants to chat about it."

"I can't—I'm brunching with the SAS and I'm going to be late."

"Have a cup of tea and then take a shortcut over Connery's lawn. He won't mind."

"You know his house is named 'Out of Bounds'?"

"Who Dares Wins, Robin," said John.

"Oh, ha ha," said Robin. "Get a move on. And tell Marsha to brief me as soon as she can."

"Will do," said John. Thirty seconds later he was depositing his golf clubs in his mudroom, wondering if, two hours after he'd left, Marsha was still discussing baby prep with their daughter.

"John?" came Marsha's voice from the laundry room, which was mudroom adjacent.

"Yup. How was Marguerite? Robin says hi, by the way, and asks the same question."

"She's worried. Marguerite, I mean."

"Worried about what?" said John, feeling a bubble of concern forming in his chest.

"Not about anything in particular. Just, you know, first-time mother stuff. I want to go see her."

"Okay, I'll call the plane. Just let me jump in the shower."

"No, no, we have that dinner tonight—we gave them the date weeks ago."

"Oh, so you get to go see our daughter and I have to stay and make small talk?"

"Yes," said Marsha, giving him a peck on the cheek and retrieving a basket of fresh laundry. John sighed.

"Fine. Is there coffee?"

"Yup. It's fresh," said Marsha, passing through the kitchen on her way to their bedroom at the opposite end of the house. John was pouring himself a cup when Marsha called out, "And don't forget, it's white tie tonight!"

"*What?*" said John.

Marsha stuck her head back into the kitchen. "Ha ha. Gotcha."

John rolled his eyes. "I hope our grandson doesn't inherit your butter-knife wit."

"Our grand*daughter!*" said Marsha, who'd disappeared again into the next room.

"Yeah, yeah, keep telling yourself that!"

From the other side of the house, John heard Marsha laugh. He sipped his coffee and wondered if he did actually need to dress up for dinner. On the one hand, it was the Bahamas—shirtsleeve capital of the world. On the other hand, he was dining at the house of one of Lyford Cay's more potent potentates, the governor of a medium-sized Midwestern state. But he was a pretty low-key governor, all things considered. A sports coat would probably do. A tie would probably be overkill.

After dinner, John drove into town to buy cigarettes. (He hadn't been keeping them in stock—Marsha was worried about him living to see his grandkids' graduation. *Women,* he thought, shaking his head.) He was only a hop, skip, and a jump away from the Baha Mar casino-hotel complex—part-owned by the Midwestern governor he'd dined with—and figured what the hell, he'd have a flutter.

He got a private blackjack table, played for about an hour, and quit when he was forty-nine thousand ahead. He made a quick stop for a nightcap at the bar of the Rosewood, one of several dozen bars scattered among the Michelin star restaurants that spilled off the edges of the big gaming rooms.

The Rosewood bar was (a little on the nose) paneled entirely in rosewood. The seats were overstuffed leather and Louis Armstrong sang from an old bubbler jukebox. It felt like a wartime men's club in London. John ordered an old-fashioned, the bar's specialty; it was made by pouring the whiskey, et al, into a decanter filled with freshly combusted wood smoke. The bartender asked if applewood would be okay, and John told him it would.

The handheld woodstove was shaped sort of like a pistol, with a flexible tube coming out the barrel, to shoot the smoke wherever you wanted it to go. It went into some nice cut crystal, followed by the whiskey and the bitters and whatever else, where it was stirred (not shaken) until the drink had absorbed the smoke. Then it was poured onto a spiral of orange skin and a single large, perfectly cubic ice cube.

John took his drink and sat down on one of the overstuffed couches, and drank it contemplatively while he listened to Louis sing "Do You Know What It Means to Miss New Orleans."

Despite attempting to evince, as he approached his grand-daughter's due date, a staid and mature facade—the calm voice of reason—John had been compulsively checking his phone every two minutes since Marsha had left. He was just sliding his phone back into his pocket, and, with the other hand, bringing the old-fashioned up for a sip, when an old familiar face walked into the Rosewood. Petr Kovac, whom he hadn't seen in twenty-five years.

He'd never intended that he and Petr should lose touch; it had just happened. Every once in a while, John saw Petr's name in the paper. Petr had built himself a remarkable fortune, one of the largest in Eastern Europe. But, as a rule, he kept almost as low a profile as John. No megayachts, no space exploration.

Since planting his feet back in Texas, John hadn't done much business in Europe, and Petr's business was more or less entirely European (though John seemed to recall hearing that he was now branching out into China).

The Gazneft deal wasn't something John thought about every day anymore—though he'd been thinking about it more lately than, say, five years ago. Gazneft was now powering most of Germany while Trump was objecting to paying for NATO to defend Germany from Russia while Germany spent the money it didn't spend on defense to buy gas from Russia instead of the US. And Gazneft, perhaps, playing a much greater role than anyone had guessed in funding the "Green" movement, paradoxical though it might sound.

But of course, the stronger the environmental influence in politics, the less drilling countries did (countries other than Russia). Since this didn't actually reduce the amount of fossil fuels those countries needed, it just meant that instead of digging up their own oil and gas, they paid for Russia to dig up *their* own oil and gas.

And then there was the successful lobbying, worldwide, against nuclear power. Gazneft's biggest triumph had been Germany's decision to close its nuclear power plants. In a truly remarkable display of the shortsightedness of politics (or perhaps, the usefulness of bribery), "Green" replacements for nuclear energy had been hoped for but not actually planned for.

Prior to denuclearization, fission had provided a sixth of all German energy. A friend of John's had described it to him this way: "Germany has jumped out of a plane with some thread and a book called *How to Build a Parachute*." In the end, Russian energy would be their only option.

It was the opinion of John's parachute-analogy friend that either Russia was going to end up owning Germany, or Germany was going to have to rebuild its anemic postwar military. Either way, he guessed that war was in Europe's not too distant future. For NATO to continue to exist, the European members either had to start paying their own bills or find a new way to persuade American voters to go on subsidizing rich first-world countries that had free health care instead of armies.

The first option was unpalatable both to Europe and the US military-industrial complex (not to mention the politicians the complex funded). So the question was, would Europe agree to pay higher gas prices and buy American, or would they gamble on the military-industrial complex having their backs and continue to buy Russian. This friend (himself a German) guessed Europe would gamble—and lose.

Of course, this guy had been wrong about things before. He'd told John confidently that Vladimir Putin had terminal colon cancer. Even so, John was glad his European investing days were behind him.

Except here were his European investing days, walking into the bar at the Rosewood. And John was very glad of that.

"Petr!" he said loudly, getting to his feet and walking toward the bar. "Petr Kovac!"

Petr turned around and saw John; his face broke into an ear-to-ear smile. He spread his arms wide.

"John! Well, I'll be damned!"

"Get him one of these," said John, holding up his old-fashioned to the bartender, who nodded. "Petr, God, it's been a long fucking time. A quarter of a goddamn century, Jesus. What are you doing here?"

He stuck his hand out and Petr shook it vigorously.

"I'm meeting a friend of a friend about a land deal. It's sort of a courtesy thing, a stopover. I'm on my way to Alaska to do some skiing."

"That's great. Jesus. It's so strange seeing you again after all this time."

"Yes—what's the English expression? A sight for sore eyes?"

John nodded. "Yeah. When was the last time we talked?"

"Well, I know after *The Wall Street Journal* article came out, I was embarrassed to call you. So probably not since then."

"Ugh. That fucking thing."

Petr was shaking his head. "And it was such bullshit. Not the tiniest bit of fact-checking. They said I grew up in Moscow, that my father was a Czech diplomat there. My father worked in India and I grew up in New Delhi. Easy mistake, right?"

"Well, they got all their shit wrong because no one who actually knows anything about it—*really* knows anything about it, or about Gazneft's ultimatum to us—'your stock or your life'—is going to talk about it. Not after what happened to George Menshikov."

"God," said Petr. "George."

"Yeah," said John, finishing his drink. "Let's not talk about it. Where are you staying?"

"Here," said Petr. "Upstairs."

"Come and stay at my place. My wife's away, there's plenty of room. We can get nostalgic."

Petr accepted his drink from a bartender who'd appeared at his elbow. "Thanks." He clinked it against John's empty glass and took a sip. "Sure, what the hell. Where do you live? I have a meeting at Lyford Cay tomorrow."

"Lyford Cay," said John.

"That's handy," said Petr.

"Perfect. Are you alone?"

"Yeah," said Petr. "My wife's with the kids in Prague."

CHAPTER 33

When George Menshikov started publishing his insider-dealing, voucher-privatization Russian-oligarch stories, he started getting death threats. By the late nineties, he'd had to get full-time bodyguards. Finally, Forbes brought him in from the cold, back to his home in New York.

His large, stylish apartment resumed hosting the parties he'd thrown for Russian émigrés and New York intellectuals. Vodka, caviar, Tchaikovsky, deep conversations about Tolstoy and Chekov and Pushkin.

George's great-great-grandfather had been a friend of Pushkin's, one of the Decembrists who'd been exiled to Irkutsk. His grandfather had been an officer in the White Army, fighting against the Bolsheviks to preserve the dream of a liberal democracy in Russia. George had been born and raised in New York City but at his core he was a Russian patriot. When he ran the New York marathon, he would energize (and entertain) his fellow runners by singing—in English—old Czarist marching songs. "We run for Mother Russia."

In 1999, Putin had been elected and Russia seemed to be getting back on track. Yeltsin had been a vital first step away from Communism but his government's corruption had overwhelmed its republicanism. Five years into Putin's administration, George was still optimistic. In late 2003, Forbes asked him to go back to Russia to head up a new Russian edition of the magazine. His wife was adamant he refuse. She remembered the death threats. But fighting for a free Russia was something he had to do. By the beginning of 2004, he was spending three weeks a month in Moscow.

Building the new magazine took up most of his time but in the little spare time he had he made enemies everywhere. He started a campaign to rebuild churches all over the country that had been turned into municipal buildings, to help rebuild the Orthodox Christianity that had once been the country's backbone. He fought developers in Moscow and St. Petersburg who wanted to tear down Russia's architectural heritage. Most of all, he fought to expose corrupt businessmen and politicians. He picked up where he'd left off in the nineties.

On July 9, 2004—a Friday—he worked late in the *Forbes* offices. By the time he finally called it a day around ten P.M., all his staff had gone home. The only people left in the building were some reporters for the Russian edition of *Newsweek*, which shared some of *Forbes*'s office space. George waved goodbye to them and stepped outside. He was sufficiently optimistic about the New Russia that he had gotten rid of his bodyguards.

When he saw a Lada with tinted windows begin to roll down the street toward him, he might have regretted that. The driver's window came down, and George Menshikov was shot four times. He collapsed, but didn't lose consciousness. He tried to crawl back to the doorway. A reporter from *Newsweek*—Alexei Fisher—had come running when he heard the shots. He called for an ambulance and while they waited fifteen minutes for it to arrive, a *Newsweek* editor asked Menshikov if he knew what had happened.

"No," said George. "Someone was shooting."

"You don't know who?"

"No," said George.

The ambulance arrived. George needed oxygen but the ambulance men said they didn't have any, so they called a second ambulance, which did. George was put on a stretcher and loaded into the back. Fisher got in with him. The driver radioed the ambulance dispatch to ask what hospital to take George to. They sat outside the *Forbes* offices for another fifteen minutes while the driver waited for an answer. No one seemed to be in a hurry, except for Fisher, whose urging was ignored. While they waited, George began to drift away toward unconsciousness.

When they arrived at the hospital, George was rolled into an elevator to be taken to an operating room on a higher floor. The orderlies wouldn't let Fisher get into the elevator with them, so he ran up the stairs to meet it at the other end. It never arrived. Fisher tried to find out what was happening and a nurse told him that the elevator was stuck on the ground floor. Fisher ran back down the stairs. He couldn't get the elevator doors open. He begged the on-call doctors and nurses to help. They ignored him. He smashed a chair and tried to use the leg to pry open the elevator doors. He got through the outer doors, but couldn't get the inner doors open. Finally, a superintendent arrived with magic elevator tools and the inner door was opened. Menshikov was dead.

The Lada that the assassin used was found abandoned a few miles from the site of the shooting. As of 2023, his murder remains unsolved.

CHAPTER 34

B ack at John's house, out on the veranda, with a view of the pool and ocean beyond it, John was pouring Petr a postnightcap nightcap.

"So," said John, handing Petr a glass of slivovice. "What have you been up to for the last quarter century?"

"Oh," said Petr. "A little of this, a little of that."

"I hear you're doing pretty well these days."

Petr smiled. "I make a living."

John laughed, and said, "You know, I see your name in the papers occasionally, connected to all these movers and shakers in the EU, and I always think to myself, why aren't you in politics?"

Petr shook his head. "I've been involved in politics in the Czech Republic, but I can't run for anything."

"Why not?" said John, lighting a cigarette and holding the pack out for Petr. "Camera shy?"

"There's a Czech think tank," said Petr, accepting a Camel and a light, "that meets every year to discuss the world and the future and Czechia and Europe and so forth. Some years ago we were

discussing Ukraine, and a senior Czech in the EU bureaucracy
was giving a speech about why Europe should help create a
split between the Ukraine and Russia. I said that Russia pays
Ukraine three and half billion dollars a year, and asked, 'Is the
EU going to pay them that money instead?' He got angry and
said no, of course we weren't going to pay it, but freedom from
Russian influence and closeness to Europe and maybe new trade
deals would more than compensate for the loss of Russian revenue. I said, 'What will Ukraine do until then?' And he said I
didn't know what I was talking about and refused to speak to
me again. The very next day, I get a call from a friend at the
foreign ministry—"

"The Czech foreign ministry?"

"Yes," said Petr. "A friend at the Czech foreign ministry, who
tells me to be aware, this guy who gave the speech has just asked
that I be investigated as a potential Russian agent."

"You're kidding."

Petr shook his head. "So they investigated me. Went through
all my emails and texts and bank information. Probably listened
to my phone calls. Maybe they still are. Of course the point was
never to find anything, it was just part of the process of harassing
people who weren't on board with getting rid of the Ukrainian
president Yanukovych."

"That must have been a while ago, now."

"Yes, but once people get the idea you're a Russian spy, or any
kind of spy, there's no way to convince them you're not. People
there remember Communism. Though it's maybe ironic because
this kind of 'denunciation' was the number one form of eliminating
political enemies under Communism. But it's nothing new. You
have character assassination here too."

"Well," said John, taking a long drag on his Camel. "At least it's better than real assassination."

Petr laughed. "Yes. Though of course we have that as well. I mean, look at George. Or Browder's guy, the lawyer Magnitsky. You know someone tried to kill my accountant?"

"What'd your accountant do?" said John.

"Well, nothing, of course. This was back, oh, in the late nineties. I was a Conservative, but the Czech Conservative Party had become extremely corrupt. And they'd been in power too long. So I decided to make an anonymous contribution to the left-wing candidate. A very large amount of money, especially in those days, but I was doing okay. It actually wasn't so long after the Gazneft deal.

"Anyway, I didn't want people to know the donation came from me; I didn't want people to think I was changing sides to buy influence. So I did it through my accountant. All perfectly legal, but completely anonymous. Anonymous even from the candidate. So this left-wing candidate wins, in large part thanks to my money, and he comes to my accountant and says, 'I want to know where the money came from; it's dangerous for me not to know.' And my accountant says, 'I can't tell you.'

"I should tell *you*," said Petr, gesturing to John with his cigarette, "that my accountant had a year earlier had a brain tumor removed. He was in a coma for months. Everyone said he'd never wake up and then one day he did. It was like nothing had ever happened; he was totally normal again. So he went back to work, handled the political donation, and then tells representatives of the newly elected president of the Czech Republic that he won't disclose private information about a client. So the next day, someone walks up to him on the sidewalk, puts a gun to his head, and," Petr made the sound of a gunshot.

"Jesus Christ."

"Yes," said Petr. "But it didn't kill him. He had an operation and they took the bullet out and fixed his skull but he fell into a coma again—but then, a few months later, again, he just woke up like nothing had happened." Petr laughed. "He's an incredible man."

"They ought to put him in a superhero movie."

"Yes," said Petr. "Fortunately it doesn't happen so much in the Czech Republic. But it happens everywhere. You remember, last year, or a couple years ago—when was it?—the Novichok poisoning in Salisbury, in the UK."

"Yeah," said John. "I think it was last March."

"That was done—overseen, I mean—by the head of the GRU. Igor Korobov. And, you know, using a chemical weapon, a nerve agent, in a foreign country—it's an act of war. And Colonel General Korobov made the decision to assassinate Sergei Skirpal—who'd been a double agent. He worked for GRU but he was also working for British Intelligence, MI-6. Korobov made the decision to have him killed *without* consulting Putin. He just did it on his own. Decided to use a chemical weapon in a little town in West England. And so Korobov died, suddenly, a few months after the Salisbury incident."

"Jesus."

"People said it was because he'd made a mess of the operation but that wasn't it at all. At least, not what people tell me. The mistake he made wasn't in how he carried the operation out—it was thinking he could perpetrate an act of war against a foreign country on his own authority."

"Jesus," John repeated.

"Yes. It's a dangerous job, being head of the GRU. I don't know all the details, but when Putin didn't push for all of Eastern

Ukraine after Crimea, there was an attempted coup in which Korobov's predecessor was involved. Colonel General Igor Sergun."

"The GRU only hires 'Igors,' huh?"

"Yes," said Petr, lighting another cigarette.

"So what happened to him?"

"He had a sudden heart attack in Syria, when he was thrown out of a helicopter."

"Wow," said John. "Russians do not fuck around."

"No," said Petr. "Of course, you know that as well as anyone." He took a long drag on his cigarette and looked out toward the sound of waves crashing on the beach. Then he turned back to John. "You remember Babayev Chocolate?"

John laughed, hard, struggling to swallow the slivovice in his mouth. When he got it down, he said, "I'd forgotten about that."

"One of the biggest candy manufacturers in Russia," said Petr, laughing himself. "Or the biggest? I don't remember. We buy a controlling interest in the company through the vouchers. We showed up for the first meeting with management . . ."

"And the only guy to show up from Babayev," finished John, "is wearing a butcher's coat covered in blood."

Petr laughed so hard he started to cough.

"Put your hands over your head," said John.

"He put down a contract on the table," said Petr, waving off the advice and continuing to laugh. "He put down a contract for us to sign, turning over all our equity in the company for some tiny sum of money. Less than we'd paid for the vouchers. And you just said, 'Fuck it, I've already got my ticket home,' and you gave me your stock and wished me good luck with it."

"Holy shit, I'd completely forgotten about that. What'd you end up doing?"

"I sold the whole stake to a friend I made on the Caspian Sea. You remember."

For a moment, they sat in the afterglow of an intense bout of laughter. When they'd caught their breaths, each lit a fresh cigarette.

"So—wife and kids in Prague?"

Petr got sort of a queer look on his face.

"Yeah. So, guess who I married?"

"Svetlana Stalin?" said John.

"Anna."

"Who?"

"Anna, Anna—you know, our translator? The girl on the train?"

John blinked twice and stood up. Confused anger was boiling up in his throat.

"What?" he said. "What?"

"You're not going to congratulate me?"

"Why the fuck didn't you ever tell me?"

"I don't know," said Petr. "We'd fallen out of touch. We hadn't talked in years. You and me, I mean. When I met her again, we hadn't talked in years. And, I mean—I didn't think you liked her very much. I guess it just never occurred to me you'd be interested."

John drank down his drink, turned and threw the glass—letting a slightly drunk inclination toward melodrama get the better of him. He heard it spelunk into his swimming pool. Less dramatic than the shattering glass sound he'd expected.

"Forgive me, John. I should have told you."

"Yeah," said John. "I mean . . . congratulations. That's great, it really is. I'm just a little shocked."

"Have another drink," said Petr, pulling out his wallet. "Here's a photo of us in Berlin, on our honeymoon."

John took the photo and looked at it. There she was. A beautiful girl, looking not too much older than the last time he'd seen her. Or the first time he'd seen her, in her cigarette-girl getup on the train. She was in her twenties then, thirties in the photo, forties, presumably, in real life. John and Petr were in their fifties now. Petr looked the same—exactly the same, as if he hadn't aged a day. John wondered how he looked to Petr.

"Who the fuck goes to Berlin for a honeymoon?" he said, handing back the photo.

Petr chuckled. "There was a fashion show, very chic."

John shook his head, trying to come to grips with the situation.

"So what's the rest of the story?" he said, getting a new glass and filling it. "What happened at that auction? Where was it? Tara? How did you find her again?"

"Yes," said Petr. "At Tara. In Omsk Oblast."

CHAPTER 35

In Tara, for the Omsk auction, after Anna had been pulled out of her hiding hole by the men who'd killed her rent-a-cop bodyguards, she had been dragged back to the street and thrown into the trunk of a car. They'd driven with her in the trunk for a long time—or anyway, what felt like a long time; it was too dark to read her watch.

Finally, they'd stopped in some sort of warehouse, where she'd been allowed to use a bathroom and was given some food and water. She asked what they wanted from her but they refused to say anything—they being a pair of men who she assumed were the men who'd dragged her to the car. She had no way of knowing for sure. Neither had said anything, then or now, and both had been wearing ski masks and still were. She had been telling herself that Gazneft wasn't Baader-Meinhof but in fact that's exactly what these guys looked like.

She ate slowly, afraid of what would happen when she finished. When she did finish, one of the men reopened the trunk of the big black German sedan she'd emerged from, and waved for Anna to get back in.

She hesitated; her animal instinct being to do anything other than get back into her tiny, miserable, cold, dark prison cell. But then the second of the two men shoved her toward the car and seeing that—one way or another—she was going to end up inside the trunk, she climbed back in herself, trying to look bored and indifferent. She lay down, and the trunk was slammed shut on her again. For a few minutes she fought off a panic attack. She wasn't claustrophobic—or, anyway, she *hadn't* been—but no one reacts well to being sealed inside a coffin-sized box by two men who were almost certainly murderers.

At some point she fell asleep. After an eternity, she was woken by the opening trunk and let out again. Same two men. Same trip to the bathroom, same tasteless food, and then back into the trunk.

This routine went on for a long time. A very long time. Long enough for her to have several full-blown panic attacks of banging on the inside of the trunk lid, begging to be let out, offering the men whatever they wanted, screaming, wailing, hyperventilating, and fainting. They ignored her.

At some point during her imprisonment, she began to focus on suicide as the only way out and felt around the trunk for something sharp with which to do the job. She'd had the almost-atheistic upbringing of all rural Communists; the little bit of religion that had escaped state obliteration being the folk-orthodox traditions of peasants.

She knew suicide was strictly forbidden, by God. Unable, anyway, to find a way to kill herself, she began to pray—nothing formal, mostly blank verse asking for deliverance or death and salvation. This went on, and on. Occasionally she fell asleep.

Occasionally she was let out and fed. Occasionally she reached a point so far beyond hope that she might as well have been catatonic.

This routine continued until she was woken by the blinding brightness of a flashlight pointed directly at her face. After a good thirty seconds of examination—maybe to make sure they had the right girl?—the light clicked off. Now she could see who was holding it. It was a third man, wearing an expensive-looking suit, and a ski mask of his own. He was shaking his head at her.

(Here Petr interjected: "I suspect, based on the description, that this was Krylenko. But there's no way to know because he never showed his face. It might just have been someone who worked for him." John nodded, and Petr resumed the story.)

"If only you had taken the very reasonable offers that were made to you in Omsk," said the man who might have been Krylenko, "you wouldn't be in this position now."

"I have had time to reconsider those propositions," said Anna. "And would now be willing to accept." She wasn't being funny; she was much too badly rattled for that. She just wanted to go home.

The man laughed.

"It's a little late, I'm afraid. We bid your vouchers, so you've really nothing left to offer us. And now people are calling me, asking if I can locate you, find out what happened to you. I told this nosy person that you were dead. And I'm afraid I'm going to have live up to that report."

Anna said nothing.

"Get out of the trunk, my dear," the man said, taking her by the arm and pulling her upward. She'd used her legs so little for, what, three days? Five days? A week? She had no idea how long she'd been in the trunk, but her legs would barely support her weight. The man in the suit led her to a concrete wall and told her to sit down. She lowered herself gingerly down the wall into a seated position, pulled her legs up to her chest, and rested her head on them.

Then the man took out a Polaroid camera and took a few steps back, trying to find an angle he liked.

"Hold your chin up, my dear. I want to get a clear look at your face."

Anna was past the point of resistance. She did what she was told and hoped it would lead to some sort of relief.

"Good," he said. He pulled a Makarov pistol out of the back of his waistband, flicked off the thumb safety, and aimed it at Anna's face. She went white.

"No, no, don't worry, it's just a joke." He kept the gun pointed at her face and pulled the trigger. She flinched so violently she almost dislocated her hips.

"See?" said the man, pulling the trigger a few more times. Clicks from the double-action hammer. Anna was shivering.

"No, I just want you to pose with it." He walked over to her and placed the gun in her hand, and then raised her hand and arm until she had the gun pressed against her own temple.

"Good," said the man. "Don't move."

The camera flashed and buzzed and a picture printed out its front. The man in the suit waved it back and forth a few times, waiting for it to develop. It did, and he examined it.

"Good. You look beautiful. All finished my dear—you can put the gun down now."

Anna lowered the gun and placed it gingerly on the ground, pointing away from her.

"So," said the man. "I wanted to make sure we understand each other. You've heard the Spanish expression *plata o plomo*? This is the picture I'm going to send your family, along with one of your dead body, if you don't tell me exactly what I want to know."

Anna nodded.

"I don't want to be ungenerous. I don't need your vouchers anymore, of course. What I do want is to know who you're working with, who they're working for, what banker they use, how they're incorporated—everything. And if you tell me everything I want to know, then you'll be fine. In fact, you'll be better than fine. Because after that I'm going to take you to the airport and buy you a one-way ticket to wherever you want to go—so long as it's out of Russia, where you won't be in anyone's hair."

Anna kept her eyes down; she was looking blankly at the floor.

"How do I know you won't just kill me afterward?"

"Even here, killing people is inconvenient, and I have nothing to gain from it. You don't know who I am, or who I work for—even if you think you can guess. Of course, it's academic, since you have nothing with which to bargain—all you can do is hope I'm telling the truth. Luckily for you, I am."

"You killed the policemen who were guarding me."

"Well, not me personally, but, yes. From killing them, I had something to gain. Kidnapping you. But from your death, I would get nothing except maybe some people wanting revenge. And you must know the proverb, do not make an enemy without a good reason."

"Yes," said Anna. "Ask me your questions."

◆

"How did you find all this out?" John asked, cutting into Petr's story.

"From Golokova," said Petr.

"*What?*" said John. "You met with Golokova again?"

"Yes," said Petr. "I was summoned to her office after that *Wall Street Journal* article came out."

"Jesus Christ," said John. "Why?"

"Because the source for the story was an idiot American kid in my office."

"Jesus Christ," repeated John. "How?"

"After you left the company, you know, we continued on in Russia for years. I mean, we still have an office there and, until the *Journal* piece, I worked in it pretty regularly. I was going back and forth between Moscow and Prague.

"I was in Prague when a *WSJ* reporter called the office. He wanted to ask a few questions and I wasn't in the country, so our youthful receptionist thought, naturally, she'd put the call from the American reporter through to the one American I had working in the office. Who was also youthful, and stupid. Someone's nephew. His uncle asked me to give him a job and I had him doing research on undervalued assets in central Asia, or something. Basically it was busywork.

"So the reporter asks him about how we bought Gazneft, and this kid—who didn't start working there until three years after it happened—this was 1997, I think—so he'd heard a little about it, around the watercooler, so to speak. So he just told all that to the reporter. He gave them the caveat that this was all thirdhand stuff, but they didn't publish that part.

"So I wake up in Prague, a few days after all this happened—not knowing it had happened—open *The Wall Street Journal*, and there it is, front page of the business section. I was reading it a third time when I got a call from Gazneft—Golokova's assistant told me to be in her office at 15:30 Moscow time. I said I was in Prague. He just repeated, 'Be in her office at 15:30 Moscow time,' and hung up.

"I call the office to find out what the fuck happened and then rush off to the airport, grab the first flight to Moscow, change in Amsterdam, and I'm there about a half hour early. She makes me wait for about two hours, and then calls me in. 'How did this happen? This violates the confidentiality portion of our agreement.'

"And I said, 'It was a stupid fucking American kid. That's why they got all the details wrong. But what do you want me to do, have him killed?' and she says, 'No, not him.'

"I say, 'What, you want me to kill myself?' And she says, 'No—if this ever happens again, if one more word about this appears in print, you're going to disappear. And it won't be the light-touch kind of disappear, like your little girlfriend.' I say, 'What are you talking about?' And she says, 'That girl Krylenko grabbed in Tara and sent to Istanbul.'

"I was . . . speechless. I made my obeisance, promised it wouldn't happen again, she repeated her death threat, and I got the first plane to Istanbul."

"Mary, Mother of God, Petr," said John. "Why the fuck didn't you tell me about any of this?"

"When I didn't hear from you after the *Journal* piece came out, I figured you were mad about it too."

"I wasn't mad, no," said John. "I was out of it and I just wanted to keep my head down and *stay* out of it."

Petr nodded. "I can't blame you—getting called to the head-mistress's office wasn't fun."

"Makes me shudder to think about. So what happened in Istanbul? You found her?"

◆

At the airport, waiting for his plane, Petr called the office and told them to find a private investigator in Istanbul and have him track down Anna Lydiovna Scherbatskaya. Also to make a reservation for him at the Pera Palace Hotel and have a car meet him at the airport.

The plane landed as the sun was going down. The Bosporus looked like a river of molten silver flowing into the golden horn, dotted with black. Freighters making their way from the Black Sea into the Sea of Marmara. And vice versa.

At the airport, Petr bought a carton of domestic Camels and began chain-smoking, not stopping until he fell asleep in his hotel room three hours later. He was across the hall from the room that Agatha Christie wrote *Murder on the Orient Express* in. When he fell asleep, the cigarette fell out of his mouth and burned a hole in his undershirt.

When he'd checked in, he'd told the front desk to call and wake him the moment a message came for him. He woke up naturally midmorning; no call from the front desk. He called down to be sure and, when the maître d' confirmed that there were no messages, he asked for a tailor to be sent up to his room. He hadn't brought any clothes with him to Moscow so he hadn't brought any to Istanbul either.

The tailor tailored, left to cut the suit—Petr gave him five hundred million lira (about 2,500 dollars, American) to make it a rush job—and then sat down to wait. When he got tired of waiting, he attempted Turkish television and, when that proved to be a bust, he sent down to the front desk for a copy of *Murder on the Orient Express*, which he'd never read. They didn't have one. So he asked them to send up a copy of every European and American newspaper they had that wasn't *The Wall Street Journal*. Then, on second thought, he asked them to send up *The Wall Street Journal*, to see if there was anything new that had leaked about the Gazneft deal. There wasn't. He read it cover to cover and continued to chain-smoke.

His suit arrived in the late evening. Still no messages at reception. He called his office to make sure they had actually hired the private investigator and, when they confirmed they had, he ordered dinner, killed a bottle of wine, and went to sleep.

The phone woke him up at ten the next morning. It wasn't the front desk, it was a direct call from the private investigator—he introduced himself in Russian and Petr rushed him to the substance of the call.

"I've located Miss Scherbatskaya. She's teaching Russian and East Turkic languages at the Austrian-Christian school in Karaköy, Sankt Georg Avusturya Lisesi. It's a well-known school, a cab driver will know where to take you, but if you have a pen I will give you the proper address. Her home is a small apartment four blocks away from it. I will give you that address as well. She is unmarried and lives alone."

Petr was writing all this down, took the addresses, thanked the investigator, and hung up. He showered and shaved and before eleven A.M. he was standing outside the school, looking at its yellow masonry facade—decked out with a Turkish flag beside an Austrian one—trying to decide if he should go in and look for Anna, or ask if she was teaching today, or ask what time she'd be done, if she was.

He burned through half a dozen cigarettes trying to make up his mind. Eventually he went inside and up to a little desk that was tucked behind a small ticket-window-sized window, as if the school were a movie theater. He asked what time the school day was through and if the teachers would exit through the front. The receptionist—such as she was—didn't speak Russian. Petr repeated the question in German and she said yes, the teachers left by the main exit, and school was over at three.

There was a coffee shop on the other side of the street, and Petr went there to wait. He barely tasted the genuine Turkish coffee, something of which he was normally very fond. He tried several times to read the paper, but it couldn't keep his attention.

The coffee shop had its radio tuned to an American music station. It began to play a new Weezer album—*Pinkerton*—and Petr found himself drifting back to his absurd sturgeon excursion on the Caspian Sea. The slightly nasal voice of Weezer's singer repeated over and over again, something about how he'd be good for some girl and she'd be good for him, but when the next song started it turned out the singer had made a little mistake, that he was dumb and she was a lesbian. The coffee shop changed stations to some traditional Turkish music.

Petr heard a school bell ring at three and spent about fifteen minutes watching kids in school uniforms slowly trickle out of the school. Some went on their way, some stood around in groups chatting, a few came into the coffee shop. And then, suddenly, there she was. Walking straight toward him, toward the coffee shop. Looking just as beautiful as he remembered her, though in a formal and somewhat matronly dress. Probably to fit in with a teaching staff that included a lot of nuns.

She opened the door to the coffee shop and walked right past Petr without noticing him and got in line to place an order at the counter. Petr folded his newspaper and, using it to discreetly dry his clammy palms, stood up and walked over to her. He tapped her lightly on the shoulder. She turned around, expecting to see one of her students.

They locked eyes. Her mouth fell open. For a beat, she just stared at him, slack-jawed. Then she threw her arms around his neck and buried her face in his shoulder and started to cry.

He hadn't expected that. He stroked the back of her head and told her everything was all right. He felt her breath—for a moment so rapid that he worried she might faint—start to slow down.

The school kids in the coffee shop were all watching now, looking uncomfortable, whispering to each other. Petr kissed Anna on the top of the head and she rolled her head to the side and kissed him hard on the lips, pulling him in as tightly as she could. He dropped the newspapers and pulled her in even tighter. Now the school kids started to giggle.

"Come on," he said. "Let's get out of here." He used his thumb to wipe away the dampness on her cheeks and she answered his suggestion with a nod.

They spent the next three days in his hotel room.

"We lived together for a year in Prague," said Petr. "And then we got married. Three kids."

CHAPTER 36

The next day—nursing only a relatively mild hangover—Petr went to his meeting. Afterward he and John played a round of golf, during which John shanked a ball into Sean Connery's swimming pool. Neither had grown sufficiently rich not to joke about the absurdly high green fee. Afterward they had lunch at the club's restaurant on the beach, and then John drove Petr to the airport. They shook hands and promised to keep in better touch. John wished Petr good luck skiing and Petr wished John good luck with a first grandkid.

Marsha was already on her way back, so John waited at the airport, sitting on the hood of his Japanese-import Honda. Like Japan, the Bahamas drive on the left side of the road, but all the cars on the island were American and had left-hand drive, which was an irritating combination. The Japanese Honda had been Soichiro Yamamura's idea—suggested in their last conversation before Soichiro had died a few years earlier. John wished he'd thought to ask Soichiro to translate some of the Honda's buttons for him while he'd still been alive, though the car's indecipherable interface lent it an amusing air of mystery.

Jim Schultz was dead too. He'd died a few years earlier, aged ninety-five. The last of the postwar diplomatic titans. (Or actually, second to last—John was pretty sure Kissinger was still alive.) John thought he really ought to call Donny Dietrich. Petr had got him in a nostalgic mood. Donny was still in Hollywood, working on another new fortune—he'd been one of the first guys into big-budget streaming movies. He already had some Golden Globes to show for it, though when John had last seen him the thing Donny'd been proudest of was being the only guy in attendance at Ricky Gervais's Golden Globe massacre who'd really enjoyed it. He told John, with great relish, that unlike the rest of Hollywood, the only skeleton in his cupboard was the dinosaur he'd bought from Nic Cage.

Forty-five minutes later, Marsha landed at Lynden Pindling International Airport (the hardest of all international airports to pronounce), and fifteen minutes after that they were back at the house. And life went back to normal, for eleven days.

Twelve days after Petr left the Bahamas, John's cell rang. It was a number he didn't recognize so he ignored it. The number called him twice more over the next two hours. John answered the third call. It was Anna from the train. She introduced herself as Anna Kovac. John recognized her voice immediately and could hear immediately that she'd been crying. He felt a shiver up his spine. Petr's had a skiing accident, he thought—his mind instantly going to the Michael Schumacher case. One day, the world's greatest driver, the next day a trip to the slopes and he's a vegetable undergoing experimental stem cell treatments.

"Anna, what's wrong? Are you okay?"

"Petr told me he'd seen you and gave me your number, wanted to invite you and your family to Prague."

"Did something happen?"

"Petr's dead."

"God . . . My God." So much for getting reacquainted. Petr. Excellent shape; fifties but looked ten years younger. Young wife, young kids. His whole life ahead of him. "What happened?"

"He was in a crash."

"Oh, Anna. God. A skiing accident?"

"A helicopter crash. He was helicopter skiing in Alaska. There was a weather warning, and all the other helicopters came back, but his stayed out . . ."

She trailed off and there was a long silence. Finally, John prompted her. "He got caught in a storm?"

"No," said Anna, and then after a long and pregnant pause. "The weather was perfect. Though there had been a weather warning and all the resort's other helicopters had been recalled."

John let that hang in the air for a moment. "Anna, do you think he was murdered?"

"No one will tell me anything," she said. "They say it's for legal reasons. But Petr has a friend who works there who called me to offer condolences. He told me some things."

John said nothing, letting Anna collect herself and continue.

"He wasn't killed by any sort of . . . blow. Any trauma," she said, after fighting down the tears in her voice. "He didn't die *from* the crash. He was suffocated, smothered. 'By snow' is apparently what the official report says. It says that the helicopter caught one of its runners on a ridge and flipped, slid down the side of the mountain. It filled up with snow and smothered everyone inside.

"There were five other people aboard, including the pilot. Four of the others died too. I haven't been able to find out who the survivor was. Whoever he is, he's not talking to anyone.

"Petr's friend who called me said Petr didn't leave from the lodge where he was staying, but joined the helicopter flight from some other . . . from a third location. He said that the weather at the location of the crash, at the time of the crash, was perfectly clear. And that from the time the helicopter's . . . tracker went off, which told the ski lodge people that there had been a crash—from then until the time the emergency rescue team was informed, there was a two-hour delay. And then another four-hour delay before anyone actually made it to the crash site. At which time the bodies were removed from the scene without any police involvement or, uh . . . forensic? Forensic investigation."

"Lord," said John. For a few more, long moments, neither said anything. "All this European energy stuff . . . while he was here, we talked about it in sort of a vague way. He didn't tell me if he was involved in it or not."

"Today," she said, by way of answer, "the Czech government will expel sixty-three Russian diplomats from the country. Someone who didn't give his name called to tell me that." She paused again and added, "But I don't know if he was murdered. I guess all we can do is wait and see what happens next. But I thought you should know the story. Just in case."

John resisted the impulse to ask, "Just in case of what?"

CHAPTER 37

On April 22, 2021, sixty-three Russian diplomats were expelled from the Czech Republic.

A little more than a week later, in May, 2021, "John" started telling me this story.

ACKNOWLEDGMENTS

I t's tricky writing acknowledgements for a book where nearly all of the real characters' real names have been redacted, but some have given their consent to be thanked sans pseudonym. Thanks to Peter Fellegi, a truly fascinating guy, who formed much of the composite Petr character. Thanks to Bernie Sucher, another truly fascinating guy and the basis for the Benny Sheldon character. Thanks to nightlife icon Doug Steele, who was the basis for the Doug Steele character. Thanks to my editor Otto Penzler, a literary giant whose enormous reputation is well deserved. Thanks to Tom Jenks, another literary legend, and to his wife Carol, who were instrumental in getting this whole thing going. Thanks to my exceptional agent Warren Frazier, who made this book happen. Also, though they're not technically my agents, Warren's colleagues Moses Cardona and Anne Hawkins have been extremely helpful with advice and support; thanks to them too. Thanks to Charles Perry, who's Otto's publisher and righthand man. Thanks to Managing Editor Will Luckman and copyeditor Kathy Strickman, who did an outstanding job polishing the book. Thanks to Derek

Thornton at Notch Design, who worked with Charles on the wonderful cover art. Thanks to Julia O'Connell, an all-around problem solver at Mysterious Press. Thanks to Tanya Ferrell who did the PR—if you're reading these acknowledgements, that's probably because of her. And, because acknowledgements have to be written quite a while before a book's actually published, thanks to everyone else who worked on the book in the interim. You will have been much appreciated.